MOONSHOT

LM FOX

MOONSHOT

LM FOX

MOONSHOT

Editor: Readers Together

Proofreader: Cheree Castellanos, For Love of Books4 Editing

Formatter: Shari Ryan, MadHat Studios

Cover/Graphic Artist: Hang Le

Cover Photographer: Wander Aguiar

Cover Model: Kyle Kriesel

To my Granny, who was my biggest cheerleader.

Ask, believe, receive, and be immensely thankful for all is possible when we live in gratitude and joy.

CHAPTER ONE

Mick

Staring down at my Montblanc Summit, it's now 12:25 p.m. My ass has officially fallen asleep in this brutally hard metal chair. I've probably gazed at my expensive watch twenty times since I sat down over an hour ago. Initially surrounded by patients both young and old, I now find only one person remains in this orthopedic clinic waiting room. And that poor sap would be me. A twenty-seven-year-old ex-ballplayer turned medical device salesman, constantly seated amongst the torturous thoughts of what might've been.

The fancy timepiece I received for securing a full ride on a baseball scholarship years ago seems to mock me as I turn to look toward the receptionist. As Joanie places the phone receiver down, she peers up from her paperwork and quickly realizes she's not alone. Giving her a tired smile, I push my black horn-rimmed glasses back up my nose. It's not her fault I'm still here.

"Hang tight, Michael. I'll check on them again for you. Thank you for always being so patient," the sweet middle-aged clerk encourages. The petite woman's well-coifed blonde bob barely moves as she jumps from her seat smiling, a bit embarrassed, in my direction.

Normally, I bring a book or something to work on while I sit here. The lengthy wait time to meet with one of the providers in this clinic is predictable. Of all of the offices I visit, this one's the one that always leaves me hanging. They aren't any larger than the rest, but there's an air of pretentiousness at this particular location I don't encounter elsewhere. While my product is important to their livelihoods, seeing me is another story. It's as if I'm the serving of leafy green vegetables their mother is forcing upon them.

Meeting with these clients is beneficial, ensuring any questions they have are answered, and the devices they need are readily available for their surgical cases. Surgical cases that put a lot of money in their pockets. You'd think that'd be worth eating your veggies without complaint. Yet this is a part of the job I've come to accept.

"I don't have time to deal with some sales guy today. It's been a busy morning, and I want to grab some lunch. I'm sorry he had an appointment, but no one asked me. Get Ava to see him."

I overhear the unmistakable pitch of Dr. Stark's arrogant voice. Dr. Joseph Stark is an orthopedic surgeon specializing in shoulders at Central Virginia Orthopedics. In his mid-thirties, he's educated, certainly skilled in the OR, not a bad-looking guy, and one pompous asshole. Every interaction I've ever had with this man has been condescending. It doesn't matter that I'm also a trained professional, here to do a job. *We are all beneath him.*

I've worked with FlexPath for over a year now. The work isn't bad, as far as sales jobs go. I do quite a bit of traveling, but for the most part, my product sells itself. Our company supplies partial knee replacement hardware to the hospitals that perform these procedures. This product has found wide appeal with surgeons in my area. I rarely have to answer any questions, but the high dollar item requires regular visitation to the hospitals to ensure they have the correct stock on hand and routine calls on the orthopedic clinics to be available to address any concerns. When I first started with the company, I was frequently asked to be in the operating room, directly available to the surgeons to answer any questions. This can be a high-stress environment and requires a lot of training. It's an adrenalin rush being in the OR, yet this is no longer necessary as the procedure has become routine. So until a new device hits the market that requires intensive interoperative education, I make 'house calls.' Typically, a monthly visit to each office will suffice, however, the busier practices I call on every other week.

This was never my passion. I didn't wake up in high school one morning dying to sell prosthetic parts. The only thing on my mind back then was chasing a childhood dream. I was going to be a major league baseball player.

I'd played ball my whole life. What's more, I was fucking good at it. I'd spent the majority of my youth on a field in one town or another. Juggling school baseball with travel leagues, my focus was one hundred percent on the game. All with the elusive goal of hitting the big leagues one day. I was getting on a baseball card come hell or high water.

My family was overjoyed when I received a scholarship to play at my local University. Not only had I gotten a free ride, but I was close enough they could easily attend games and I could still be home for Sunday dinner when I wasn't on the road. The world was my oyster.

My mom had worked two jobs for as long as I could remember to put away money for college. She splurged on my graduation gift, purchasing this ridiculously overpriced watch. Fumbling with the dials, I can still hear her sweet voice as she presented the gift to me, her overworked hands trembling. "I know when you're a big shot ballplayer, you'll be able to buy your own fancy things. But I wanted you to have something special to remind you of us back home when you're up at bat miles away." I feel a slight lift to the corner of my mouth as I recall the proud look in her eyes.

Business was my chosen major when I began my college career, but only because I couldn't declare baseball as my primary course of study. It seemed like a good backup plan, but when you're young and invincible, you never contemplate you'll actually need one. Yet my dream crumbled at the end of my freshman year when I blew out my shoulder. Batter's shoulder, they called it. Well, whatever it was, it crushed every hope I'd held for my future. And I've been trying to pick up the pieces ever since.

"Ava should be out in just a minute," Joanie advises as she leans into the receptionist window. There's a twinkle in her gray eyes. Is she proud she managed to convince someone to see me, or is it something more?

"Thanks, Joanie. I appreciate it. I know they're busy."

Ava. Or, Elsa as I've named her in my fantasies. Now there's a silver lining to this wasted hour and numb ass. Ava's a physician assistant in the practice, seeing patients in follow-up postoperatively in addition to regularly scheduled clinic patients.

A Nordic beauty, Ava's tall, statuesque, and fair-skinned with almost platinum blonde hair and ice-blue eyes. Yet, more striking than her physical beauty is her personality. Her Elsa external vibe may be icy cold, but her nature is warm and endearing. She's never without a bright smile and appears genuine in her conversations. I'd know because when she makes direct eye contact with you and bestows one of her smiles, it'll take your damn breath away. Even a beauty queen like Ava couldn't fake her enchanting interactions. Her persona is a glaring contrast to the self-righteous, arrogant surgeons in this office. Even some of the other physician assistants can be a little haughty at times. But never Ava. I'm sure she's this way with everyone she meets, but it's easy to get caught under her spell.

I've spent many a night envisioning Ava in my bed. In my head, we're perfect together. Then I wake up. Sure, I'm attractive, fit, and financially secure. But I'm no match for the highly educated, successful surgeons with impressive bank accounts she's surrounded by daily. I make a decent living, but I'm well aware I'm a salesman with a bachelor's degree. Returning to school to obtain my MBA is an option I've considered. But I don't enjoy business. Not too motivating when you're only contemplating this feat to *keep up with the Joneses*, so to speak.

My job isn't bad. Working hard and remaining flexible, I've surprised myself by surpassing the sales goals set by my company. I make a better income than many of my peers, and I keep baseball in my blood, coaching a local little league team. The only thing missing from my life is companionship.

Due to my frequent traveling, a dog isn't even an option. I've wanted one for years, but it wouldn't be fair to have it couped up all day. And honestly, I'd much rather curl up with someone a lot less hairy.

It's been years since I've been in a relationship with a woman. But that ship has sailed. When my baseball career went up in smoke, so did my girl. As much as I'd love the chance to date someone as beautiful and kind as Ava, I'm not willing to risk another letdown. Losing my girlfriend of five years and my dream of playing in the big leagues was enough devastation for one decade.

I meet plenty of attractive women in my travels. My ball-playing days may be over, but this ex-jock can still score. I stay in shape, dress to impress, and my mom raised me to know how to treat a lady. Then once the evening's events move somewhere private, all gentlemanly behavior vanishes once the clothes come off.

On the road, calling on out-of-town clinics at least twice a week, I'm thankful to have plenty of new options for occasional company. New options who aren't looking for a long-distance relationship. There hasn't been anyone who's tempted me into anything beyond one night since college. But, if anyone could…

"Hi, Michael. It's good to see you."

Looking up at this regal blonde-haired beauty, I try to keep my cool.

Ava

Walking to the reception area, I happily greet Michael. Except for the awkward fact he's been sitting in our waiting room for over an hour, I'm excited to see him. I look forward to his visits to our office. He's kind, respectful, and hot as hell. This man has starred in many a fantasy of mine. I bite my lip, realizing it's taking effort on my part not to let him see the effect he's having on me.

"Michael, I'm sorry you've had to wait so long. Do you want to follow me to my office? If nothing else, the furniture's more comfortable." I hold out my hand to shake, as is customary, but have to steady myself at the jolt of electricity that shoots from his warm, masculine hand into mine.

It's terrible the way Dr. Stark and many of the other providers treat

Michael and the other sales reps who visit our office. They have a job to do and are providing our group a service. It wouldn't have taken Dr. Stark five minutes to say hello and sign that damn form Michael needs for his boss, showing he was here today. That type of behavior is so unattractive. Who cares about your career success, your wealth, or your looks if you're a dick?

"I feel awful about not grabbing you sooner. I went out to get patients on two different occasions and noticed you were there but thought you were waiting on one of the docs." I wince.

"Ah, it's okay, Ava. It's part of the job. I make appointments each time I come to make it easier to fit into everyone's busy schedule, but it doesn't always work out. I appreciate you seeing me." He gives me that megawatt smile I've come to dream about. The man should honestly consider doing toothpaste commercials for a living. He's just radiant. But it's probably every bit as much the buff bod and the charismatic banter, as it is the movie star teeth. He's the whole package.

"Hey, I have an idea." I quickly interject, placing my finger to my lower lip in thought. "Unless there's something specific you need to meet with one of the physicians about, why don't we just set up a standing appointment to meet every other Thursday at 12:30. You'd be my last appointment before lunch. I don't run late often. Hopefully, it'll ensure you spend less time sitting in a hard chair, hoping someone will stop what they're doing to speak with you." *Plus, I get to look forward to a little eye candy, all to myself, every couple of weeks.*

"Wow, really, Ava? That'd be awesome. It's rare anyone has any real questions for me. I just have to visit to be sure everything with the product's going okay. You'd be doing me a huge favor." He beams down at me, and I can almost feel the current crackling between us. I could get lost in that smile. *God, is it just me? Can he feel it too?*

"Of course, I don't mind at all," I almost whisper, realizing my gaze is probably bordering on unprofessional. But those molten brown eyes are practically turning me into a puddle.

"Plus, I'd much rather meet with you than any of those guys." He winks, causing me to blush. With my pale skin, that doesn't take much and is impossible to hide once it begins.

All right, I know he's just being flirty. He's an unbelievably handsome guy. And he's in sales. Isn't that part of their training? Lay it on smooth to close the deal. He probably uses the same technique when he's trying to pick up women. So, if I know this, why are my lady parts suddenly all abuzz? I feel my cheeks warm a little more and scold myself for allowing him to have this effect on me. *I probably look like a tomato on heels.* "Thanks, Michael. You're sweet." I quickly sign his form and hand it back, knowing he's already spent too much of his day with us.

"I'll see ya in two weeks, Ava. I'll let Joanie know to pencil me in. Thank you, again." He waves goodbye and heads out my door to the reception area. Unable to stop myself, I allow my eyes to casually drift down his torso to appreciate the nice way his well-fitted trousers hug his muscular ass. I guess that's one good thing about sitting in the waiting room for an hour. He'd removed the suit jacket giving me an unobstructed view. *Maybe I can crank up the heat in there in two weeks, just before he arrives. See if he'll take off his shirt.*

Giggling, I sit down in my office chair and can't help but smile at our recent interaction. He's so attractive. He's kind of the boy next door but with a touch of smolder. He's always dressed in business attire, but I'd seen him in the OR when he first started working with FlexPath. The colorful tattoos climbing up his arms had my mouth watering. I was mesmerized. And I don't know which had me more captivated, the arms or the art. With or without the ink, the chorded muscles extending from his sleeves were panty-melting. I'm not sure if the rest of him looks like that, but those puppies were impressive. He must spend plenty of time in the gym.

It'll be nice to have something to look forward to at lunch once in a while. Typically, my lunch breaks are spent with the door closed, the lights off, and my head down on my desk. I've been plagued with debilitating migraines since the onset of my menstrual cycle at age thirteen. It's a gift of my DNA as my mother spent the majority of my childhood in bed with migraines. Her mood swings were like night and day. She was either miserable and in pain or a live wire. I no longer consider it a psychiatric issue. Since my headaches began, I've had first-hand knowledge of their debilitating effects. But I refuse to let them take over my life as her migraines had.

My mother is beautiful and smart but a slave to her vices. She smokes, drinks large quantities of caffeine, and indulges in wine and cheese. All of these, I've learned, often contribute to frequent migraines. I've made a painstaking effort to modify my lifestyle and diet to limit the headaches as much as humanly possible. I try to reduce stress where I can and do yoga. I've also embraced meditation as part of my daily routine. However, I still find the severity of the headaches more than I can bear several days a week and have to spend my lunch hour trying to curb the unrelenting tension. I've found if I take a prescription medication that doesn't cause drowsiness, turn the lights off, and meditate, it will often get me through the rest of my day. I can't afford to lose my job over this. I've already watched my mother lose so much.

My father had hung in there for years with my mother's chronic pain but finally waved the white flag and surrendered via divorce. I initially saw him every other weekend, but this soon trailed off once he met his current wife and started a new family. I've never had any relationship with my stepmother or stepsiblings and just accepted that's how men are. They're in your life until something better comes along. Then they're gone.

I love my mother. However, we don't often see eye to eye. She's focused on my looks, and I want to be taken seriously. She wants me to meet a nice man and settle down. I want to be able to stand on my own two feet. I'm determined not to end up the way she has. She'd been abandoned with a child, often bed stricken by her migraines. I quickly learned to fend for myself and her. Dad's alimony and child support got Mom through financially, but between the constant headaches and raising me, she never entertained a relationship with a man. There was the occasional date, but nothing lasting.

This reality inundates my thoughts. Could there be someone who'd want to care for me at my worst? Someone who I didn't fear would leave when something better came along?

CHAPTER TWO

Mick

"Thanks, Ava. I appreciate you taking time out of your schedule to meet with me." It's been a month since we established the set appointment times at the clinic, and every time I return, I worry I'll be banished back to the metal chair.

"Oh, I'm happy to do it, Michael. It's no trouble."

My eyes drop down her form as her slender hand dips into her starched white lab coat pocket, pulling out an ink pen to sign my paper. Unable to help it, I lean a little closer while she's distracted, inhaling her scent. Peppermint. She always smells like peppermint. It figures. Everything about this enchanting woman is sweet.

"Any questions?" I laugh. No one ever has questions for me. I pray that the sheer quantity of surgical prostheses used by this clinic will be enough to keep me coming back. If my bosses get wind of how little I have to do to keep the sales coming, I could get sent to another region or given a different item to hawk.

"No." She giggles. She's so fucking cute. "Maybe I should come up with a list in case your job ever asks what you do when you're here."

"Hell, you're a mind reader. I was thinking the same thing. Thank goodness my sales are so good. I don't think they care so long as that keeps happening." I grin back at her. She probably thinks I'm a little crazy. It seems I'm always smiling at her. But she probably gets that from every man she meets.

"Well, I'll work on it all the same. Brightening my day will be at the top of the list," she says, placing her pen safely away.

As I reach for the form, my eyes connect with hers. Her translucent ice blue eyes are hypnotic. Between her beauty and the kind words, I'm a little star-struck as a frisson of current warms my fingertips as they graze her hand. For a beat, I stand there motionless. Just watching her eyes on mine. Noticing the soft way her lashes dance as she blinks. There's the finest stray lock of hair lying against her cheek I'm dying to tuck behind her ear. *Shit*. I have to take a steadying breath. "Thanks, Ava. I'll see you in a few weeks," I manage to get out. My voice feels thick. *Jesus, what's happening to me?*

"Bye, Michael." Her eyes seem to sparkle with the salutation.

There's a strange pull in my chest as I turn toward the door. Every other Thursday, I come to the Central Ortho clinic and sweet Ava's in the waiting room to greet me within five minutes of my arrival. Like clockwork, I can count on her to usher me in and out. I'm finding I wish I didn't have to be shepherded out quite so quickly. Granted, I'm thankful to avoid endlessly sitting in the uncomfortable chairs of the waiting room. Yet, I discover I'm looking forward to returning almost before my current visit's over.

I'd love to ask this amazing woman out. Everything about her makes my spirits soar. She's gorgeous, kind, intelligent, and sexy as hell. Yet there's no way around it. I could never date Ava once and walk away. She's a forever kind of girl, and I'm just not sure I'm ready for that.

The sting of Paula's betrayal had left a scar. We'd met in middle school and had become fast friends. She was a cheerleader, and I was the star leadoff hitter of the baseball team. The friendship quickly morphed into teen crushes and later, love. It was always comfortable. She was one of the prettiest girls in school. She'd made all of the Homecoming courts and as cheer captain, was one of the most popular girls in school. I was fairly popular, given my baseball reputation, but the school social class system tended to make me uncomfortable. I preferred the company of my family and my friend, Zach, to hanging out with a bunch of jocks and their backstabbing girlfriends.

With Paula, there were no deep conversations or feelings of longing. We didn't sit up all night on the phone, both waiting for the other to hang up first as I'd heard others speak of. But it'd been the two of us for so long, it simply felt right. Until it wasn't.

After the devastation of my Batter's Shoulder injury and multiple failed surgeries, I had to face the music. My major league baseball career was over. It was one of the worst moments in my life, coming to terms with the decision to walk away. The next few months were like grieving a death. But I guess that's exactly what it was. The death of the future I'd held so tight.

I attempted to shield how much I was struggling to prevent the people around me from feeling uncomfortable. No one ever knows the right thing to say. Why put them through it? Yet there was no need to try to comfort Paula, as she was absent much of the time. Her visits to the hospital after my injuries or subsequent repairs were rare. The one time I can recall her bothering was when she had a friend along. In retrospect, I suspect that visit was all for show. I admit this wasn't shocking. Paula had always been a bit superficial. Deep and meaningful our relationship had never been. Despite this, I still expected more from her.

Instead of the soothing reassurance that everything would be okay from my girlfriend of five years, I felt abandoned. I made excuses for her. It was our first year in college. The transition from high school academics to the grueling requirements of college hadn't been easy. Yet it seemed, in hindsight, much of her absence was due to partying into the wee hours versus pulling an all-nighter. More and more, she began to pull away. Until one day, I discovered she'd seemingly left and forgotten to inform me.

It was near the end of my freshman year when I walked into the campus library, arm in a sling, looking for a book to complete a class assignment. As I rounded the stacks, I heard familiar giggling. Assuming I'd find Paula and a girlfriend gossiping over the latest college shenanigans, I was instead stunned speechless to find her in a compromising position with Brett, the team pitcher. As I leaned back behind the end of the shelving, I observed them laughing together with his arms wrapped about her waist. He was whispering into her ear, and based on her facial expression, she was eating it up. My stomach churned. Beyond the betrayal, I couldn't recall a time she'd ever been like that with me. Giddy and playful. Even when we were younger. Seeing them like this was a real blow. But the hits kept on coming.

I didn't want to start a brawl in the middle of the library, so I retreated to my dorm to confront her about it later. We'd been friends before we were more, and I didn't want to ruin that with a public spectacle. Once back in my room, I opened my laptop and logged in to social media to find the relationship between my girlfriend and Brett had been going on for some time. There were multiple pictures posted on both of their social media pages as if they'd been an unofficial item for months. Hell, my page still said, 'in a relationship with Paula Patterson.' *What a schmuck I was!*

Trying to put my game face on, I called Paula asking her to come by. I wanted to have this conversation in person. She owed me that much. There was no point in trying to justify this as something other than what I observed with my own two eyes. There was no way she could claim their closeness today, coupled with all of the pictures I'd found, was innocent, friendly behavior.

When Paula came to my dorm hours later, I'd laid it all out there. Yet, my committed girlfriend of five years merely shrugged her shoulders at the images and said, "It's college. You didn't think we'd really make it through four years of college together, did you?" Something tells me if I was still hitting grand slams, we would've made it just fine.

There was no I'm sorry. I never meant for this to happen. Not even a 'it's not you, it's me.' Just a blank expression like I was in the wrong for even bringing it up. She turned and walked out the door that day as if we were never anything more than acquaintances and never looked back. If she'd been this callous after spending this many years together, I have a feeling marriage vows would've meant little more.

As painful as that time remains, I know I dodged a bullet that day.

How much longer would she have hidden that relationship. How many others had there been during high school that I was too blind to notice? My gut said Brett was akin to a relief pitcher, waiting in the wings for his turn. Paula was beautiful and could have any man she wanted. And it appears she was more than ready for a replacement. Maybe that's all there ever was between Paula and me. I was the shooting star she'd hitched her ride to. I was going places, and she wanted to be there for it all. When it appeared my limelight had faded, and the career was over, she moved on to the next shimmering beacon to try again.

Jock chaser or not, Paula left a bitter taste in my mouth for women and relationships. I'd already lost my major league baseball dreams and the girl I thought I'd eventually marry. I wasn't ready to deal with another blow. The women I'd met in my travels for business had provided all the connections I needed. One hot, steamy night at a time. I made it clear I wasn't looking for more. That I was purely in town for business. There were no numbers exchanged, and often I never even learned a name. It was a warm body to fall into when I needed it. Nothing more.

Ava is not that type of woman, and I know it. If I wanted to ask her out, I'd have to be all in. Plus, if it didn't work out, I'd still have to see her in the office. Could I handle returning here if it went sour? Because I was damn sure it'd be her rejecting me if it ended. There's no way I'd be able to walk away from a woman like Ava.

This woman is the stuff movies are made of. She's poised and articulate. She makes you feel as if you are the most important person in the world when she has your attention. I know our interactions are purely business, but I try to flirt a little when I can get by with it. Yet, she's surrounded by attractive, wealthy men with impressive degrees. I could never compete with the likes of them. Nor would I want to. I'm done trying to prove myself to a woman just to be replaced when I don't meet their expectations. One-night stands give me what I need without dealing with eventual heartbreak.

Pondering this is fruitless. When Ava's surrounded by multimillionaire surgeons and the like, why would this breathtaking woman consider going out with someone like me?

CHAPTER THREE

Ava

It's been a horrendously stressful day. The clinic got a late start when an impromptu fire alarm went off. After standing outside for almost an hour, we were cleared to return to the building and had to try to do what we could to move patients along a little quicker. Otherwise, we might not get a lunch break today.

Dr. Stark is on call for the ER today, causing him to be more irritable than usual, barking at everyone in his wake. But as usual, I'm his most convenient target. Not to mention, he's been pulled from the office multiple times, leaving me to pick up the slack. I've tried to take it all in stride, reminding myself he's just an asshole, Ava. Don't take any of this personally. But it's still beyond unpleasant.

I manage to complete my work responsibilities, plastering on a smile, despite his condescending attitude. I've seen twice as many patients during the first four hours of my shift as usual. This should make me feel accomplished. However, the added stress has brought on a familiar aura.

My migraines are almost a customary part of life now. I don't know which days they'll arrive, but expect at least two days a week will be torturous. But regardless of avoiding triggers, stress can induce one hellish headache. And around here, I spell stress with a capital STARK.

My usual migraines will slowly creep up as a feeling of tension or pressure in my head and neck, but they're usually centered behind my left eye. Light and unpleasant noises aggravate the discomfort, and extreme nausea usually comes along for the ride. I've found that mint seems to help with an upset stomach. I should own stock in peppermint candy for the amount I regularly buy. You can find them almost everywhere you find me. In my lab coat pocket, my purse, my coat, my desk, and all over my home. To someone unaware, it looks like I need an intervention. Yet, popping one into my mouth or placing them in a cup of herbal tea seems to keep nausea from intensifying into full-blown retching.

The truly treacherous migraines present with an aura. I'll see a gold halo behind my closed lids and know it's coming. There's no sense fighting it once the aura appears. I've learned getting upset about it only makes it worse. Thankfully, I have a few non-narcotic prescription pain medications on hand which don't elicit drowsiness. While these can still be addictive, I only use them when it's absolutely necessary. If the pain builds too quickly and the nausea is more than a peppermint can abate, I have some nondrowsy nausea pills as well. Ultimately, rest is what works best. The last patient before lunch has left, and I'm grateful to be able to lie my head down on my desk for thirty minutes. For all the therapies I've tried, rest in a dark space often works better than any chemical.

"Ava, honey. You don't look like you feel well, but Michael's here. Would you like me to send him away? He's such a dear, I'm sure he wouldn't mind coming some other time if he knew you weren't up to it," Joanie asks, stroking my arm.

Had I fallen asleep? I didn't even hear her come in. "No, no. It's fine. He never stays long anyway. I should be fine." I rub the back of my neck instinctively. "Could you just ask him to give me like five minutes before you send him back?"

"Of course, dear." Joanie exits my office, heading to the front of the clinic, and I sit down at my desk to look through my purse for my pill bottle. She's such a kind woman. It wasn't long after I began working at the clinic that my headaches started wreaking havoc. I'd discovered back then that I had a hard time with a scent Joanie wore to work. I tried to distance myself from her but worried she'd feel I was being rude. After much internal debate, I shared that bright light, harsh noises, and some smells could aggravate my symptoms. I assured her the headache was already there at that point. Her perfume had not caused them, just made my nausea a little harder to bear. I apologized for always smelling like a walking tin of Altoids as my way of broaching the subject, and she was such a dear about it. Never once did she make me feel bad. She rarely wears anything beyond a mildly fragranced hand lotion now. I hate that I could've stolen something from her she enjoyed wearing, but she insisted I needn't give it another thought. She's looked out for me when they get bad ever since.

As I swallow the little white pill, I consider momentarily what it'd be like to come home to someone like Michael if I had a headache such as this. He's so gracious and good-mannered. Not to mention mouthwatering. He'd probably be all the medicine I needed. It's dangerous to contemplate such things. I don't need a reason to become sad or depressed at my current circumstances. It'll only make the headaches worse.

It's been a long time since I've been with a man, and none of them looked like Michael. Most of them were intelligent businessmen I'd met online or had been acquaintances of friends or work colleagues. My relationships never seem to last. I've not experienced anything deep and meaningful with someone. In the beginning, it was all my doing. I lived in fear of ending up like my mother. Of being tossed aside for someone who wasn't so complicated. It was easier to just accept being alone. Yet after a while, that existence is miserable too.

So I've tried to put myself out there. I date if you want to call it that. Yet, every man I go out with seems so superficial. Initially, meeting someone new is loaded with possibilities. I'm sure I'm not everyone's cup of tea, but I have a shelf full of beauty pageant trophies to prove some find me physically attractive. *Thank you for that, Mom.*

When I meet someone new, usually there's excitement as we get to know one another. Often it's forced excitement on my part. But they appear pleased I haven't catfished them once we meet in person, and

I'm pleased for the chance this time could be different. This time could lead somewhere. It's not a lot to ask for. That I might hope for a significant other versus a superficial other for a change.

Yet very often, it turns out to feel like I'm a challenge in some way. There's no real connection beyond the physical. I'm simply arm-candy. I equate it to what an escort might feel. Spending time with someone where there's no spark. No chemistry. Listening to them go on and on about their accomplishments as if they're interviewing for a job. I hang in there with each man, thinking the common denominator here is me. Yet, once I finally tear down my defenses and sleep with them, they're often out the door, never to be heard from again. *Maybe I'm just really bad in bed?*

There've been a few men who've taken an interest that felt genuine. But unfortunately, I felt nothing romantic in return. It seemed wrong to get their hopes up by continuing to date. Knowing they held unrequited feelings made it difficult to entertain anything physical. Sure, I have needs. But I'd prefer to have purely carnal, unemotional sex with someone where we both know the score. I'd never want to give false signals to an otherwise nice guy. Nothing is appealing about that scenario.

Knock, knock.

Looking up into the rugged face of the attractive man standing before me, I no longer have to force a smile. He's wearing charcoal gray slacks, a crisp white shirt, and a black silk tie. His soft, brown curls are styled to perfection, and he's wearing the black horn-rimmed glasses that make me weak in the knees.

"Hi, Michael. How are you?"

His deep brown eyes give me a warm sensation. An affection I appreciate right now. "I'm good, Ava. How are you?"

"Fine. I'm afraid I don't have long today, as I have something I have to get to as soon as you leave. I hope you'll forgive me if I simply sign for you this time." I look up from my desk at him apologetically.

"No, of course. I understand. You're always so accommodating." He slides the form across my desk, so I can pen my name, and continues. "I did want to ask you something, though."

"Oh?" Of all days. Any other day I'd be dying to answer any

question he had. *Yes, I think you're the hottest man I've ever met. Yes, I'd love to sleep with you. Yes, we can do it here. Is the desk good for you, or would you prefer up against the wall?* Today, however, I'm just trying not to puke on his shoe.

Pushing the paper back across the desk in his direction, I lift my eyes to him once more. The headache is getting worse as I can barely focus on the strong jaw, dreamy smile, and the gorgeous strands of dark hair I'd love to fondle. *Damn Dr. Stark and his overbearing stressful self.*

"Are you okay? You don't seem like yourself today."

"I'm fine. It's just been a stressful morning. Was that your question?" I toss back to him, trying and failing to offer flirty banter. Why did this headache have to come when he's here? Is it too much to ask to have a few unhindered minutes with this thirst trap?

"No. I. Well…"

I've unknowingly dropped my head down under the force of my extreme discomfort and gently raise my head to make eye contact with him once more before he leaves. I should just tell him about this headache. He'd understand. He's so darn sweet. And it's not like I have to worry about him ditching me because of them. Hell, he's paid to come here. It's not like he's coming here for me.

"I was—"

"Ava, there you are. After you're done doing…" Dr. Stark looks between Michael and me before continuing his sentence. "Whatever it is you're doing, will you look at the afternoon schedule and figure out how you can manage to see my patients without rescheduling. I have to take an ER case to the OR. You can move your patients if needed."

"But—" There's no need finishing the sentence as he's already left and wouldn't care what my current circumstances were. I drop my head in my hands and pray for a miracle to help me get through the remainder of this day.

"Tool," Michael mutters.

My head snaps up, and I catch his shocked facial expression. You know this headache is bad when I'd almost forgotten he was here. Between Dr. Stark and the migraine, it's almost hard to remember *I'm* here.

"I'm sorry, Ava. That was terribly unprofessional of me," he interjects.

"Well, maybe so. But it's the best thing that's happened to me all day." I laugh. Ugh, even laughing hurts. What I'd give to go home and lie down. *Think I could ask this incredible hunk of a man if he'd take me home? Hell, he'd think I wanted a lunch date booty call. Not that I'd turn that down any other day. If I got fired, it'd be worth it.*

"I hope not," he answers, catching me off guard.

I try to sharpen my focus. What had he been saying? Oh yeah, we were talking about how it was the best thing that had happened to me all day. I simply got distracted by this vice-like grip on my skull. *Well, that and the thoughts of lying naked underneath the god of a man standing in front of me.*

"What do you mean? It's honestly been the worst day ever." I drop my head back into my hands, not even caring that he's still here. I just don't have it in me to pretend everything's okay anymore. I'm so overwhelmed at this moment. If only something good could break through this misery. Something that could get me through the next few hours here before I go home and crawl into bed.

"Well, I was wondering…"

Michael stops talking, and I realize how rude I'm being. If I'm not going to tell him about this headache, the least I can do is try to be attentive while he's here. If I can't focus on his handsome face and beautiful eyes, I can at least point my gaze in his direction so he knows I'm listening. That his presence is important to me. Lifting my head in his direction, I wait for him to continue.

"I was wondering if you might join me for lunch when I come back in two weeks?"

CHAPTER FOUR

Mick

"Yes," Ava blurts out.

I can't help the chuckle that escapes. That was the last thing I was expecting from this staunchly professional goddess. "Well, okay. It's a date." I watch as her smile widens, and my heart nearly stops. *This could be dangerous, Mick. There's no walking away from this beauty.*

"I'm sorry, Michael. It's been an absolutely hellish day here. You've been the one bright spot in an otherwise bleak morning." She stops speaking to rest her hand on the nape of her neck, extending her porcelain throat. God, she's beautiful. "Thank you. I'm really looking forward to it."

"So am I, Ava. See you in a few weeks. Bye." I move toward her door and can't help briefly looking back over my shoulder at her before walking away, noticing an odd expression on her face. She almost seems pained. Was she simply trying to get rid of me? She initially seemed so excited with her utterance of 'yes.' *Hell, Mick. You're just being paranoid. Get your shit together. She said yes. This is a good thing.*

～

It's been two weeks, and I'm as nervous as a groom on his wedding day. *What the fuck is wrong with me? Jeez, I go out with beautiful women all of the time.* Why am I acting like this date is anything more than lunch? Because a girl like Ava doesn't come along every day. That's why.

I admit I'm reliving my youth. All of the stereotypical behaviors I've witnessed from John Hughes' movies like "Sixteen Candles" and "The Breakfast Club" where teens go through the trials and tribulations of their newfound crushes. I never experienced this with Paula. We just went through the motions. But this girl is putting me through all the feels.

Ava is like pin-up girl material. She's the beauty queen with a heart of gold. You can't help but wonder how a dream girl so beautiful could be standing in front of you in the flesh. Giving you her undivided attention. Although she's definitely the most engaging, articulate woman I've had the pleasure to meet, I'd be lying if I didn't admit I've been thinking about her a little more often without any conversation. Unless the two of us moaning could be counted as meaningful dialogue.

I've known Ava for over a year and always felt she was out of my league. Yet, she's never acted like it. Beyond what she does to me in my fantasies, she's a beautiful soul. And that fucking spark I feel every time my hand grazes hers isn't something I've ever felt before. If she can make me feel like that with something so small, what else could there be between us?

I really want to make a great impression on her. This lunch date I've planned has to be perfect. I've made a call to Luigi's to make sure they have a table ready for us. I know she has a short break, so I've ordered ahead. I figure whatever she doesn't like, I can take home.

Luigi's is a hometown favorite. It's a small, locally-owned restaurant with fantastic food and is reasonably priced. I've come here since I was a kid and dare anyone to find better authentic Italian food. I asked Luigi if I could have a table in the corner for privacy. After all of the ribbing about 'a special lady' was over, he agreed. Now I just need to stop by the office to get Ava.

∾

As I approach the office, I note Ava's standing outside the front doors. It suddenly dawns on me that my asking her out isn't terribly professional, and she may want to limit anyone's knowledge of our plans. I wouldn't want to do anything to make her uncomfortable.

"Hi. Have you been waiting long?" I ask.

"Oh, no. I just came out, actually." She grins up at me. For the first time, I assess she's probably about five foot ten, comparing her to my six foot three frame. Granted, she's wearing heels, but I'd bet she's at least five foot eight or nine barefoot. "I only have about forty-five minutes. I usually only get a thirty-minute break for lunch, but Joanie said she'd cover for me." I watch as she covers her mouth with her small, delicate hand and giggles. *Fuck, I could eat her up.*

"Well, let's head out then. I parked close, knowing we wouldn't be here long." I escort her to my Silver Ford Explorer and open the passenger door. She's dressed in a loose-fitting, pale yellow blouse and a navy blue pencil skirt that falls about mid-calf. There's a slit in the front of the skirt, which exposes some of her creamy soft skin. I watch as her slender legs curl into the car and have to calm myself. *It's only lunch, man.*

We drive the few short miles required to reach Luigi's, and I ensure she's okay with Italian. *If not, I guess she's eating a salad.* I detect a hint of mint floating between us in the car together and can't help but notice the effect it has on me. There's a slight warmth and a tingle in my chest as if I'd just consumed one myself.

"Oh, I love it. And Luigi's is my favorite."

Standing a little taller, pride filling my chest, I walk around to her side of the car and open the door for her, gently placing my palm against her lower back. Sparks jolt me again, and I can feel it all the way to my dick. I need to down a tall glass of ice water and get my shit together before I completely embarrass myself.

"Ah, Mick. Good to see you. And who's the lovely lady?" Luigi greets us as we enter the cozy space.

"Hi, Luigi. This is Ava. She's apparently a big fan of your food too. Don't let her size fool you." Looking at Ava, I notice her eyes are ping-ponging back and forth between Luigi and me. "I've been eating here a long time. Luigi and I go way back."

"Oh, I see." She giggles.

"Right this way, Mick. I have a very special table ready." He winks. "I know you're under a time crunch. Is there something special you'd like to drink?"

"Oh, just water for me, please," Ava responds.

"Same." I pull the chair out for her and take a seat at the four-top table. The restaurant is quiet, with only a few other patrons. "I knew you didn't have much time, so I called ahead and ordered a few of Luigi's classics. There's also salad and bread. I hope that's okay."

"It's more than okay. It's so thoughtful. Thank you." She beams.

Luigi brings our water with two servers in tow who present the salads, plates of antipasto, cheese ravioli in marinara sauce, fettuccine alfredo, and penne ala vodka. She's glowing at the service and the luscious food. Luigi's for the win! After Ava instructs which entrees she'd like to try, the servers spoon helpings of steaming pasta onto our plates and offer freshly grated cheese before departing.

"Holy cow, this is amazing, Mi—" I notice she stops abruptly, and I lower my fork to assess what's wrong. "Luigi kept calling you Mick. Is that a nickname, or have I been calling you the wrong name for almost a year, and you're too polite to correct me?"

"No, Mick's a nickname. My little sister couldn't pronounce Michael, and so it stuck. All of my friends and family call me that."

"You have a little sister? That must be nice."

"Wasn't always. The last thing you want is babysitting duty when you're eleven years old, but she's a pretty cool kid. I can't believe she's driving now."

"Wow, an eleven-year age gap," she questions as she takes a bite of ravioli, closes her mouth around her fork, and moans.

There goes my dick again. Focus, Mick. "Yeah, my dad left when I was young. It was just Mom and me for a long time. My mom met Rob when I was nine. He's a good guy. I'm glad she found him. Anyway, she remarried about seventeen years ago, and Emmaleigh came along a year later." I take a large bite of pasta and wipe my mouth of any lingering sauce. "How about you? Any siblings?"

"No, just my mom and me. My dad left when I was young too. But my mom never remarried." I notice she's slowed down on eating as she's appearing to push the food around her plate now. She is thin, so maybe she doesn't eat much. "I think about it sometimes. It would've been nice to have a sister or a brother. Emmaleigh is lucky to have you."

"Did your father remarry?"

"Yep. I saw him some after the divorce, but once he started having kids with his new wife, he kinda forgot about me." She shrugs, reaching for her water. I hope I haven't stepped into something painful with this line of questioning.

Trying to assure her I understand some of our shared histories, I push forward. "Yeah, I never saw my dad again after he left. All I have left of him is memories of playing catch in the yard. I think I got my love of baseball from trying so hard to impress him one day."

"What do you mean?" she asks, putting her fork down.

"Ah, it's silly. In my naïve young head, I thought if I played really well and grew up to be a big baseball star, he'd see me and want to know me again." I watch as she puts her delicate hand over mine and wonder why on earth I've shared something like this with her. On a first date, no less. But Ava is the kind of girl you can just relax and be yourself with. There's no pretense. She's kind and open. There's no judgment from her as she looks at me with those ice blue orbs. "I'm sorry, I didn't mean to get so heavy on a first date. Over lunch, no less."

"No, Mick. Is it okay if I call you Mick?" she asks timidly.

"Ava, you can call me anything you want, pretty girl. This has been the best lunch I've had in years." I can't control my grin. Hell, I hope I'm not scaring her with my over-the-top enthusiasm.

She laughs in agreement. "Me too."

We continue to make idle small talk. She shares how her mother had her in the pageant circuit as a child and preteen.

"I didn't mind it when I was young. Then it just felt like a great big game of dress-up. But as I got older…"

She shares how she was able to put away a sizeable nest egg for college with her winnings but begged to stop participating as it seemed to exacerbate the dumb blonde image she was trying so hard to avoid. It didn't matter that she excelled in school. All of the people in her social circle had decided her academic achievements were awarded to her based on her looks, not her merit. Her face falls a bit with this reflection, and the unfortunate enlightenment makes me sad. Judgment based on your appearance can cut like a knife regardless of whether you're considered attractive or not. I'd never contemplated this before, having assumed attractive people were merely fortunate for having good looks.

Attempting to change the subject and bring us out of the deep conversations we've fallen into, I share how I've been coaching little league baseball as a way to stay connected to my dream after my injury and career plans went up in smoke. I leave out how my team is a hot mess and will likely not win a single game this season. We've had enough depressing talk for one lunch.

"So, there was no way to fix your shoulder, so you could play again?"

"It was a labral tear. They tried twice to repair it with surgery, but it just never felt right afterward, and my hitting suffered. I knew if I kept pushing, I'd cause more damage, so I stopped playing." I deliver this information as if it wasn't the worst thing to ever happen to me. "Man, I'm just giving you my whole sob story today. I bet you're quite impressed with me now, huh?" I reply sarcastically.

"Are you kidding? I love how open and honest you've been. I'm surrounded by arrogance and superiority all day. You're a breath of fresh air, sir." She winks, and I almost choke on my bread. Her pale skin has a beautiful pink blush to it, and her tranquil eyes are like staring into the sea. *God, this woman. She's simply incredible.*

Looking down at her watch, I notice the wince and quickly turn to make eye contact with the closest server. "I've got all of this, Ava. Why don't I get you back to work?"

"What?" she stammers.

"I knew you'd have a short window of time to eat, so Luigi told me he'd pack everything up, and I could come back to settle up after I've dropped you off." I watch as she stares at me, mouth ajar.

"Mick. That's the nicest thing anyone's ever done for me."

"Well, that's sad. You deserve to be treated like a princess." I have to stop myself before I call her Elsa by mistake. "It's really nothing. I'd be willing to do a lot more than this if I could get another date with you." I grin, hoping this date has gone as well as it appears.

"I'd love to go out with you again. But you certainly don't have to go all out. Just spending time with you has been great."

Attempting to mask my pride, I turn to make eye contact with Luigi as we stand. I reassure him I'll be back momentarily before walking Ava to the car.

"Thank you so much for everything, Luigi. It was so good," she advises as she rubs her flat belly. My eyes drop down the length of her as she speaks with him, and I can't help but imagine what she'd look like with only a bra and panties, performing that same motion. My dick twitches, waking me from my inappropriate thoughts. *There will be plenty of time to consider that in the shower later.*

As we buckle up, I consider my options. I'd love to take the return trip slow or maybe go the long way to work so I can make this date last a little longer. But I know I have to get her back to the office quickly. She'd said Joanie was already covering for the additional fifteen minutes she took. I don't want to put her in a difficult position.

There's no conversation between us on the trip back. Yet we appear to be sending morse code as we continually look at one another and grin. Please tell me she's feeling this too. This is more chemistry than I've ever felt with anyone on a date. But then again, those are usually just a means to an end for me. As much as I'd love to sleep with Els— I mean, Ava, getting to spend time in her realm was more satisfying than any physical connection I'd had with a woman in a long time.

As I pull up in front of the office doors, I take a quick look around before opening the car door for her. As she steps onto the curb, I lift her hand, placing a chaste kiss over her knuckles. I want to be a gentleman, but it feels almost vital that I ensure she knows how attracted to her I am. As I drop her hand, I notice the same electricity is present, making my lips tingle. Hell, I might need medical care if I ever fuck this girl. If the spark between our superficial touch is this strong, I'm afraid being inside her might be deadly.

"Thanks for a great lunch date, Mick." Ava beams up at me. God, I want to reach down and cup her face. Kiss those sweet, pink pouty lips.

"It was my pleasure," is all I can say as she walks back into the office.

As I head back to Luigi's, my cheeks begin to hurt under the strain of my intractable smile. I can't help myself. I know I'm going to get grilled by Luigi upon my return, but I don't even care. I really want to take a chance with Ava. If I fall, it'd be worth it. Right?

CHAPTER FIVE

Ava

"Hey, girl."

I look up to see my dear friend, Eve, waving to me from the back corner of the small bistro. She stands from her seat at a corner booth, opening her arms wide.

"Oh gosh, how I've missed you," I reply as I crush her against me. "How long have you been waiting?" Glancing at my watch, I confirm I'm on time for our much overdue dinner plans.

"You're fine. I was just anxious to get this night underway. It's been way too long, Ava. I feel like it's been forever since we've had any quality time together. Damn PA school." She laughs.

"Ha. Yeah, it's hard to have time to do anything beyond sleep and study in that program." Eve has been attending my alma mater, Eastern Medical School, in the tidewater region of Virginia. While all PA schools are competitive, Eastern is particularly so. It's a private college with smaller class sizes, allowing for more individualized instruction when needed. Midlevel providers like physician assistants and nurse practitioners are often seeing the very same patients as the physicians with whom we work. The training is grueling to ensure we're adequately prepared for our jobs. Medical school is a four-year program plus a residency requiring three additional years of study for primary care physicians. More for orthopedic surgeons and the like. The PA program, including clinical rotations, is completed in less than three years. Thus, there's a lot of information to learn in a very short amount of time.

"How's it going?" I ask, reaching for my water.

"It's intense. The amount of material you're trying to absorb is insane. I don't think I had any idea what I was in for when I applied."

I chuckle. "It's probably a good thing we didn't know. I'm not sure that anyone would go through with it if they did."

"Good evening, ladies. Can I get you something from the bar before dinner?" the server asks, voice dry and uninterested, not making eye contact with us but instead looking at his Apple watch.

"Oh, I'd love a glass of Merlot," Eve replies to the tall, thin server whose face remains expressionless.

"I'll just have water, thank you."

"Oh, Ava. You're going to make me drink alone? Is it the migraines?"

"Yeah, it's usually better if I abstain. But if we go out later, maybe I'll get a drink then." I hear the distinct sound of a voice clearing above me and glance up to see the obvious annoyance of the gentleman holding his pen and pad of paper. *Really?*

"Would you like to hear the specials, or are you ready to order?"

Jeez, what's your hurry, man? The place doesn't close for hours. My eyes connect with Eve's, and a knowing smirk crosses her face. Oh, no. This gal has no filter.

"Oh, I'm sorry. Were we not going fast enough for you, Edward?" she asks, looking at his nametag. "Could we have a few more minutes to look at the menu, please? Then, when you return with our drinks, you can share the specials, and I'm sure we'll be ready to order," she adds with obvious sarcasm. Granted, Eve had put herself through undergrad waiting tables and made huge tips doing so.

I quickly return my attention to Edward, whose face is anything but expressionless now. He looks like he's sucking on a lemon. Or constipated. He spins with a flourish and briskly walks into the kitchen, the door slamming closed behind him.

"Really, Eve? He's probably going to go spit in our food!"

"He had it coming. He was being rude. I didn't say anything inappropriate. I just encouraged him to try a little harder to do his job." She shrugs her shoulders and begins to read her menu like she's glancing over the Sunday paper at the breakfast table, completely unaffected.

"Oh my god," I utter as I drop my head in my hands. *This girl.* Eve is a gorgeous girl with blonde hair that falls to her shoulders in beachy waves. Her hair is a rich, golden hue, unlike mine that almost appears white. She has big brown eyes and the most incredible complexion. Hell, I'm not into girls, but I get a little captivated by her sometimes. Her give-no-shits attitude about the world around her only adds to her allure, in my opinion.

I quickly decide on a small chef salad and the crispy roasted Brussel sprouts, if nothing more than to enjoy the look on Eve's face when I order it. She's a stunningly beautiful petite blonde who never seems to gain a pound but abhors vegetables. Brussel sprouts, I'm quite sure, top the list.

"So, clinicals must be getting close. Are you staying in the tidewater area to do them or coming back home?"

"I'm doing a little of both. I'm not in a hurry to get home to my meddling brothers, so I'm going to do a few in tidewater and a select few here. I'm hoping to get my ER rotation at St. Luke's."

I can't control my giggle at this. Eve would constantly remind me of the contrary, every time I'd wax poetic about how much better my life would've been had I had brothers like her. Eve was the fifth of six siblings and the only girl. She wasn't able to sneeze without one of her overprotective Manning brothers checking her temperature. She was rarely out of their sight. Parties and dating had been nearly impossible. No boy would garner the approval of any of them individually, much less the group as a whole.

Despite her protests to the contrary, I still thought her situation sounded like the more appealing option. Growing up an only child had been isolating. I couldn't bring friends over because they might be too loud and aggravate my mother's condition. It didn't matter anyway. I wasn't sure I wanted to risk sharing my circumstances with my friends. They didn't need to see what life was like at my house. Doting on my mother as she lay in bed or lifeless on the couch, wearing her depression like a cloak.

"Have you ladies had a chance to review the menu?" Edward's terse greeting interrupting my depressing thoughts of yesteryear.

"Ah, yes. I'll have the chef's salad with a side of ranch and the roasted brussel sprout appetizer," I quickly reply. My eyes snap over to Eve, who's making a gagging gesture with her mouth and index finger. *Classic!*

"Yes, Edward. Thank you for asking. I'd like the breakfast burger with the works." The years of being surrounded by testosterone have shaped her eating habits. Thank God she's got a great metabolism. Eve quickly closes her menu, grabs mine, and hands them both to our stoic server with a sickeningly sweet grin on her face. A tooth could pop out from the strain of that cheesy smile. *Lord, this girl.*

Edward turns toward the kitchen without a word, not quite as dramatic as his last exit.

Eve leans in, her beautiful brown eyes suddenly looking deadly serious. "If I smell so much as bad breath on my burger, I'm calling the News on Your Side reporter to get them to investigate this place."

"Oh, lord." I hoot. "You're a mess." I take another sip of my water. "So when do your clinical rotations start?"

"Very soon. I have my first one already scheduled in tidewater. They like us to do the first one close to the school for some reason. Who knows why. In case I get scared and want to come home to Mommy?" Eve again shrugs her shoulders and takes a sip of her wine. *God, I miss wine.*

"When would your ER rotation take place?"

"That one is next. Oh, I hope I can get it at your hospital, Ava. I've always dreamt of working in the ER there. When I volunteered as an EMT, I always liked the atmosphere at St. Luke's. A lot of the other emergency rooms in town act like you're a taxi service. They'd seem annoyed to have to take report from us about the patient. Like our care didn't matter. It's never like that at St. Luke's."

"So the emergency room is where you ultimately want to end up?"

"Well, I'm not making any commitments until I finish all of my rotations, but yeah. I'm pretty sure that's where I want to be when I graduate. I'm hoping I can make some connections while I'm doing my clinical rotations to help secure a job once an opening presents itself."

Edward returns with our food and silently slides it onto the table in front of us. And when I say, on the table, that's about the gist of it. Our plates are deposited in the center of the table for us to retrieve. As if this is supposed to demonstrate his disdain for our still being here. Hell, it's his tip on the line.

"Why, thanks, Ed," Eve croons, pulling her man-sized sloppy burger in front of her tiny frame. She leans down as if she's going to take a big bite while he's still standing beside us but instead looks up at him and takes a loud, nasally whiff of her food.

I almost spit out my water. "Thank you," I manage to get around my snort.

Again, I watch the runway spin as Edward whirls away from us and stalks back toward the bar.

"You're killing me, E."

"Ah, he can try that shit on someone else. So enough about me. What's been going on with you?"

"Well..." I drawl, unable to keep from grinning.

"No! What? We've been here this whole damn time talking about PA school and fucking Edward!"

I quickly look about the restaurant to make sure 'fucking Edward' hasn't heard her outburst before continuing. He's stealthy in his arrival at our table, and I don't need a cold pitcher of water dumped in my lap when he finally snaps. "I had a lunch date with the dreamiest guy, E. He's beyond handsome. He's... well, I don't even really know how to describe him," I say, clutching my hands under my chin, feeling like a Disney princess explaining her prince to small woodland creatures.

"Jesus, Ava. Well, you better try. I need deets," she says before digging back into her messy burger.

"Okay, okay. He's a sales rep that visits my clinic. He's been coming there for about a year. He's this mix of sexy bad boy on the outside and the sweetest guy you can imagine on the inside. He's so kind and thoughtful—"

"Yeah, yeah… get back to the sexy bad boy on the outside part. What's he look like?"

"He's tall. He has smoldering brown eyes and dark hair. He's got a smile made for a Colgate commercial and…"

"And what?"

"Well, when he first started coming to the office, he'd have to be present in the operating room in case there were any questions about the device he was selling. When he was scrubbing in one day, I was there to ask Dr. Stark about a patient and noticed the colorful tats on his arms. Gah! I've been fantasizing about seeing the entire art show ever since."

"Hmm. That does sound enticing. So how did the date go?"

"It was quick but great. He took me to Luigi's for lunch, but I couldn't stay very long. You know my stupid boss. God forbid, I enjoy one long lunch break. But Michael ordered ahead so we could spend as much time together as possible, and I'd still have time to eat. He even drove me back to work and went back to pay and get the leftovers so I wouldn't be late."

She raises a brow at me while wiping her face. "Wow. Okay, maybe he is kind and thoughtful. You deserve that, Ava. But I really hope he gives you the sexy bad boy stuff even more than the good guy routine. I can't wait for you to call and tell me someone's finally rocked your world."

"Uh, hmm."

My eyes slowly creep upward toward the snickering expression on Edward's face. Is he gloating that I've never gotten my world rocked? What is up with this guy?

"Is there anything else I can get you?" The asshole has the nerve to wink at me. *What the hell?*

"Just the check and some manners, please, Edward. Thank you," Eve interrupts.

The server walks away with a little less bravado as if he's won, catching us at a moment of weakness.

"I'll be right back," Eve advises as she shimmies off of her bench seat. She saunters over to the hostess stand and leans in to have a conversation with the young lady at the podium. The girl returns moments later with who I assume is the manager. I watch as Eve takes money from her purse and hands it to him, curious as to what she's up to. As she slides back into the seat, I await details as to what has just transpired, but nothing.

"Well?"

"Well, what?"

"What was that?"

"I just told the manager that I was so impressed with the food and the establishment that I wanted to present my tip in person."

My mouth drops open at this.

"I told him that everything had been perfect from the hostess to the food and the lovely setting."

I continue to look at her, mouth agape. Had some alien invaded her body?

"What? It's the truth. My food was great. I like the place. I enjoyed everything but the waiter who'd gone out of his way to antagonize us. I wasn't going to let the fact that Edward was on his period ruin my evening. I told him to make sure everyone but Edward received part of the tip and gave him a hundred dollar bill." She lifts her chin proudly. "I was going to use it to pay for our drinks later but decided it was more important to make a point." She takes one last nibble off of a french fry before wiping her hands on her napkin. "Guess I'm going to have to flash my boobs at a few unsuspecting guys at the bar now."

"Oh, god." I shake my head.

"I can be the better person. The rest of the folks shouldn't be penalized because Edward clearly didn't want to do his job well today. Now, come on, girly. Let's go get that margarita that has your name on it!"

Mick

Standing at the pitcher's mound, I try to get the attention of the fifteen kids running about the infield. It's like herding mice.

"Okay, guys. Let's get it together. The sun will go down before we even get practice started at this rate."

"What's the point, Coach Mick? It wouldn't matter if we practiced twice a day. We'll never win a game," a ten-year-old sporting a very worn baseball cap states emphatically.

"Yeah. We suck!" another faceless player shouts behind him.

"Awe, come on, guys. Look at the bright side. We've got nowhere to go but up!" I grab a couple of players, encouraging them to pair up in the outfield to throw balls to one another until I can make my way to them, then corral a few more to suit up for batting practice.

I'm the only coach who's committed to being here for this team on a regular basis. There are a few assistant coaches. Parents who were already planning to be here for some practices and games but not fully committed to the team as a whole as much as killing time while their son's here.

"Barton, suit up in the catcher's uniform," I yell across to the kid pouring red clay from the field into his sister's solo cup while her back is turned. *Jeez. What a mess.* Luckily, the season has barely started, but this team is at a significant disadvantage. Most have never played baseball before. Some have never participated in any organized sports. It's hard to discern if any of these kids possess any natural talent, as it's hard to get them to take practice serious enough to assess their skill.

What's more, no funds are coming in to help with uniforms or equipment. Most of the fundraisers have benefitted the older boys whose parents are more invested. Many of the kids on this team couldn't afford to pay the full-price league fee to participate. I've tried to work 'scholarships' into the process to underwrite some of the boys whose families couldn't otherwise afford to be here. It's a shame local little league sports have to be this expensive. I get the travel leagues fees. But every kid should have the opportunity to play if they want to. The downside, however, is that this team looks like the Bad News Bears.

I'm sure I could probably get one of the offices I call on to support the team by making a meager donation. It wouldn't take a lot to help get these boys in matching jerseys. But I don't want to do anything that would compromise my job. So, for now, we work with what we have.

If I have to, I'll go by some T-shirts at the craft store and make some damn uniforms myself.

"Ben, toss Marcus the ball. This is baseball practice, not lawncare 101." Ben just looks at me with a blank expression holding a handful of clover he's picked from the outfield.

"Tell me again why you put yourself through this," a gruff voice rumbles behind me.

I turn to see my best friend, Zach, and his dog, Otis. Zach is a domineering presence, standing almost two inches taller than my six foot three height. And he's a wall of muscle. His long hair is pulled back today, with a few stray strands dropping to his shoulders. A trail of colorful ink extends from his left sleeve. Zach spends his workdays with the fire department and his free time divided between the gym and the fishing hole.

"Come on, man. They're not that bad."

I watch him crook one eyebrow as he looks over my shoulder. Cringing, I slowly turn and follow his gaze to two boys who are in the outfield, pants down, each trying to pee farther than his opponent. *Fuck's sake. They're ten, not two.*

"Bryan, Sean, put your peckers away and get back to work. We're playing the Devil Dogs at the next game, and I can bet they aren't goofing off right now. This is serious business to them." The majority of the boys on that team are travel ballplayers in addition to playing little league. They're every bit as dedicated to the game as I was growing up. It's in their blood. I'm not really sure what's in these kids' DNA. As this thought crosses my mind, I hesitate to turn back around, knowing what's coming.

"Are you a glutton for punishment, or what?"

"Oh, shut up. They'll come around." I walk over to Otis to give him a scratch behind the ears, and the mutt rolls over to present his belly before I can start. Otis is one lucky bastard. A stray hound dog Zach took in years ago. Now, unless Zach's at work, they're practically inseparable. "This is one spoiled dog."

"Yeah, well." Zach shrugs.

I get it. It's only him and the dog. Might as well spoil it. Zach has sadly become quite the loner over the last few years. He barely resembles the larger-than-life boy I idolized growing up. But sometimes, life throws you curve balls you aren't ready to catch. Or, in Zach's case, a torpedo.

There wasn't a time I could remember when Zach wasn't in my life. Growing up, he lived right next door. My mother and his were best friends. Still are. A relationship that grew based on their shared circumstance. Both became single parents after their husbands walked away without a second glance. Mrs. Henry had been alone for several years before my father abandoned us. It felt as if Zach and his mother made it their mission to look out for us during those early transitional years. It was hard, but he gave me the male role model I needed.

Zach is almost twelve years my senior. He's always felt like the older brother I wish I'd had. He stayed in his family home as he prepared for the fire academy and remained a constant presence in my life. Even during our darkest days, as my dream career went up in smoke and his family life crumbled, ending in divorce, we tried to keep the lines of communication open.

But while I've tried to rejoin the living, coaching this team, and at least questioning taking a chance on a relationship, Zach stays put in his self-imposed exile. I don't push him. It's not worth risking that I could be the next casualty in his seclusion. It's his life, and he needs to decide what's best.

But for me, I'm growing tired of the isolation. I've never felt as alive as when I spent that lunch with Ava. I don't want to end up like Zach, lost and alone. I'm ready to live again.

CHAPTER SIX

Ava

God, this one's bad. It's been a long while since I've had a migraine so intense I had to renege on a commitment. Yet, here I am still in bed, lying in the dark. Allison, our office manager, was so kind when I called to tell her I might not make it in today. Somehow, I doubt Dr. Stark will be as understanding.

I've showered, taken several prescription migraine pills, and hydrated with so much water I think I could float. The headache has started to ease somewhat, so I contemplate my schedule and consider my options momentarily. If I go in at lunch, I only have three hours to see patients before I can turn my lights off and finish up my day. This could be doable. I'm sure my musing has nothing to do with the fact Mick is coming today. But what better medicine could there be?

Looking at the clock, I notice I have only forty minutes before Mick is due to arrive at the office. Jumping from the bed as if I'm suddenly on fire, I hastily dress, try to apply a little makeup to conceal the discomfort I'm dealing with, and race out of the door.

~

Practically sprinting into the clinic, I drop my things in my office and approach Joanie.

"Hi, love. You feeling any better?" she asks.

"Yes, a bit. I'm sorry I had to inconvenience anyone. When the headache started to ease off, I got here as fast as I could."

"Ava, don't be silly. You've managed to work around your headaches for so long. You push through when anyone else would've gone home. You're one of the toughest people I know. It's okay. You just missed Michael, though."

My face falls at this news before I can remember I have an audience.

"Yeah, I thought you might be sweet on him. He's awfully cute." She taps her finger against her chin with a knowing grin.

I can't help smiling back. "Yes, he is." The grin quickly fades as it dawns on me the one highlight of my day is gone. Damn headaches. Trudging back to my office, I try to make the best of the remainder of my afternoon and not focus on the fact that it'll now be another two weeks before I see that 'awfully cute' guy. Why hadn't he asked for my number at lunch that day? If I had his, I'd text him to let him know I'm here. Not too desperate, right? I have his business card from prior visits, but calling his work number feels a little over-eager. *Gah! The next two weeks can't go by fast enough.*

～

"Ava, would you mind joining me for lunch? I need to go over a few things with you, and I don't want to put this off. Unfortunately, my afternoon is full, so I can't do it later in the day." Dr. Stark asks from the doorway. Nothing he asks ever really feels like a question. It's more of a command he's waiting for me to acknowledge. *Tool.* I try not to laugh at the term of endearment Michael gave him.

The last thing I want to do is join this horrid man, but I feel like I owe it to him after bailing on my patients this morning. "Sure, Dr. Stark. Are you eating in your office or going to the physicians' lounge?"

"Neither. I'm headed to the cafeteria. Felt like something from the grill today. We can eat outside in the atrium." He waves his hand at me to pick up the pace.

As we approach the cafeteria, Dr. Stark heads for the grill line to grab his food, and I look for a table under the overhang to prevent direct sunlight. The combination of bright light and Joseph Stark are about the two worst things I can come up with to soothe a migraine. Luckily, the cafeteria line doesn't seem too long today, and it's only a few minutes later when I see him leaving his place in front of the cashier. I watch as he spots where I'm seated, carrying over his food and water. *Nice of him to ask if I wanted anything. Asshole.* I reach into my pocket and grab a peppermint. Removing the plastic wrap, I pop the minty treat into my mouth. Something tells me this interaction will bring on the need to hurl.

Before sitting down, Dr. Stark drags the black wrought iron chair across the cement and then lurches forward toward the table with his seat, creating a horrific sound in its wake. Is he completely unaware that I called out this morning due to a headache? Knowing this troll, he likely just couldn't give a shit. I mean, I've had them repeatedly over the years that I've worked with him. Never once has he asked if I was okay.

Joseph Stark is a menace. He doesn't hide the fact that he treats the male physician assistants quite differently than he treats me. I'm surprised he doesn't ask me to fetch his coffee for him each morning. He's probably worried one day I'll snap and put something in it. I'm shocked he's married. If he treats his wife the same way he treats the women here, well, I don't know why anyone would put up with him.

He takes a large bite of his sandwich before putting it down on the paper wrap in front of him. Placing one arm around the back of my chair, he leans in. The pungent odor of tuna melt on his breath practically smacks me in the face, and I try to focus on the peppermint in my mouth. "So, Ava, I was disappointed to hear we had to move several patients this morning. That's not like you to be so unprofessional."

My head abruptly snaps in his direction, mouth falling open in consternation at his statement. "Dr. Stark, I called out sick this morning because I had a debilitating migraine. It was so intense it wasn't safe to drive, much less provide optimal care to any patient I evaluated." I deliberately stop my rant to calm myself before continuing. "I'd thought I might need the entire day off, but when the pain eased a bit, I decided to come in so I could prevent having to reschedule any more patient appointments. I've worked here for years, and I've never called out sick." I hate that it happened. *But I'm only human, for God's sake.*

"I understand, Ava. I'm just saying that a little more notice might be appreciated. Most of these patients are people you're seeing in follow-up of surgery I performed. Your unprofessionalism can be a direct reflection on me." He digs into his foul-smelling lunch as if what he's said isn't the most magnanimous, insulting thing I've ever heard. *I'll try to plan in advance of an incapacitating migraine in the future.* "I'm sorry you weren't feeling well, but I felt it was my duty to remind you how your actions can affect my practice."

I suddenly feel his hand caressing my back, and I fight the urge to rip his arm off and shove it down his throat. *Maybe if I take a big whiff of his food, I can just barf on him and call it a win.* Whatever mild relief I'd received with my earlier attempts to medicate this migraine has completely evaporated. I'm sure the fact that I'm fuming isn't helping. I make a mental note to start considering other options for work if this behavior continues and hold my tongue for now. It certainly won't help my headache to go off on this asshole in the middle of the crowded atrium. And if my reaction to him continues to escalate, he's going to see yesterday's lunch in his lap whether I try to prevent it from happening or not.

Turning away from him, I try to count to five and take a cleansing breath in through my nose. *Focus on 5:00 p.m., Ava.* "I understand, Dr. Stark. Now, if you don't mind, I'm going to return to the office. I want to get a handle on the afternoon caseload before they arrive because I'm heading out immediately after my last patient of the day to get some rest." Standing up from the chair, I spin on my heel to get the hell away from this man before I tell him exactly what I think of him.

∾

Mick

Walking toward the Orthopedic office, I have a spring in my step that's been missing for weeks. I've been chastising myself. Why on earth hadn't I asked for Ava's number after that lunch date? It's been torture wanting to see her or hear her voice, knowing I had to wait until this appointment.

That date was over in a flash. I kicked myself immediately after getting back into my car for not asking for her cell number. But I was too preoccupied with the desire to lay one on her in the middle of the parking lot. Giving her a soft kiss on the hand seemed like the safest option out in the open. Hell, it'd be my luck that Joseph Stark would walk up on us and give her a hard time. For what? *Because he's an asshole, that's for what. Because he can.*

I was so excited to come here today, you'd have thought I was meeting the likes of Derek Jeter. Like any woman could rival my admiration for him. As far as I'm concerned, he's one of the greatest players of all time. Laughing at the absurd analogy, I shake my head.

I've tried to stay busier than usual, hoping time would pass more quickly. I visited my mom and my sister, met Zach and Otis at the fishing hole, and tried to jot down some drills to perform with my little league team to get them into gear at practice. I've also gone to the gym every day since our date, attempting to distract myself from the constant thoughts of her and dispel some of the extra energy. Well, that and jerking off. Despite that, I find I have more vigor than I can contain and decide to climb the steps to the clinic instead of taking the elevator. Reaching the top, I slow my roll so I don't look over-eager and take a deep breath before opening the door to the clinic.

"Hello, Joanie. How are you this fine afternoon?" I greet the always pleasant receptionist, unable to hide my joyful anticipation at seeing Ava.

"I'm great, Michael. You look chipper," she replies.

Tone it down, Mick. "Oh, it's just a beautiful day outside. What's not to be chipper about?" I try to cover. "Is Ava here? We have an appointment at 12:30."

"Oh, no." She hesitates momentarily as if she's unsure how to proceed. "She called out sick this morning. I'm sorry. I didn't think to let you know ahead of time. I should've called you."

"Oh. I'm sorry to hear that. I hope she's okay." My face falls. I realize I'm probably not masking my disappointment well.

"She'll be fine," she quickly returns, no evidence of concern. *What?* Her statement seems odd for someone who called out sick, particularly someone as sweet as Ava.

"Would you like me to reschedule with one of the other providers?" she prods.

"Um, wha—" My internal thoughts are distracting me from her questioning. I force myself to replay what she's just said. "Oh, no. I'll just come back in two weeks."

"All right, dear. Enjoy the rest of your day," she returns with a curious look on her face.

Yeah, right.

Taking the elevator to the first floor, I try to reorganize my day. I have another orthopedic practice at this hospital that's been flexible with visits in the past. I'll head there before proceeding to the OR to review the current inventory. I'm usually pretty regimented about my sales visits to make sure I can fit in all of the necessary stops each week. But this could work.

Having accomplished a lot despite the haphazard change in my schedule, I give myself a little pat on the back for knocking those things out despite my disappointment in the day's turn of events. *God, I was looking forward to seeing her. And getting her number. Maybe I'll call the office tomorrow and check on her. Tell her how sorry I was to hear she was sick and ask for her number.* As I walk down the hallway toward the adjoining building, I pass the cafeteria with a lift in my spirits at my new plan. Unexpectedly my stomach growls, reminding me of the hour. *Maybe I'll just stop and get a bottle of—*

Looking through the glass that separates the cafeteria seating from the outside courtyard, I notice Ava sitting with her back to me and rat bastard Joseph Stark sitting entirely too close, arm around her chair with his face practically buried in her hair. *What. The. Fuck?* Had I been given the brush off? Did she not want to deal with me today and so asked Joanie to tell me she was sick? My muscles all tense, and my once pangs of hunger are gone as my stomach lurches. Familiar waves of anger and rejection wash over me as I take in the ice princess and her arrogant mate.

That's what I get for taking a chance.

CHAPTER SEVEN

Ava

"Hey, cous." Carson bends down to offer a kiss to my cheek before sliding into the seat beside me. Placing his hand over mine, he gives it a gentle squeeze. "How've you been?"

"I'm okay. How are you? Time's really gotten away from us. We used to meet up regularly, but I feel like I've been letting our dinners slip because of my job."

"That bad, huh?"

"Hi. My name is Tabitha. I'll be your server. Can I get you anything to drink?"

"Hi, Tabitha." Carson winks. "I'll take a Grey Goose and tonic. And my cousin will have water. Thank you."

Oh, god. He's always on. "For goodness sake, can't you tone it down? You're not leaving here with her number, Carson."

"Who says? She's cute."

Ugh.

"So, you were saying. Is the job causing you to work longer hours, or is it just wearing you out?"

"The latter. I'm having a lot more headaches than ever before. I honestly attribute most of them to my surly boss. Most nights I come home, and I'm in bed by 8:00."

"Hell, Ava. You're only twenty-seven. Please don't turn into Aunt Carolyn."

"It's not like anyone chooses this, Carson. I've been doing pretty well, all things considered. I haven't had to go to the ER for any treatment in a long while. Up until recently, I'd never missed a day from work. And even then, I came in at lunch to try and prevent any more of the patients from being inconvenienced. Not that my boss appreciated it."

"What do you mean?"

"He basically shamed me for having the nerve to be so sick I'd have to miss work."

"Fucker. Give me his license plate number. I'll find a way to get him," he threatens. For all of his bravado with women and about his power as a police officer, I know my cousin. He'd never do anything sketchy. He's very upfront about his playboy status. If a woman gets her feelings hurt when he doesn't call back, that's all on her. And he loves his job and would never do anything questionable. He's wanted to be a police officer since we were kids and played cops and robbers. I recall desperately wanting to dress up in the police costume and use the plastic handcuffs with the little toy key, but Carson was always the cop. It was in the cards from the beginning.

"Oh, you'll do no such thing." I laugh.

The polite server returns with our drinks, quickly taking our entrée orders before returning to the kitchen. She's jubilant and professional, a stark contrast to Edward at the café recently. I shudder at the thought. Then again, this young lady may have already fallen under my handsome cousin's spell. *Lady killer.*

"So, how's your love life, Av? You finally let anyone special in?"

Taking a bite of my salad, I glance around the place. "Well, I'm not sure. I had a lunch date recently. It was here, as a matter of fact. It was a quick date on my lunch break."

"Oh, yeah. How'd that go?" he asks around a bite of lasagna.

"I thought it went great. He was so polite and charming. There was never a lull in our conversation. He works as a sales rep for a medical device company and has been visiting my office for about a year now. I've been interested for a while, so when he finally asked, I was thrilled."

Wiping his mouth, he drops the napkin to his lap, giving me his full attention. "Why does this feel like there's a but coming?"

"Well, that's just it. He seemed as excited about the afternoon as I was, saying he'd pull out all of the stops once more if I'd agree to go out with him again. We grinned at each other like teenagers the whole way back to my office. He kissed my hand, said goodbye, and I haven't heard from him since."

"What? That doesn't make any sense."

"I thought so too, but maybe I'm missing something. Is it odd he didn't ask for my number?"

"Well, sure. A little. But you said it was a quick date. Maybe the time got away from him, and he didn't think about it until after he left. But…"

"But, what?"

"He knows where you work. I'm just saying, Av. If it'd been me, I would've called there and asked for you or come by if I hadn't gotten your number. But then again, that's me. I'm a player. You know how my mind works. I'm always thinking ahead on how I can seal the deal."

Taking a sip of my water, I can't help but agree. I've considered this myself. If he'd really had that great a time with me and wanted to see me again, it wouldn't have taken much to get my number.

"Come on, Ava. Cheer up. I bet there's more to it. This guy sounds like he liked you. Maybe work's been tough for him too."

"Maybe. I think he travels for work also. So I guess that could be it. I was supposed to see him again the day I called out sick. By the time I got to work, I'd already missed him."

"Just be careful. Guys who travel…"

"Guys who travel, what?"

"Ava. A lot of guys who are out of town several days a week for their job like it that way. They can meet a different woman in every zip code. They don't have to worry with a relationship. If this does work out with him, just be careful. I know every guy isn't a player. But I don't want to see you hurt." Putting his fork down, he swivels slightly in his chair in order to face me. "If he hasn't tried any harder than this to reach out, it could be because you're more interested in this relationship than he is. Because he's getting his dick wet on the road, and you're just the local girl. I mean, if I liked a girl, I would've found a way to get in touch with her by now."

My brows scrunch together in a pained grimace, and I feel my stomach summersault. I hadn't considered this. Putting my fork down, I've suddenly lost my appetite.

"Babe. I could be wrong. I just want to warn you because you're too fucking nice. I don't want to see anyone take advantage of you." He lays his hand back over mine, and I try to swallow the lump in my throat.

"How are you enjoying everything—"

I look up, wondering what's interrupted this person's inquiry, when I notice Luigi standing beside our table. His expression is unreadable, but I'm aware he could be trying to place where we've met before.

"Luigi, hi. It's Ava. We met recently when Michael... I mean, Mick brought me here for lunch. I was telling my cousin, Carson, about it." I'm sure I've shared this detailed information too quickly, pointing at Carson as I rattle on, but I don't want to risk Luigi thinking I'm on some date with another man.

What appears to be relief now crosses his face as his serious expression relaxes into a kind smile. "Ah, Ava. I remember. It's hard not to remember such a beautiful girl. Thank you for joining us tonight." Luigi turns to Carson, extending a hand.

"It was fantastic, sir. Always is," Carson adds.

"Can I bring you a coffee or some dessert?"

"Oh, none for me. I need to be getting home."

"Well, speak for yourself. Could I have some tiramisu to go? I'll enjoy it this evening." Carson grins past Luigi at Tabitha, who is twirling her hair, making goo-goo eyes at him as she stands next to the hostess station. *Oh, good grief.*

"Of course, sir. I'll have Tabitha bring it right over. It was good to see you, Ava."

"Thank you, Luigi. You too."

As Luigi walks away, I reach over to grab my purse. "Do you mind terribly if I head out? I think I need to lie down."

"Oh, no. I didn't mean to upset you."

"No. It's okay. You were just being concerned. You're right. I have a habit of being a bit too naïve and trusting sometimes. The reminder is appreciated. I think the week's just caught up with me."

As I start to stand from my chair, I see Tabitha coming toward me with a white to-go box in her hand and hear Carson whisper, "Like taking candy from a baby. Think I can get her to feed it to me when she comes over later?"

Good lord.

～

I wake the following morning feeling out of sorts. Not only could I not shake the conversation I'd had with Carson over the 'local girl' possibility, I just didn't like feeling so out of control. I'm a strong, independent, modern-day woman. I don't need to sit back and wait for some prince to ride up on a white horse and pronounce that I've been selected as his significant other. If Michael is interested, he should say it. Carson's right. There's no reason he couldn't have reached out by now to the office. It wouldn't have taken much effort to call and ask to speak with me long enough to get my number.

I've showered and dressed, had a cup of tea, and still feel agitated. I consider my exhausting weeks of late and realize my routine has fallen to shit. I used to be very regimented about meditating and going to yoga. When had this stopped?

Grabbing my phone, I look through my contacts for my favorite yoga studio. The Hot House. They offer barre yoga for all skill levels. I enjoy the hot barre yoga. It could be the sensation that I'm cleansing my aura. But then again, I'm always cold, so there's that. Quickly hitting the button before I come up with an excuse not to, I pour another cup of tea as the phone rings.

"The Hot House. This is Liza."

"Hi, Liza. I know it's last minute, and a Saturday no less. But by any chance, do you have any yoga classes with availability today?"

"Hmm. Let me look." I can hear her tapping away at her keyboard as I sip my peppermint tea. "Yes, you're in luck. There's a hot barre class at 10. It's an advanced class. Is that okay?"

"Yes, I think I can handle that. I've been doing yoga for a long while. I'll be there. Thank you," I reply, disconnecting the call. Looking through my phone's calendar, I decide to schedule my next appointment before I leave to ensure I keep this healthy habit going. I feel much better when I meditate daily and include yoga in my regular routine. I'm not sure how I let this slip, but I decide it's mandatory if I'm to continue working with Stark and letting hot men play with my head.

~

Arriving at The Hot House, the place seems busier than I recall. Although, I don't usually come on a Saturday morning, opting instead to come before work when the studio's more serene. I check-in at the counter and head toward my class.

I still have several minutes before the lesson is underway, so I find a location in the center of the room and place my mat on the floor. Pulling my arms up over my head, I do a few stretches to prepare my limbs for the poses that will be occurring amidst the high heat of the space.

As I twist my trunk to elongate my spine, I catch a glimpse of an odd sight. It's rare to see anything beyond women clad in various shades and styles of lycra in this area. But at the rear of the room, a male, in his mid to upper thirties, I can only describe as *holy hell is he hot,* is sitting on a yoga mat. He's sporting a five o'clock shadow, dark inky hair, and deep blue eyes that would almost rival mine. I realize I've been caught staring when I witness an eyebrow rise in my direction and a tantalizing dimple pops from beneath his dark whiskers. I quickly spin around to face the front of the class before my imitation of a human tomato returns.

Reaching for my water bottle, I take a large gulp. Not only has seeing this Adonis behind me gotten me flushed, but the temperature in the room is starting to affect me. The class hasn't even begun, and I'm already a hot mess.

"Good morning, class. I'm Jade. Welcome to advanced barre yoga."

We offer good mornings in unison before Jade thankfully gets the class underway. At least I'll have something positive to focus on while I'm here. I assume the first pose, watching Jade closely. The heat is starting to really catch up with me. With each new position, I can feel the intense stretch as the sweat trickles down my skin.

Over and over, as if on repeat, I contort my body in ways that should feel unnatural, then release the pose to allow increased circulation while ridding toxins from my body. I love how I can get lost in the experience, focused only on my breathing and the pull of my taught muscles instead of the constant stressors and insecurities at war with my brain.

But the best part of yoga for me is the steady release of feel-good hormones. The delivery of endorphins, dopamine, and serotonin brings happiness. A sensation of joyfulness that's hard to describe. However, today feels different than the last few visits.

I'm feeling proud of myself for keeping up with the complicated poses until I turn and catch sight of the man candy behind me and realize I've been bent forward much of the time I'm here, with my ass as his primary view. *Ugh.* Well, it's yoga, and he chose to sit there. Hmm, is that why he's here? No. Certainly, he wouldn't have signed up for an advanced class with poses of this intensity in a sweltering room just to pick up women. Hell, that guy could get lucky while standing in the drug store aisle buying cream for jock itch.

"And relax," Jade instructs. Her voice makes me suddenly aware I've been stuck in my own head. Wow. This class went by faster than expected. I try to sit still, taking some cleansing breaths before I gather my things and head to the showers. As I stand, I can't help but look over my shoulder. But the class's star pupil is no longer behind me. Turning my head, I notice he's at the front of the room, surrounded by women. *Go figure.* Our eyes lock briefly, and he gives me a saucy wink, again confirming he's caught me looking. I no longer have to worry with the color of my face giving my embarrassment away, as the heat and the constant exertion have caused my entire body to look like a walking Twizzler. I'll probably be red from head to toe until hours after I shower.

I intentionally wait until the surprise hottie and his harem have departed before exiting the space. Between his antics and the conversation with Carson last night, I'm questioning why I'd want to even consider entering into a relationship with a hot traveling salesman. The scenario is ripe for constant apprehension unless I decide to trust him. But what's the alternative? Begin a relationship with someone you aren't attracted to? Have no chemistry with? Or take a chance and hope for something electric?

I don't want to be a doormat, but I'm tired of living in fear. Carson's right. I just need to be aware of the possibility, but that doesn't mean I shouldn't put myself out there. All men aren't unabashed hot yoga playboys or single police officers looking to pick up their next sweet treat.

I stand in the cool shower, trying to bring down my body's temperature as well as let go of the images of attractive men only looking to score. The yoga and the heat have caused me to feel electric. You'd think I'd be exhausted by what I just put my body through. Yet, I feel the opposite. I'm wound up. As the water trickles over my skin, there's a buzz. It's as if I'm hyperstimulated. I'm sure it has nothing to do with the hot guy in class and everything to do with the hormones my body's releasing.

My hands drift down my hot skin, spreading body wash over my sensitive flesh. I suddenly picture Michael's hands doing the same. Running down my arms, gliding sudsy soap over my supercharged body. Stopping to tease my responsive nipples and caress my hypersensitive breasts, I imagine him applying shampoo to my hair and massaging my scalp before turning me to face him and devouring my neck, my mouth, my collarbone. As I can feel the thrumming between my legs, I have to get myself together. I can't believe I've let these images taunt me in a public place. But I want him. I've never been so attracted to anyone. I've never felt the chemistry I experience with Mick.

Turning the temperature a bit cooler, I need to get myself together.

As I stand under the now frigid water as it strikes my hair and skin, I suddenly feel a renewed sense of power. If I really want this guy, I need to put myself out there. The next time he's scheduled to visit the office, I'm going to be ready. I'm not going to mince words. He's going to know how much I enjoyed our date. That I'm interested in more. Then I'll leave it up to him where we go from there.

I'm not going to beg. And if he's not interested, I'll walk away with my head held high. But I refuse to end up all alone like my mother. All because I was too afraid to take a chance.

CHAPTER EIGHT

Ava

It's been a month. A solid freaking month since I last saw Mick. I can't believe how much I've missed him. The day I arrived late to work following my migraine had been a bear. Every day since had been more of the same. Busy days with the constant looming of Dr. Stark around me like a pesky fly at a spring picnic. Continually imparting his uninvited opinion and pressing for me to perform additional work. I've enjoyed working with this practice, but if his behavior keeps up, I'm going to have to look for something else.

My thoughts are immediately brought back to the here and now as my phone dances across the desk. Momentarily, my heart speeds up, thinking it could be him. Then I remember he doesn't have my cell number. Looking at the screen, my face brightens at the sight of Eve's pretty face on my screen.

"Hey, girl. What're you doing calling me mid-day? Did they actually give you guys a break today?"

"Ha! We've had a little downtime today. The professor for my last class was out sick, and they couldn't find a replacement in time. You'd think someone told us we all won the lottery. I'd never seen so many grown-ass people try not to hoot and holler!" She almost squeals at her unexpected delight. "I called to tell you my news. I got it!"

"What? The ER rotation you wanted here at St. Luke's?"

"Yes. I'm so excited, Ava. I know it's just a six-week clinical rotation and with it only being my second clinical, I won't have the ability to impress anyone. But this feels like a game-changer for me. Like all of the hopes for this to happen one day are finally coming true."

"Oh, Eve. You're going to impress them just fine. You're a hard worker, and you'll jump right in and be willing to do whatever procedures they have available. If you can just manage to keep that sassy mouth shut until you land the job, you're all set." I giggle.

"You're not wrong." She chuckles. "I know I won't get to see much of you, being so busy there. But I hope if I'm ever doing a day shift, we can meet after work for dinner. I'm so excited about this, Ava."

I can practically feel her exuberance through the phone line. I'm so tickled for her. "Oh, Eve, we'll make sure it happens. If not, we'll plan it on our day off so I can hear all about how it's going."

"Okay. I have to go. There are a bunch of us going to lunch to celebrate our short-lived freedom from our orthopedic lecture."

"Hey. I resemble that remark."

"Oh, sorry. There goes my mouth again. I'm sure it's completely different there, Ava. It's just sitting in this class all day—"

"Oh, honey. I'm teasing. I completely get it." And some days, it's *not* completely different here. But it all seems so much more exciting when you're still in school. "Go enjoy your lunch. And thanks for sharing your news. I can't wait to see you in scrubs and a lab coat. I'll be so proud."

"Thanks, Ava. Bye."

Hanging up the call, I make a mental note to text her regarding her graduation date and ask off for the Friday before. Wouldn't want to wait until the last minute, and suddenly Dr. Stark says it's too late to have the day off because he's already claimed it for himself.

Knock, knock.

My head flies up immediately, wondering if somehow I'd lost all track of time. I barely catch sight of Joanie at my door before I'm looking down at my watch.

"Oh, it's not time yet, dear."

Busted. "Oh. Yeah, sorry."

"A little excited to see him, are you?"

"Yeah. More than a little. I feel pretty silly about it. I mean, I think this is probably one-sided. That lunch date with him was amazing. It's not like he doesn't know where I work. If he were interested, he would've called here. Maybe between the fact he hasn't and that he didn't ask for my number that day... well, I need to face he's not interested."

"Oh, beautiful girl. If you'd seen the way he looked when he practically skipped into this office two weeks ago for his appointment with you. When I had to tell him you'd called out sick, it was like watching a hot air balloon deflating. It broke my heart, the timing of that darn migraine."

"Really? You're not just saying that to make me feel better?"

"No, Ava. That boy really has a thing for you. I just know it. I'm rooting for you two," she adds with a sweet, fairy godmotherly expression.

I can feel my cheeks pink and reach up to feel the instant warmth there. "Thank you. I hope you're right."

"Now. The reason I came in here. Allison and I were talking. The weather has turned absolutely beautiful, and we tossed around the idea of going to a Flying Squirrels game. You know, like a girls' night. Nothing better than a gorgeous evening, good girlfriends, and some hot guys in baseball uniforms."

Oh my god. I wasn't expecting that from her. Joanie's almost old enough to be my mother. But everything about this sounds great.

"Yeah, I'm in. I'd love to go with the two of you. Are you guys big baseball fans or something?"

"No. Allison scored a few tickets in a giveaway basket for a little league fundraiser. I couldn't care less about sports. But the uniforms..."

I can't help laughing out loud. "Well, thank you for including me. I can't wait."

"Okay. I'll let Allison know. I best get back to my desk."

As Joanie returns to the front of the clinic, I think about my favorite baseball player and swoon. God, I've missed him. It feels like the longest month of my life since that lunch date. I feel my heart rate pick up as I recall getting dressed for work this morning with renewed vigor. You would've thought I was going on a blind date, instead of my usual day's work at an orthopedic clinic, the way I was laying out clothes on my bed trying to find just the right outfit for the day. I'd chosen a light blue V-neck top that clung to my chest a little tighter than I normally preferred for work attire and the same navy blue pencil skirt from our date. I'd caught the look on Mick's face as I slid my legs into his car that day and had to bite my lip at his reaction. It didn't take a rocket scientist to see he appreciated the view. Today Mick is scheduled to return, and nothing is going to prevent me from seeing him.

Looking at my watch, I note it's 12:20. Mick's always early, so I take a chance and glance out into the waiting room. There are a few people scattered in chairs, left waiting for their loved ones to exit their appointments, I suppose. But no one matching the description of a hot, dark-haired, smooth-talking baller in a business suit.

"Can I help you with something, Ava?" Joanie flashes me a knowing glance. *Gah, busted again.*

Giggling, I feel a flush cover my cheeks as I look back at her. "Um, just checking to see if Michael's arrived yet. Didn't want to make him wait." There's no sense pretending. Good grief, I'm acting like a girl with a high school crush instead of a grown-assed, independent woman. *What is happening to me?*

"Well, I'll send him right back." She smirks.

Turning back to my office, I sit down at my desk, trying to control my silly schoolgirl nerves. My hands are actually sweaty. When had I ever felt this way about a boy? No boy, or man, had ever filled my thoughts as he has. I try to calm the jitters by lying back in my chair and closing my eyes momentarily. I recall the vision I'd enjoyed last night of Mick grabbing me to him with his strong arms, pulling me against his chest before planting his delectable mou—

"Hi, Ava. Joanie said to come straight back."

The timbre of his voice causes my stomach to flutter. Jeez,

everything about this man makes me weak. What I'd give to have that sexy voice rumbling in my ear as he fondles me. "Mmmm—"

"Uh, hm."

My eyes fly open as the utterance interrupts my saucy thoughts. Mick's standing by my door, with an odd expression on his face. Disoriented by the disrupted fantasy, I rub my legs with my clammy palms and try to gather my senses.

"Hi. I'm sorry. I didn't hear you come in." I jump up from my seat and round my desk to stand in front of him in anticipation... of what, I'm not sure. I look up at him in awe. God, he's so handsome. He has his contacts in and his hair seems more tousled today. I fix my gaze on his molten eyes. But they look different, somehow. Almost hollow.

I watch as he pulls the signature form from his briefcase and reaches around me to lay it upon the desk. "No questions, I assume."

Startled by his flat affect and my apparent solo feelings of excitement over this meeting, an anxious feeling settles over me. There's a sick feeling in the pit of my stomach replacing the arousal there only moments ago. Am I getting the brush off? How could I have gotten this so wrong? Jeez, men usually waited until they slept with me before they gave me the cold shoulder.

"Mick? Is there something wrong?"

I watch as a blank stare is returned to me. *What the hell? Were we even on the same date?*

Puzzled, I continue. "I was excited you were coming to the office today. I've really missed you. I was so upset when I got here after you'd left a few weeks ago when I wasn't feeling well."

I watch as a peculiar expression crosses his face, one brow lifting in an almost menacing countenance. He stands rigid, continuing to remain painfully silent in front of me. *What is happening here? Have I done something?*

"It's so not like me to call out. I didn't think I'd make it to work that day, but I started to feel a bit better and didn't want to miss seeing you. I think I broke every speed limit trying to get to the office just to find you'd already left." His expression is flat. I'm trying not to plead. *What's wrong? Talk to me.* "Joanie said I'd just missed you. I was so disappointed," I continue. I pour out my explanation, rapid-fire. Still nothing. I need to stop this. I've done nothing wrong. Had he met someone else and that lunch was a one-off?

I give it one last attempt before I need to face the music. "I had to spend my lunch with Dr. Stark instead of you." I try to make a silly gagging face, demonstrating my disgust at eating with smarmy Stark to lighten the mood. His shoulders seem to relax a bit, and I have renewed hope whatever's bothering him is improving.

Lifting his hand, running it through his gorgeous artfully disheveled dark strands, he finally looks me in the eyes. "I'm sorry you weren't feeling well. It's good to see you too, Ava."

"Ava, I had to add another patient to your caseload before lunch," Dr. Stark rudely interrupts my long-awaited visit with Mick. I watch as his gaze bounces from me to Mick and back again. A look of irritation now notable on his stern face. "I'll sign whatever Michael needs."

My mouth drops open at this unwelcome change in events. I've waited a solid month to see this man, and this isn't going at all how I planned. I spent an hour getting ready this morning, picking the perfect outfit. I'm finally recovering from the fact he didn't immediately sweep me into his arms and kiss me like I'd been hoping. Instead, I take solace in getting him to finally speak to me only to have this asshole barge in and ruin everything.

"They're patiently waiting for you in exam room three," Dr. Stark interjects.

My eyes bounce from Dr. Stark to Mick, and frustration takes over. I feel defeated. Angry, disappointed, and defeated.

"Sure, Dr. Stark," I say as I head toward the door. I need to face the music. This day isn't going to end as I wanted. No sweet, brief interlude with my dream man. No phone numbers exchanged. Just more disappointment. Turning slightly, I let out a quiet, "Bye, Michael." Unable to make eye contact with him before heading to room three.

I can't let him see the tears I'm trying to push back. No one gets to see me hurt. I've at least got my pride. I made it abundantly clear how I felt. If there's going to be anything beyond business with this traveling salesman, he better make it very clear next time or I'm done with these games.

CHAPTER NINE

Ava

"Ava, Dr. Stark just called. He asked if you could bring some more of his business cards to the OR," Joanie states knowing every bit as much as I do, this is not really a question.

"I have a patient in ten minutes," I respond dejectedly.

"I know. I told him that. He said you'd better make it quick then." She scowls while repeating his usual ostentatious directive.

"Fine. I guess the brisk walk will do me good, right?" I'm trying desperately to maintain a positive outlook in spite of this despicable man. "I'll head over and be right back. Could you make my apologies to Mr. Brown if I'm late?"

"Of course, Ava. Don't rush. He'll understand."

I head into Dr. Stark's office and grab a handful of cards from the holder at the corner of his desk. I'm not about to waste any time rummaging through his things looking for the box of cards. This should hold him until he gets back and can get more. Walking swiftly down the hallway to the stairwell, I fly down the two floors to the bottom, knowing I'd still be standing by the elevator doors otherwise.

As I traverse the bustling corridor that leads to the surgical wing, I smile and wave at a few familiar faces.

"Hey, Ava. Long time no see."

"Hey, Ryan. Yeah, I don't get out of the office as much as I'd like. I had to bring Dr. Stark some business cards. I guess he gives them to family to contact him with any questions. Do you know what OR suite he's scheduled to be entering?"

"Ah, let me look."

I follow the tall, blond-haired surgical tech I've known for several years toward a large dry erase board that's mounted on the wall. The various operating room suites are listed along with patient last names, times of surgery, the procedure to be performed, and the surgeon. As I'm looking for Dr. Stark's name, I feel an odd presence to the right. Turning my head slowly, my eyes connect with a tall man dressed in scrubs and a blue surgical gown, all gloved and ready to enter his OR suite to begin a case. What is it about that guy that looks so familiar? Even from here, I can make out the deep blue eyes. Not much else is visible past the mask and surgical cap he's wearing. It's odd, really. This isn't some quick look to check out someone new in the hallway. His gaze is penetrating.

"Did you hear me, Ava?"

"Um, what?"

"I said Dr. Stark is in OR 4."

"Oh, okay. Thanks, Ryan."

Looking back over my shoulder before heading toward Dr. Stark's surgical suite, I notice the unknown surgeon must've entered to begin his case as there's no one standing by the sinks any longer. Shrugging my shoulders at the odd encounter, I head in the direction of my nemesis.

Lifting the business cards from my pocket, I realize the card Michael had left is sitting on top. Joanie had given it to me after he left last week with a mischievous look in her eye. Grinning at the hope things could be back on track between us, I pop it back into my lab coat and make a mental note to place it in my purse when I return to the office.

~

"Hey, Joanie. I got back as fast as I could."

"You're fine, Ava. Mr. Brown was late himself. Bonnie just took him back to the exam room. Take a minute to catch your breath. I don't want you wearing yourself out. We have a game to get to tonight."

I perk up a bit at this, having almost forgotten due to my chaotic morning. "Oh, I can't wait, Joanie. Who knew I'd get so excited about a baseball game? I simply haven't done anything fun in a while, beyond dinner and drinks with friends. I'm so thankful you guys included me."

"Me too. It'll be fun. Are you meeting us there or did you want to ride with Allison and me after work?"

"No, I'll meet you. I didn't bring a change of clothes with me this morning. But my last patient is at 3:00 so I'll have plenty of time." Walking toward exam room three, I take a deep breath and collect myself before knocking on the door. "Hi, Mr. Brown. It's nice to see you."

The day has continued to move at a fever's pitch, running from one patient to another as if I'm running the bases, desperately trying to slide into home. Home would be 4:30 p.m. Quitting time. Today's typical of any day when Dr. Stark's scheduled in the OR. It's as if he has Joanie double-book my patients to include his. But I've tried to remain focused on the evening in front of me. I'm not letting Joseph Stark or any other man get in the way of my having a carefree girls' night.

"Ava, could you come here a moment?" Dr. Stark calls from down the hall.

What? It's 4:20. I was so close to making a clean getaway. I briskly walk to his office, hoping I can take care of whatever this is and head out so I have time to get home and change before heading to the ballpark.

"I wanted to introduce you to Dr. Lee. He's a hand specialist at Mary Immaculate but is generous enough to come to St. Luke's to offer his services when Dr. Morgan's out, or there's a case that'd benefit from his expertise." Dr. Stark rattles off this information as if Dr. Lee's about to begin a lecture. I reach out my hand, hoping to make this short and sweet until my blue eyes meet his. *Holy shit. This is the guy from—*

"Yoga girl."

"What?" I ask, stunned momentarily. This is obviously the surgeon from earlier today.

"I think you may have been in a yoga class I attended recently," he adds. There's a sauciness about his greeting. His voice is deep and rich, and there's the hint of a dimple in his left cheek. Everything about this man screams player.

"Oh. Yes. I think you're right." I notice an odd expression on Dr. Stark's face and decide to make a quick exit, so he doesn't have to worry that this sexy surgeon will be an issue for me. "It was nice meeting you, Dr. Lee. I'm heading out, Dr. Stark. I'll see you in the morning." With this, I turn and exit before he has a chance to interrupt. His behavior tends to be a little better in front of strangers, so I'm hoping I can use this to my advantage.

Grabbing my things, I dart for the door. "Bye, Joanie. Meet you guys at the gate at 6:00."

"We'll see you there, dear."

Mick

Heading to the reception area, I shake my head. I don't know what to make of this. Ava seemed genuinely excited to see me. Could she have been telling the truth about missing me? God, I really like this girl. But seeing her with Dr. Dick in the courtyard fucking hurt. I have no right to be possessive. We've had one date. She honestly doesn't seem to be the type to string a guy along, but neither did Paula. Obviously, my radar on such things is not finely tuned.

Before I can think better of it, I stop at the desk and ask Joanie if she can give Ava my business card since we were interrupted.

"Did no one sign your form Michael?"

"No, Dr. Stark signed for me," I answer hesitantly, unsure how to explain why I'm leaving the card for her. Quickly jotting my personal cell number on the back, I hand it to the inquisitive receptionist. "In case she has something come up in the future and needs to reschedule." I smile, more at thinking quickly on my feet than for being polite. I feel good about this recovery until I watch Joanie flip the card over and notice a smirk on her face as she looks back up at me. *Busted.*

"Got it. I'll make sure she gets it, Michael," she adds with a teasing wink.

~

"Michael, it's good to see you," Luigi greets as I walk toward the bar.

Shaking his outstretched hand, I take a seat. "I ordered takeout on the way here. I'm sure it's not ready yet. It's good to see you too. How've you been?"

"Good. Business is very good."

"Oh, I wanted to thank you again for the donation of the dinner for two for the little league fundraiser. It was very generous of you."

"I was happy to do it. I think it's great what you are doing for those kids. Was it successful?"

"The fundraiser? Yes. I got my sister, Emmaleigh, and my mom to make gift baskets we raffled off. They all did better than expected. I think the one with your dinner and the Flying Squirrels giveaway earned us the most money. At least I can get the boys matching hats and some much-needed equipment."

A server dressed in a starched white shirt and black vest brings a to-go bag to the bar that smells heavenly. It'll be a chore not tearing into the veal piccata before I get home.

"Looks like your food is ready," Luigi says, inspecting the ticket. "Here you go. Enjoy."

"Thank you. I will."

"You know what would go well with that?" Luigi interrupts as I'm pulling my credit card out of my wallet.

"A good red?"

"No, a fair blonde."

Stopping with my card mid-air, I look at his serious expression.

"She was in here the other night, you know. Your girl."

"Oh," I answer curiously.

"And she wasn't alone."

I can feel my brows pull together in a scowl. It's one thing to have your suspicions, but to have it confirmed—

"Don't go thinking the worst, son. She almost tripped over her own tongue trying to introduce the young man. Her cousin, I believe. She seemed almost frantic to clear the air."

The immediate relief at his statement takes me by surprise. Why had one date with this girl had such an effect on me?

"Haven't you two been seeing each other?"

I just shake my head. Unable to explain why I haven't tried harder to reach out to her and how stupid I feel at letting my insecurities get the best of me.

"I've been working here a long time, Michael. I'd like to think my place is very romantic. I see a lot of couples enjoying a special occasion here. Some first dates, sure. But you two. I don't think I've seen a couple so drawn to one another. I worried you wouldn't have a chance to eat for all of the talking and smiling you two were doing."

"Oh, so you watched the whole thing, did ya?" I laugh awkwardly.

"Not the whole thing. Enough. Don't let that one get away, son. I think there's something magical between you. You reminded me of my Maria and our first date."

"Well, that obviously worked out well."

"Thirty-seven years and counting. Ah, go home. Your food will get cold." He slaps me on the shoulder and walks away before I can say another word.

~

It's been a week since I've seen Ava, and she hasn't left my thoughts. Am I making a mistake by even entertaining another date with her? Maybe I should just clear the air about what I saw. But I don't want to come off as some possessive stalker. *We've had one fucking date.* Hell, she probably hasn't thought about me since I left her office, regardless of what Luigi thought he saw.

But she did seem pretty excited to see me before we were so rudely interrupted by Dr. Dick. I don't know what to think anymore. Who knows if she even received the business card I left? Internally, I struggle with this as Joanie seems like a meddlesome woman, and I can't imagine she wouldn't have taken great joy in pointing out my number on the flip side of that card when she presented it to Ava.

Lying in this generic hotel room in southwest Virginia, I lie back in the bed with my head propped up on several pillows. There's always a game on, but I find I'm too preoccupied to enjoy it. Usually, I'd be searching the bar for a different distraction. However, I haven't been interested in looking for pussy when all I can think about is Ava. Does she ever think of me when she's alone?

Taking a swig of my nearly empty beer, I place the bottle down on the bedside table and shrug off my pants and shirt. Climbing into the bed, I lie back down and remember how sweet Ava looked when she made that silly face of disgust regarding having lunch with Stark.

I'm choosing to believe her. I have no reason to doubt her beyond my own misgivings. She seemed flushed when I first arrived at her office. Was she still feeling bad? I'd managed to control my physical response to her until she practically ran around her desk to greet me. Having her beautiful body so close was perplexing. I was angry at what appeared to be her dismissal of me, but my body was on high alert. She smelled heavenly. Not as much of a minty aroma as it was fresh. Her pheromones probably smell like the arrival of a first winter's snow. Clean, crisp, beautiful. Making you want to snuggle up with her to keep warm. *Good lord. What's happening to me? I'm officially losing it.*

It was a struggle to keep one hand in my pocket and the other on my briefcase with her so close to me. I recall wanting to grab her and pull her to me, bite that succulent lower lip and slide my tongue into her sweet mouth.

Lying in this bed, recounting memories from that odd day, elicits more arousal than awkwardness. I can feel myself growing hard, as I always do when alone with my thoughts of her. This is nothing new, as jacking off to visions of my sweet Elsa has become commonplace. I can picture her pale skin, imagine her sweet dusky nipples, and her swollen, pink pussy all laid out for me. A buffet beyond the likes of anything Luigi could offer up. I pull rigorously at my hard cock as I picture her plump, soft, pink lips wrapped around my shaft. God, what I'd give to fuck her mouth. My dick is so engorged, it's becoming painful. Reaching down, I use my left hand to cup my balls and stroke my pulsating cock with my right.

My mind shifts gears, picturing her on her back, her long blonde locks tousled about her on the pillow. I fist my cock harder, pretending she's underneath me as I pump my dick and reach out to stroke her soft, wet folds. I won't last a minute once I'm nestled into her hot center. Lining myself up, I push in and picture her face awash with endorphins. Fuck, what I'd give to see her come while my heavy cock was nestled deep inside her. Spreading my legs wide, I pick up the pace, beating my swollen rod with ferocity now. I'm nearly there. *Fuck, this girl.* Feeling the pressure build, I know I'm about to unload. In my mind, I watch as I withdraw from her tight body and spurt ropes of come across her pale chest and belly, marking her. Attempting to slow my ragged breaths after another lonely climax I've given myself, I peer down at the mess I've made. I've never had difficulty finding a warm body to share my evenings with while I'm away. Yet it appears I now prefer the visions of the ice princess to real-life orgasms with anyone else.

Ten minutes later, I return from the shower and think I might finally be able to doze. As I reach for the bedside lamp, I notice there's a message lit on my phone. Worried my mom has attempted to reach me while I've been preoccupied with fantasies of *Elsa*, I quickly open the phone and check for any missed calls.

Returning to the messaging app, I open it to find a picture. Ava's sitting beside Joanie and another woman I don't recognize wearing a Flying Squirrels T-shirt and a radiant smile. Her hair is pulled up in a high ponytail, and there's a bit of pink staining her cheeks. The Richmond Flying Squirrels are a minor league double-A club affiliate of the San Francisco Giants. While not the big leagues, attending their games is still a lot of fun. They tend to be more engaging, with lots of crazy antics and giveaways for the fans. Finally able to pull away from the vision of this woman's face on my phone, I look underneath the picture at the text.

Ava Kennedy
8:20 p.m.
Ava: I wish you were here. No, really. I don't know a thing about baseball. Winky face emoji.

I cannot stop the grin from taking over my face. This girl. She *was* thinking about me. Well, obviously not the same way I was thinking about her. I try to gather my thoughts before attempting to text her back.

10:20 p.m.
Mick: I'd be happy to teach you. Wish I was there too.

I decide to leave off the eggplant emoji and put my phone down before I risk saying anything inappropriate. Thankful for the unexpected end to my day, I turn off the lights and head to sleep with a goofy grin on my face.

CHAPTER TEN

Ava

It feels like forever since Mick's been to the office. I couldn't stop thinking about him at the Flying Squirrels game last night.

The evening had been such fun. Our seats were great, close to the field, between home plate and first base. We had an amazing view of the players as they traversed back and forth from the dugout and prime placement for catching various objects shot out to the fans from the team mascot. A hot dog practically bounced off of my head into the lap of a fan above me at one point.

Joanie and Allison really let loose when they're out for a good time. I think I laughed more at their shenanigans than I have in a very long time. Who'd have thought these two mild-mannered married women from the office, one with a grandchild on the way, could be so raucous? They had no trouble voicing their delight as the players would exit the dugout one by one to take their turn at-bat. Apparently, while Allison's big into muscular athletes, Joanie's an ass man. They rated each player as if they were unknowingly starring in a *Mr. Baseball* cover model contest. I've never laughed so hard.

Yet all the while, it was Mick I was imagining on the field. I kept trying to picture him, decked out in a baseball uniform. Other than in scrubs a long time ago, I've never seen him in anything but a suit. Oh, what I'd give to see him in tight baseball pants, his muscular arms on display. And I bet he looks hot in a baseball cap. Suddenly, I feel my skin warm. *Gah. Is it hot in here?*

I've finished cleaning up after dinner and brought a new book to bed. I admit I can't help but picture a dark-haired, strong-jawed, muscular ex-ballplayer as the hero of this story. Given the steam is starting to pick up in this billionaire office romance, I can't help but let my mind wander to what it'd be like to fall into bed with Mick.

I'm no virgin, but I haven't had the most adventurous sex life. I don't do the one-night stand thing, so it's been a while. When I dated my last boyfriend, the sex was okay. Much like the men before him, it was simply a release with someone other than my battery-operated boyfriend. *While my B.O.B can always get me there, I'd like a little more dirty talk.* But I've never been with anyone like Mick before. I can imagine a night with him would top anything I've ever experienced.

Bᴢᴢᴢ. Bzzz.

Grabbing my phone from the nightstand, I'm shocked when I take in the greeting.

Michael York
9:20 p.m.
Mick: Hi.

I read the message again. Ensuring I'm not imagining this. It's as if he knows I've been thinking about him. I guess it shouldn't be surprising he's texting while he's on my mind. Lately, he's always on my mind.

9:22 p.m.
Ava: Hi.

Michael York
9:25 p.m.
Mick: I hope it isn't too late. I couldn't stop thinking about you.

9:29 p.m.
Ava: No, not too late. I was just thinking about you too.

Michael York
9:32 p.m.
Mick: Oh yeah. What were you thinking about?

9:38 p.m.
Ava: Um, I'm embarrassed to tell you.

Michael York
9:40 p.m.
Mick: What? Now I must know.

9:44 p.m.
Ava: When I was at the game last night, I kept trying to picture you in one of those baseball uniforms.

Michael York
9:50 p.m.
Mick: Is that so?

9:54 p.m.
Ava: Yes. I only see you in business suits. You can't blame me for picturing you out of them.

Michael York
9:58 p.m.
Mick: That's fair. I've pictured you out of your clothes plenty of times.

Wow. Wasn't expecting that. I'm not sure how to respond to this. We've only had one date so far. I'm not sure that I'm ready for sexting.

Michael York
10:10 p.m.

Mick: You're beautiful, Ava. I hope I haven't offended you. But I'd have to be blind not to picture what you look like naked.

10:12 p.m.
Ava: Saying thank you to that feels weird. Laughing emoji.

Michael York
10:13 p.m.
Mick: Occasionally, I picture you wearing something.

10:16 p.m.
Ava: Oh, yeah. Wearing what?

Michael York
10:19 p.m.
Mick: Me.

Gulp. Okay, so at least I know we're on the same page here. But I'm not sure I want to
encourage this to go any farther just yet. Hell. I want a real kiss before I start touching myself to dirty texts.

Michael York
10:25 p.m.
Mick: I'm sorry, Ava. Have I upset you?

10:30 p.m.
Ava: No. I've pictured the same thing. Just embarrassed to admit since we've only had one date. I haven't even kissed you yet.

Michael York
10:33 p.m.
Mick: Well, I need to take care of that then. Good night, Ava.

Putting down my phone, I close my book and slink into the bed linens. I can't stop smiling. Staring up at the ceiling, I think, *how am I supposed to sleep now?*

~

"Joanie, I've got to run down to the ER for about thirty minutes to see a patient of Dr. Stark's. Please tell Michael I'll try to get back as soon as I can. I didn't bring anything for lunch today and need to stop by the physician lounge on the way, but I'll make it quick."

"Oh, Michael already called ahead and said he was bringing lunch for the office today. And don't worry, Ava. I'm sure he'll wait as long as he needs to see you." She beams.

I feel a blush hit my cheeks. "Wow. That's so nice of him. Well, I'll try to be fast."

Taking the stairs to the ground floor, I head for the emergency department. I have to admit, I get a thrill whenever I'm able to evaluate an acute orthopedic patient in that setting. Most of my patients are pretty run-of-the-mill. They've either done what they were asked to do to ensure proper healing, or they didn't. Sure, occasionally, there'll be a patient with an unexpected post-op course. They may develop an infection at the surgical site or have some nerve damage. But for the most part, they're pretty mundane.

I never really know what to expect in the ER. As exciting as this is, I know my limits. I'm a strong woman who's managed a career in medicine I can be proud of. I'm financially independent and don't need to rely on anyone. Yet my headaches are still a fact of life. Sure, maybe in a career without Joseph Stark, I wouldn't have them quite so often. But I know the stress of the emergency room would be more than I could keep up with. And there's no going to a dark room to rest there.

As I approach the locked doors to the ER and reach for my badge to allow access, the doors suddenly swing open, and none other than Eve Manning stands before me.

"Ava," she squeals as she comes in for a hug. "I'm sorry, Dr. Harris. I know this isn't very professional. Ava's my best friend. I didn't mention the visit today because I knew I had to head back to Norfolk."

"What're you doing here?" I ask, still shocked at her presence.

"Dr. Harris was orienting me to the place since I'll be starting on Monday, and he'll be off."

"Hey, Ava. It's been a long time. I don't think I've seen you down here in almost a year."

Jake Harris is the ER director and one of the nicest physicians I've had the pleasure to meet. "You're right. They don't let me out much upstairs." I laugh. "How've you been?"

"Busy. We're glad to have Eve aboard. I'll probably have her working alongside Kat while she's here."

I only know of Katarina Kelly in passing. I've never worked with her, only the ER docs. I hope she's ready for Eve. I have to push down my internal giggle, so they don't think I'm crazy.

"Well, I'm sure Eve will learn a lot from both of you. You know, if there's ever anything I can do, I'm happy to help."

"You know, there might be now that you mention it," Jake replies, surprising me. "I was thinking about setting up an educational opportunity for some of the techs in our department. Many are EMTs or paramedics who sling and splint patients in the field with makeshift temporary materials. But quite a few of them have expressed interest in a class where they could learn how to place various OrthoGlass splints correctly. It'd be a huge help to our department if you could swing it."

"Oh, I'd love to help with that. Just name the time. If you call the office, I'll let Joanie know you may be reaching out."

"Thanks, Ava. That's great."

"Well, I better go. I have to see a patient and run back upstairs. It was good to see you again, Dr. Harris. And you…" I point at my dear friend who's following our every word. "You need to let me know when you're here and when you're off so we can get together." I give her another quick squeeze before scanning my badge to reopen the doors and attempt to find Dr. Stark's patient.

∽

Looking at the clock on the ER wall, I find it's 1:35 p.m. That took far longer than it should have. I lost some time seeing Eve and Dr. Harris, but the patient's noncompliance is the real cause of my delay. They haven't followed the post-operative instructions and have stressed their shoulder. Luckily, the x-rays look okay, so hopefully, they'll continue to wear their immobilizer to prevent any further problems. I walk swiftly back to the clinic, realizing Mick's been waiting. Looking at my watch, I confirm I only have about ten minutes before I need to resume seeing patients.

Practically running into my office, I notice a covered plate, utensils rolled in a white napkin, and a bottle of water. But no Michael. The disappointment I feel is instant. I drop my head and bite my lower lip to contain my chagrin. Oh, don't let me spend the next ten minutes trying not to cry.

"Ah, there's my girl." His deep sultry tone thrums against my back.

I feel him behind me, almost before I hear the words. Spinning on my heel, I look up to the man of my dreams. It almost doesn't feel real, moving from disappointment to delight so quickly.

"Go on, sit down," he encourages with a sweet, sensual tone. As I feel him lightly push me toward my chair, the sensation of his hand on my back instantly causes a familiar current to travel along my spine. As I take my seat, he lifts the cover from my plate and hands me the utensils. "You need to eat." Abruptly, Michael darts from the room, and I sit wordlessly, wondering where he's gone. I don't contemplate his departure long before he returns with his plate and a bottle of water. Pulling a chair up to the opposite side of my desk, he starts to dig into his food.

"Thank you," I whisper. I admit I'm still reveling in his being here. I was so worried he'd have to go before I returned. Looking at this handsome man before me, I'm a bit overcome. Is it simply relief that he stayed? Could it be from having renewed faith he's interested? Or is it merely his presence after all this time? I'm finding it difficult to relax enough to enjoy my food. I only want to sit and stare.

"You're welcome. I can't stay long. But it wouldn't be a date unless we ate together." He winks.

Smiling back at him, I tease, "Well, this may be the fastest date in history. Makes the speed lunch at Luigi's feel like an all-day affair."

He chuckles, and I pick up my fork, grateful for the food and the undeniably appealing company. As we quickly eat our lunch, it's as if we're in his car on the ride back to the office from Luigi's again, unable to stop smiling back and forth at one another in silent communication.

"I know this date isn't quite over yet," Michael clears his throat, "but I wondered if you'd agree to a third?" The hopeful look in his big brown eyes is more appetizing than anything on this plate.

Giggling, I smile back at him. "Why, yes. Could it be a tad longer?"

"Yeah, at least nine innings long. I thought maybe I could teach you about baseball at a Washington Nationals game."

Looking incredibly ladylike while quickly swallowing a mouth full of chicken Caesar salad, I blurt, "Yes. I'd love that."

Sitting a little taller in his seat, I watch as he reaches for his drink and takes a big gulp of water. His Adam's apple is hypnotizing me, bouncing along the column of his throat, beckoning my stare with the way his neck is arched. "Great. I'll pick you up next Friday. Any chance you could get off work a little early? The game is at 7:00, and DC traffic can be rough at that time of day. If not, we can go some other time."

"No, I think I can manage that. Dr. Stark's actually out of town next week, so I don't think it'll be a problem."

I watch as he stands, reaches for his plate and utensils, and leaves the room momentarily. Returning empty-handed, he comes around to my side of the desk and sits on the corner next to me. A tremble settles into my limbs at his nearness. There's a noticeable crackle of electricity between us. It's almost palpable. I have to put down my fork and take a gulp of cool water to steady myself. I'm giddy being this close to someone I've fantasized about in the way I have Mick. After he made it abundantly clear via text that he's had similar thoughts only makes me more wired.

As I look up at his beautiful face, he cups my cheeks and leans down little by little. Almost at a snail's pace. It's like this is happening in slow motion. I feel his strong, soft lips press to mine, and I could faint from the headiness of it. The kiss is soft, gentle, and warm. He pulls back slightly, and I feel his tongue dart out to lick my lower lip before nibbling on it. Mick drops another tender kiss to each corner of my mouth before placing one last soft peck on my lips. I can't speak. The kiss alone feels like the most intimate thing I've ever experienced. Pulling away, he smiles at me and stands.

"Thanks, pretty girl. If I don't leave now, neither one of us is going to get any work done." As he walks to the door and turns, I can't help reaching up to glide my thumb along the now sizzling flesh of my lower lip. I'm sure my face is bright pink. "I'll talk to you later, okay?"

In a daze, I try to find words. My voice comes out scratchy. "Okay."

And with that, he gives me one last panty-melting smile before walking out the door.

CHAPTER ELEVEN

Ava

I admit it. I feel like a love-struck teenage girl. My mind is constantly drifting to a buff ballplayer, heart fluttering at the possibility this could be real. Excited about taking a chance but trying to push down my eagerness so I don't fall headfirst into disappointment and heartache. I know he'll be meeting me at the office in a few days for our date with the Washington Nationals, but I just can't get the thought of that dreamy kiss out of my head.

Mick's called once to say goodnight while he was away and sent some sweet *I'm thinking of you* texts. Little notes to share how he's equally excited about our upcoming evening together. But try as I might, I can't seem to focus on anything else tonight.

I've had a full day at work and had an enjoyable meal with Carson this evening. I'm tired, but thoughts of a naked Michael in the shower with me after I returned home have gotten me feeling too aroused to settle in. The text messaging the other evening was about as close to sexting as I'm ready for with him yet. But maybe just knowing he's thinking of me too will allow me to finally drift off to sleep. Reaching for my phone, I bite my lower lip. *Oh, what the hell…*

9:40 p.m.
Ava: Hi. Can't stop thinking about you.

Michael York
9:47 p.m.
Mick: Hi. And I can't stop thinking about you.

There. That should be enough to get to sleep, right? Wish him goodnight and tell him you look forward to—

Michael York
9:51 p.m.
Mick: What are you wearing, princess?

What is it with men and this? I guess they're visual creatures.

9:54 p.m.
Ava: A crown

There. I'm not answering that predictable question the way he wants.

Michael York
9:57 p.m.
Mick: Just a crown. Fuck, that's hot.

Oh, lord. So much for that.

10:00 p.m.
Ava: You're ridiculous

Michael York
10:09 p.m.
Mick: Hey, grab my butt (a snowman emoji, three laughing emojis, and a carrot)

Okay, what's he talking about? Is he drunk?

10:11 p.m.
Ava: What on earth are you going on about?

Michael York
10:21 p.m.
Mick: Anna said shoe size doesn't matter. But it does (eggplant emoji)

Oh, jeez. Really? How am I supposed to get to sleep now? Wait. Who's Anna?

10:24 p.m.
Ava: What did you do tonight?

Michael York
10:28 p.m.
Mick: It was hot. Too hot.

Um, what? My stomach starts to churn a bit. This doesn't make sense. My gut tells me he's been drinking. Because none of this conversation sounds like Michael. Maybe I should just call him, so I don't make myself crazy worrying about this all night.

Dialing his number, I chew the inside of my cheek as I wait for his sultry voice to come across the phone line, reassuring me he's okay.

"Hello?" His voice sounds thick. Still sexy, but different from our recent conversations.

"Um, hi. The texts were getting weird, so I thought I'd call."

"Oh?" Silence.

"Mick?"

"Hmm?"

"Is everything okay?"

Silence. Is he alone? *No, Ava. Don't start down that path. You're letting Carson get into your head.*

"Have you been drinking?"

"No." Again, I hear nothing but heavy breathing across the phone line. This is so odd.

"I'm not sure what's going on tonight. But I guess I'll see you on Friday."

"Okay. Goodnight, El—"

"Hello?" Pulling my cellphone back to look at the screen, I quickly discern he's hung up on me. What on earth? Did he even realize he was talking to me? I start to replay the conversation in my mind as I open the messaging app to review the texts again. Does he call everyone princess? *Maybe that way, he doesn't get all of his girls confused.*

I slam my phone down onto the bed in front of me and decide I need to put these crazy doubts out of my head. That conversation with Carson about men who travel is starting to niggle me. I need to get some sleep. Fretting over this confusing situation will only make me paranoid, and Mick has done nothing to give me a reason to think the worst. He's gone out of his way to be a gentleman. I'll just ask him to clarify what happened on Friday. For now, I'm choosing to believe he simply got hammered.

There is *one* thing I'm certain of. I'm not turned on anymore.

Mick

It's been a little over a week since I've seen Ava, and I can't wait to get to her office. We've spoken by phone a few times and shared a few texts, but it isn't the same as being near her. First things first, I need to clear the air with her about some of the texts I sent the other night.

I hadn't realized how hard allergy medication would affect me when Ava began texting. I'd gone to grab a bite to eat at a new place near the hotel where I was staying in southwest Virginia. It was an Indian restaurant that had received good reviews online. I can usually tolerate a fair amount of spice, so I ordered the Naga pork curry dish. I know some Indian dishes can pack the heat, but I've never experienced one that caused anything beyond a light sweat or a burning on my tongue and throat previously. But that night... that fiery curry dish shouldn't be legal for human consumption.

I'm not sure if it was simply the extreme heat at war with my body or the amount of water I consumed to douse the internal flames, but I was wrecked. I was experiencing chest pain, belly pain… but the worst of it was my mouth and throat.

I have no idea how I made it back to the hotel alive except for the fact it was only two blocks away. I do remember that at one point I considered looking up the directions to the closest emergency room on my phone but instead chose to do what any other rational man in my shoes would. I called my mother.

First, she recommended I try a spoonful of sugar or honey. This moderately priced hotel didn't have any honey at the ready, so I broke open every sugar packet in the room's coffee station to no avail.

"How about you make a peanut butter sandwich, Mick."

"Are you dicking with me, Mom?"

"No." I could hear her laughing through her hand on the phone receiver. "It's supposed to help with the capsaicin. I think the oil in the peanut butter helps, and the bread works like a mop."

"What the fuck? I'd have to eat fifteen of them," I'd yelled, pouring another glass of water down my throat. Didn't matter. There was no peanut butter sandwich to be had in the hotel, and if I'd gotten behind the wheel, it would've been to drive myself straight to the hospital. I shake my head, laughing at the recollection of walking back into the bathroom, flipping on the light, and squealing like a five-year-old girl.

"Oh my god, Michael. What's wrong?"

As I stared in the mirror, suddenly, my biggest issue wasn't the pain nor potentially collapsing to my impending death from curry, but the fact that my lips now resembled someone who'd just received a cosmetic injection of Botox. "My lips look like Angelina Jolie after a day with the plastic surgeon." My voice is starting to sound muffled.

"Can you breathe okay?" I could hear the concern and didn't want my mother to panic.

"Yes. My tongue and throat only hurt. They don't feel swollen. Just my lips. The only breathing issue is because they're so damn big."

"It could be the capsaicin is causing them to swell. Do you have any sleeping pills with you?"

What? "Are you trying to kill me, Mom?"

"No. Allergy medicine and sleeping pills usually contain Benadryl.

It'll help the swelling. I would take a few and apply some cool compresses."

"Okay. I'll call the front desk and see if someone can send them up. I'm afraid to leave the room looking like this."

"Well, don't hang up. I need to know you're all right."

Putting down the phone, I'd rummaged through my overnight bag and was surprised to find some cold medication in my toiletry kit. I read the ingredients off to my mother, who confirmed it contained medication that should help with the swelling. After popping four pills into my mouth, because no way were two cold pills going to touch this swelling, I grabbed the phone and listened to my mother talk about anything and everything until I could reassure her that I was improving enough she could hang up. I recall hearing about some boy Emmaleigh's dating that I already want to kill. I had to listen to tales about Rob's golf game last Saturday and how he never returns anything he buys that doesn't fit.

"He must have fifteen work shirts with the price tag still attached that are a size too—"

"Mom. I think I'm better. And I'm getting kinda tired." I don't know if it was the medication that started to kick in or listening to my mother go on and on for thirty solid minutes that made me feel like my head was spinning.

"Okay, Mick. Be careful and get some sleep."

I'd placed the phone down on the nightstand and gotten into bed only moments before I saw it buzzing with an incoming message. Assuming my mother had forgotten some vital detail on the great shirt debacle, I was shocked to find it was Ava initiating a text. In my groggy state, I recall attempting to participate in meaningful conversation until I woke up this morning to find the proof of what had transpired. Good lord, I'm surprised she didn't think I was drunk. Or having a stroke.

The texts had quickly turned flirty. I must've thought I was skating the edge of acceptable with her until I reviewed what I'd sent this morning. Even with help from the talk to text feature, those texts were bizarre. All of the naked Elsa fantasies must've been trying to reveal themselves. That and I'd watched *Frozen* entirely too many times with

Emmaleigh to have memorized all of that crap. The only thing getting through the Benadryl loud and clear was my obvious desire for her.

That desire has continued to grow since the impromptu lunch in her office. Ava's plush lips had been summoning me throughout our quick meal. And that mouth was even softer and more tempting than I'd imagined. The lingering thoughts of it had done a real number on my libido.

I'd been dying to kiss her. The whole damn lunch for the office had been a rouse just to call it a second 'date.' Yet once that kiss started, I wasn't sure I could stop. It took restraint to back away. Even after munching on Caesar salad, her sweetness shined through. But I knew I would've embarrassed myself had that kiss gone any farther there. I felt myself instantly get hard and knew I had to end it and head out before things got out of hand. Her boss is difficult enough to deal with as it is. I certainly didn't need to give him another reason to bark at her.

∼

Pulling up to the St. Luke's medical park, I observe Ava standing to the left of the doors to the office building. She's wearing white converse tennis shoes, denim capri pants, a V-neck white cotton T-shirt, with a backpack slung over her right shoulder. Her shimmering long blonde hair is tied in a high ponytail. She's freaking adorable. My dream girl come to life. Pulling up, I put the car in park and run around to greet her before opening the door.

"Hi," I say before scooping her into my arms, hugging her to me tightly. God, she feels good. We've had a first kiss and some dirty texts. There's no need to hold back from touching her at this point. Hell, I couldn't do it if I tried. I pull back, grab her small backpack, and place a kiss on her nose before ushering her into the SUV. Running around the car, I try to tamp down my excitement, so I don't come off looking desperate. Hopping into the driver's seat, I start the ignition but stop short before heading toward the main road.

Turning to her, I notice a pensive expression on her face. *Fuck.* "Ava, about those texts."

"No, it's okay."

"Wait. No, I need to explain. That's not my usual behavior. I'd taken some medication after about near killing myself with the spiciest Indian curry dish I've ever eaten, and I should've given in to sleep instead of responding to your messages. I was just excited to hear from you, and… well, it should be illegal for me to operate a phone under the influence of cold medicine."

"Oh." She giggles. "I wasn't sure where you were going with some of that. But I think I can give you a pass. At first, I thought it was some weird kind of dirty talk."

"Ava, that wasn't dirty talk," I reply, voice stern, giving her a serious stare before arching my brow for the full effect. "Trust me, princess. You'll know when I'm talking dirty to you." Her entire face turns scarlet red before me. *Shit!* Guilt settles in quickly. Reaching to stroke her cheek, I attempt an apology. "Baby. I'm sorry. Did I upset you?"

"No. My skin just does this. Especially if I get turned on." Her last words are barely audible.

Well, hell yeah. I'd like to see this color on you a lot more often. Before I can let that statement sink in, she continues.

"Is it okay if I ask you one thing about that night?"

"You can ask me anything, Ava."

"Do you call all of your girls princess?"

"All of my girls?" *What the hell?* I rotate even farther in my seat, so I'm facing her directly. "I'm not sure what you're getting at, but let's get one thing very clear. You're my *only* girl." I continue to look at her until she acknowledges this. I don't need her having any doubts about where I want this to go. If I'm going all-in with this beauty, I need to jump in with both feet.

A timid look of joy crosses her face, and I feel like we're back on track. "I'm excited about this, Mick. Both the date and learning about baseball. I don't know why, but I've never really learned the lingo." Her attempt at changing the subject is commendable. But I'm not sure I'm following her train of thought.

Pulling out of the medical complex toward the highway, I push for more. "What do you mean, lingo?"

"Well, I know you get three strikes and you're out and all that. But there are a lot of terms I've heard used I don't understand. I'll admit I don't grasp a lot of the rules of the game either. What constitutes a foul versus an out? How many innings does a game have? I feel like it's different for each game I watch. Not like football where it's always four quarters."

Looking over at her as we approach an intersection, I see she's got that sweet rosy hue to her skin she develops whenever she's the slightest bit embarrassed. At least, I assume that's what it's related to. *Hell, if she gets turned on talking about baseball, I might have to fly her to Vegas.*

"I even bought this," she adds as she reaches for her backpack and pulls out a yellow book. "Baseball for Dummies."

Chuckling, I drop one hand on her denim-clad leg and squeeze. "Ah, princess, I'll teach you. You don't need that silly book."

"Oh, thank you. I really want to learn. I loved going to the game the other night. But it was hard to pay much attention with those two chatterboxes beside me. Holy cow, Joanie was cracking me up. My face hurt the next day."

"Oh, yeah? I could see her being fun to spend time with away from work. She telling crazy stories about her family?"

"Ha! No. She was giving us a play-by-play through the whole game."

"Really? Wow, I had no idea Joanie would be so into baseball."

"Um, it wasn't the game she was giving the color commentary on. It was who looked best in baseball pants and who had the hottest tattoos." She guffaws. "Joanie's one hot momma."

"Holy shit. I wasn't expecting that."

"Me either." She giggles as she retracts a bottle of water from her bag. As she drops it into the cupholder by her side, I glance over to see she's rested her hand over the top, her dainty nails painted a vibrant royal blue, drumming against the plastic in time with the music. Hell, I'd barely noticed anything was playing before now, so caught up in the enchanting girl beside me. Reaching over, I take her hand in mine and watch as her face quickly snaps in the direction of our entwined fingers. The warmth radiating from her touch continues to melt my battered heart. We're both closing in on thirty. Why am I so nervous about taking this girl's hand in mine? *Fear of rejection is a mother fucker.*

An identifiable succulent pink hue dots Ava's cheeks just as she flashes her luminous smile in my direction. *Jesus.* I didn't know a woman like this existed. One that could make me feel... what? I'm not sure exactly, but I know that I like it. I like her. *Stay cool, Mick. You have to play your cards right with this one.*

CHAPTER TWELVE

Mick

We drive the distance to the game, chatting about everything and nothing. It's so easy to talk to her. There's no pretense with Ava. I try to focus on the fact we're headed to one of my favorite things on the planet, a major league game, so I don't get fixated on how good she looks with her tits teasing me through that thin white T-shirt. I think I've asked her if the temperature is okay five times, worried I truly am turning her into the ice queen as her nipples have been torturing me through that top the entire drive. Attempting to divert my attention upward, I only get lost in how those luscious lips I've tasted are calling my name. Thank God we're going to a baseball game and not somewhere that won't hold my attention, or I'll end up mauling her in the stands.

~

As we approach Nationals Park, located southwest of the U.S. Capitol, we inch forward behind a long line of eager fans. Gazing at my watch, I breathe a sigh of relief that we've managed to make such good time.

Blessed with unusually light Washington D.C. traffic with this radiant girl seated next to me, the trip seemed almost effortless until now. But this traffic heading into the park is nothing new.

Glancing over, Ava is biting her lower lip. I lift her sweet hand to my mouth and kiss her knuckles. "We're doing well on time, princess. No worries."

Her stunning blue eyes connect with mine briefly before they drop back to her hand in mine. Does she feel this electricity between us too? Tapping the gas, I creep up a little more while we await our turn to pay for parking and gaze back at her.

Leaning across the center console, I wrap my hand behind her neck, pulling her toward me. I can't hold back from her sweet mouth any longer. Hell, the time we spend in the car to and from the game is the only part of the evening I'll have her all to myself.

As our lips collide, I can feel my hunger for her testing my control. My tongue pleads for entrance, swiping against her plush lips, and she opens for me. She's warm, wet, sweet, and my mind instantly contemplates if her pussy will be just the same. I feel my dick hardening at the thought as our tongues dance hungrily and decide to pull back to gather some much-needed restraint just as the car behind me not so gently blows their horn to remind me where we are.

Sitting with about two car lengths in front of us, I attempt to readjust the rod that is now in my pants and move forward carefully. "Sorry." Giving her a sheepish grin, I notice her cheeks are now quite red. "Baby, did that car honking embarrass you?"

"No." *Fuck. Is she as turned on as I am then?*

"God, Ava. You make me crazy. I'm going to need to apologize in advance if I can't hold back and have to touch you a lot during this game." Reaching my arm behind my head, I massage my neck, trying to get myself under control before we have to step out of this car. What I'd give to pull her into the backseat before we make our way to the stadium. But I need to take a little more finesse with this girl. I don't want to lose it and have the first time we sleep together to be in the back of my SUV that probably smells of dirty baseball gear. *Dreams for another day, maybe.*

"No apologies needed." She giggles. "I was just disappointed the kiss had to stop." Her statement comes out practically as a whisper.

There's no hiding the way I feel now. I just need to own it, smiling like a crazy-ass mother fucker or not. This night feels like a home run, and the damn game hasn't even started yet.

Having paid for parking, locked up the SUV, and now heading for the gate, I can't help but take a moment to absorb this sensation. I'm walking hand in hand with a beautiful girl to a major league baseball game. And not any beautiful girl, but one I honestly think I could take a chance with. There's nothing about her that reminds me of Paula's behavior. Letting go of her hand, I wrap my arm around her and pull her into my side as we traverse the rest of the way through the crowded parking lot to the ticket entrance. *Slow your roll, Mick. It's only your third date.*

"You want to grab snacks now or wait 'til later?"

"I had something to eat before I left work. I'll be fine. Besides, I'm too excited for snacks," she replies, beaming back at me.

Ha! Me too. "We can get some drinks from someone walking the stands. Then we'll go grab something to munch on later. Just let me know if you get hungry."

Meandering the crowded stadium, I take in Ava's bright eyes. Coming to these games is a common occurrence for me. Hell, I've come to games alone. But she looks like a wide-eyed child at an interactive exhibit, taking it all in. The noises, the vendors, colorful T-shirts, hats, and souvenirs bearing the Nationals logo, a bright red W. The air is rich with the aroma of popcorn, peanuts, and team spirit. Pointing in the direction of an overhead sign leading the way to our seats, I again take the opportunity to pull her into me. I can't get over how fucking good this feels.

We make our way down the stadium steps to our location near first base. They're great seats to take in all the action.

"These seats are incredible, Mick."

"Yeah, we got lucky." No luck about it. These are the most expensive tickets I've ever purchased for a Nationals game, but I'm aiming to impress tonight. Having a few minutes to spare before the game gets rolling, I flag down a passing concession attendant for two bottles of water and some popcorn and begin my tutoring session by reviewing everything on the scoreboard for Ava.

The beginning of the game moves along at a slow and steady pace. No one team is standing out tonight. It's all tit for tat, with the score remaining zero for both. Looking down, I see Ava's delectable hand dip into the popcorn and watch as she pops a salty piece into her mouth. Reaching over, I lift her hand to my mouth and place the pads of her index and third fingers on my tongue before sucking the remaining butter and salt from them. My eyes match hers as I place her hand back into her lap, and I watch a beautiful crimson stain her cheeks.

"Sorry. Couldn't help myself," I growl into her ear before kissing her on the temple. Oh, what I'd give to lick her everywhere.

"You're a bad, bad boy, Mr. York."

You have no idea.

❧

We've been watching the game for over an hour and having a blast. We took a short break to grab a brat and a beer for me and a soda and some sugary glazed pecans for her. It's been a great night so far. Ava's being a good sport about trying to keep up with everything I'm teaching her. It's probably a bit much for a first big league game, but I want to give her examples so she might remember some of the terms.

"That last guy hit the ball and made it to third," I say, pointing toward the base. "That's called a three-bagger or a triple."

"Got it. I feel like I can remember double plays and three-baggers," Ava responds like a serious student of the game.

Suddenly, the ball cracks sharply against the bat, and the player swings it behind him as he darts in our direction, down the first base line.

"Wow, that was good." Ava claps.

"Nah, that was a cookie. A cookie's a pitch that's easy to hit. I was a bad-ball hitter. It was why I was so good. Honestly, it's probably why I earned my scholarship."

"What's a bad-ball hitter?"

"I hit a lot of balls that were thrown outside of the strike zone. But I paid for it. The constant strain on my shoulder is what eventually did me in."

Ava reaches up to stroke my arm, and I can't help but look into her clear, blue eyes. Bending down, I place a chaste kiss on her sweet lips. Thwack. Both of us simultaneously jerk our eyes to home plate, realizing we've probably missed a few plays, lost in each other. We manage to see the batter drop the bat and run to first.

"Now, there are two ducks on the pond." I point to the players on first and second base. "They just need another good hit to bring them home."

I feel her soft hand curve around my bicep and can no longer keep my hands to myself. Wrapping my arm around her shoulders, I pull Ava into me. The contrast of her platinum locks tumbling over the dark, black and red ink of my arm makes my dick twitch. *Focus on the game, Mick.*

"Ah." I shake my head. "See how that pitch looked like it was thrown wide but then curved back in, and he missed it? That's what they call a backdoor slider."

I feel her body shake against me momentarily before I realize she's giggling.

Turning my head toward her, chuckling, I ask, "What?"

"That sounded dirty," she whispers.

My mouth drops open, stunned. "Ha, you dirty girl." I nudge her with my elbow. *Lord, I can't let my mind even go there.*

Thwaaack!

"Holy shit!" I blurt, instantly on my feet, my eyes trailing the ball's trajectory as it travels high and long. All the Nationals fans are on their feet cheering excitedly. "Yessss!" I yell, clapping wildly. One, two, three players run across home plate.

"That was the prettiest home run I've ever seen," Ava shouts above the crowd, clapping.

"Yeah, they call that a moonshot. It's what every hitter prays for."

The next player makes it to first, but the fans seem to settle down after the same runner is picked off in the following play.

"Ah, man. That's too bad," Ava mutters.

"He got caught napping."

"Ah." She giggles, lifting the sugary pecans wrapped in a paper cone up to her supple lips. I watch as she darts her tongue out to grab one, pulling it back into her mouth.

Fuck, there goes my dick again. She slowly chews before repeating the strangely erotic sight. I can't help but picture her kneeling before me, holding me tight in her hands as she flicks the head of my swollen cock teasingly before swallowing me whole. "You're killing me with that, Ava."

Her head quickly rotates to face me, tongue still outstretched toward her awaiting treat. "What?"

Leaning in, I kiss the shell of her ear. "I can't help picturing you licking me." I hear a faint gasp. "But only after I can suck all the sugar from your sweet lips." Sliding my hand further up her leg, I rest my fingertips dangerously close to the apex of her thighs, so there's no confusion as to what I'm referring. I can almost feel her mouth drop as her legs tighten around my grasp. I know this is bold, but she asked. "You keep sliding that tongue out like that, and my cock's going to be as hard as a Louisville Slugger." There's no mistaking the gasp this time. "I told you. You'd know when I was talking dirty." Briefly nibbling on the lobe of her ear before straightening in my seat, I pull a glazed nut from her container and tease it dramatically with the tip of my tongue before I pop it into my mouth, keeping my eyes trained on the field. "It's going to be delicious."

From my periphery, I can see her face now matches the vibrant red of the Washington Nationals logo. It's taking everything in me not to laugh. I'm choosing to assume it's because she's turned on. But as the next batter strikes out, bringing the opposing team up to bat, I decide to give her an out and change the subject.

"Hey, I'm going to hit the men's room and look for a Nationals T-shirt for my sister. You want to come or stay and watch the game?"

"No, I'll come." Her voice comes out shakily, in a bit of a squeak, and I again have to resist the urge not to chuckle out loud.

Taking her hand, I lead her up the stairs. Noticing a breeze as we reach the top step, I gaze up to see the clouds are turning dark. I hope we can make it through the game before it starts to pour.

Breaking my concentration from the sky to the crowd around me, a concessions attendant yells, "Coming through." He almost knocks Ava over in his attempt to squeeze by us. I manage to pull her to me just before we both collide into the concrete wall to our right.

Holding her against me, I lift my hands to cup her face and take in her gorgeous eyes. "You okay, princess?"

"Yeah. Glad he didn't spill the drinks all over me." She smiles up at me, seemingly unharmed.

I give her a tender kiss to her soft, pouty lips and place another to her ear. "I'm sorry if I was too bold earlier. I just can't help thinking about all the things I want to do to you." Dropping my mouth to the delectable column of her throat, I give her a little lick before kissing her there. A groan reverberates overhead, and I appreciate the reassurance I'm not alone in the way I'm feeling.

"I want you too, Mick. I just don't want to rush things with you."

Rush things? We aren't going that fast, are we? *Maybe I need to chill with the dirty talk. I don't want to scare her off.*

～

The game continues as it began, with both teams staying tied until the last inning. Once the Nationals are up at bat, they win with a walk-off on the third pitch. The crowd goes wild, and Ava is glowing in her enthusiasm. It's been a perfect evening.

After the excitement of a hometown win dies down, we gather our things and head toward the front of the stadium. Before we can make it to the front gate, the skies abruptly open, and a torrential downpour begins. Grabbing Ava's hand, I can hear her squealing as we run for cover under a nearby concrete overhang and snuggle up to wait for the rain to slow before proceeding to the car.

Wrapped up in this soaked beauty queen, she looks like a contestant in a wet T-shirt contest. Her thin white cotton T-shirt is practically see-through, and rain droplets hang from her lashes and cheeks. Fuck she's like every man's wet dream. Her nipples are visible through the sodden fabric, just begging to be sucked. Crushing my mouth over hers, this isn't the sweet kiss from the office. This feels like we're back in the car, continuing where we left off.

She opens for me immediately, and my tongue slides in to taste her. Our lips feast on one another, tongues stroking as I drop my hands to her ass. Rocking against her, I cannot hide how aroused I've become. God, I want her. This rain better lighten up soon, or we could get arrested for public indecency. Moving my face to her throat, I trail open-mouthed kisses from her ear to her collarbone.

"Ava," I groan.

I feel her place her hands on my chest and pull back. *Shit.* I know she's right. We've got to get control of ourselves. Whether people are distracted by the downpour or not, we're still out in public. *And she wants to take this slow.* This is going to be one torturous ride home.

"I think we're just going to have to head to the car. It doesn't seem to be letting up. Here," I say, tucking her into me. "Stay close to me."

We finally locate the car and climb inside. Poor Ava is drenched.

"I wish I had a towel or something. Oh! You can at least change your shirt. I've got the T-shirt from the gift shop in this bag."

"You got that for Emmaleigh."

"I got one for you, too." I wink. I hand her the shirt and turn my back so she can remove the saturated top she's wearing. "You decent?"

"Yeah, I'm good," she replies quietly. "Thank you."

We sit in traffic for what feels like an hour before making it out of the stadium parking lot, only inching forward intermittently. I keep adjusting the temperature as she appears to be shivering despite changing her top. Extending my arm, I grab ahold of her damp ponytail to wring any remaining water from it before removing her hair tie and fastening her hair into a loose bun.

"How'd you manage that?" Ava asks, looking baffled.

"What?"

"Do you do hair on the side?" She chuckles.

"No. I did Emmaleigh's a lot growing up. Trying to help get her ready in the morning to help Mom out. You tell anyone, and I'll have to kill you."

"Our little secret." She giggles.

Once we're on the main road, things don't appear to be getting much better. The rain continues to pummel our windshield, with the surrounding cars barely moving. According to the GPS, we still have at least twelve miles before we reach the closest highway on-ramp. Looking toward the dash, the clock now reads 11:35 p.m.

"Ava?"

"Yeah?"

"Do you want to get a hotel room?"

CHAPTER THIRTEEN

Ava

"What?" My face snaps up toward his in shock.

"It's after 11:00, and we haven't even gotten close to the exit yet. It'll probably be 3:00 a.m. before we get home. I'm happy to push on ahead, but if you don't have anywhere to be tomorrow... well, I'd spring for two hotel rooms so we could dry off and get a good night's sleep. We can probably be home within two hours when the traffic is better in the morning."

Hmm. That makes sense. Thinking more carefully about what he's said, he's probably right. Plus, I'm sure he's exhausted. I wouldn't want him to feel like he's forced to drive if he's not up to it. "Okay, sure. I don't have to be anywhere early," I answer hesitantly.

We sit in traffic for nearly forty minutes more before we're able to turn off of the main road and stop at the first hotel we see. Running inside to inquire about a room, we find they're sold out for the evening. We sprint back through the rainstorm to the car, proceeding to the next hotel to find a similar situation. Twice more, we're told there's 'no room' in the inn.

"If the next place is booked, we may have to just drive back," Mick says.

He turns the car into a Sheraton, parks under the overhang, and we exit the vehicle. The rain is coming down even harder now, if that's possible. As we approach the front desk, the clerk hangs up the call she's on and greets us.

"Hi, guys. Wow. It's really coming down out there. What can I do for you?"

"Hey, do you have any rooms left tonight?" Mick asks.

"As a matter of fact, I just hung up with a cancellation. Would you like it?"

"Yes!" We both answer in unison. Mick looks down at me with a relieved but playful smile. I'm sure he's thankful he won't have to drive back home in this monsoon in bumper-to-bumper traffic.

"Just sign here, and I need to see your credit card and driver's license," she advises.

As Mick finishes the paperwork, the kind desk clerk hands him the key. "I'll be right back. I just need to park the car."

Pacing in the lobby, I rub my hands over my arms to stay warm. The chill of the hotel air conditioning is making me tremble. At least, I think it's the temperature. I admit my nerves are a bit on edge right now. Glancing down at my reflection in the large hotel mirror, I realize my shirt is finally drying. I smile, recalling how surprised I'd been that he bought this for me. Poor Mick is going to be soaked to the bone.

As if on cue, Michael appears through the hotel's revolving doors drenched from head to toe. The dark curls of his hair are plastered to his forehead, water dripping down his cheeks and nose. He swipes his hand down his face before gliding his muscular fingers through his wet locks. Grasping my hand, we head for the elevator.

As we ride to the fourth floor, I attempt to warm his arms by rubbing my hands along his wet skin. I fear all this is doing is getting me really turned on. Suddenly, it dawns on me for the first time that we're sharing a room. I'd been so excited we finally found one, I never put two and two together. I immediately drop my hands to my sides, knowing this could get awkward. Lord, I'm not prepared for this. This has nothing to do with being shy or coy in the bedroom. But I have a track record with men. It doesn't take long for the relationship to implode once the clothes come off. Beyond the paranoia that I'm simply *that bad* in bed, I don't want to worry he's going to have one foot out of the door once we've finally gone there.

Finding our room, Mick opens the door after swiping the key card several times. "Sorry. The card's all wet." He laughs. He flicks on the light, and we both freeze. Not only is there only one room, but there's also only one bed. Mick slowly walks into the room, placing the key card onto the dresser before turning back to me.

Biting my lip, my heart rate hastens at the thought of the evening before us. Scanning his incredible physique, clinging to his wet shirt and pants, I can feel a flutter in my belly already beginning to betray me. I'm just going to accept that whatever comes our way tonight is fate. This entire day has been perfect. If this is what's meant to be, I'll enjoy every last dirty minute of it.

"Ava. I'm going to take a quick shower and hang up these wet things. Do you need to use the restroom before I do?" Mick's words interrupt my lascivious thoughts.

"Oh, sure. No, I'm fine," I answer quietly.

I start to feel a bit overwhelmed by our situation. I have no overnight bag. We're sharing a bed. I already get turned on by his slightest touch. How am I ever going to sleep next to this man? *Am I prepared to handle this… if he turns out like the rest?*

Mick exits the bath with a white towel slung low about his hips. His torso is rippled with taut muscles beneath bronze skin. *Jeez, he's even more mouthwatering than my mind could imagine.* I notice the sexy tattoo present along his right arm I recall from months ago in the operating room. The other arm's colorful artwork begins at his left pec and travels down his arm just below his elbow. My mouth goes dry at the sight of him, but lower… well, there's nothing dry down there any longer.

"Do you want to shower? I'm going to leave my clothes hanging in there to dry for the morning. Just move whatever's in your way."

My eyes widen, realizing what he's saying.

"Ava, I'll sleep in the towel. It's okay. This honestly wasn't a ploy to get you naked. It's a big bed. I won't push you."

Somehow, I believe him. He's been nothing but a gentleman with me from the very start. Well, a dirty talking gentleman, but still a gentleman. "I know, Mick. It's okay. Yeah, I think I'll take a quick shower." If nothing else, maybe it'll calm my shaking limbs.

I enter the bath and notice Mick's discarded shirt and black boxer briefs draped over the shower curtain. As I close the door, I find his jeans are hanging from a hook on the back of the door. Carefully removing my still damp T-shirt, I place it between two hand towels in an attempt to transfer some of the remaining moisture. I place them on the counter beside Mick's wet leather wallet. Jumping into the shower, I make quick work of cleaning up. I'm so on edge, I can't relax enough to enjoy the hot water as I might have otherwise. Running some complimentary shampoo into my hair, I rinse off and stand under the spray for a few more minutes hoping to soothe my nerves.

Moments later, I step out, drying off with a thick white towel before wrapping it about me. Noticing the hairdryer attached to the wall, I attempt to use it to partially dry my hair before turning it on my Nationals shirt and wet panties. I laugh to myself that my panties are wet, probably more from my reaction to Mick than the rain, but after drying them a bit, I put them and the T-shirt back on nonetheless. I don't need to help fate along tonight by going commando. I open the door to find Mick already in bed. He's lying on the far side of the king bed, almost on the edge. I know he's trying to do whatever he can to make me feel comfortable.

Climbing in, I pull up the covers and stare at the ceiling. *Lord, how is this going to work? I'm never going to be able to fall asleep with him here.*

"You okay, Ava?"

"Yeah, I'm good," I whisper, knowing it's a lie. My overcharged nerves are tapdancing through my limbs. I hope he doesn't notice how anxious I am. *Right. He'd have to be blind.*

We both lie silent for what seems like an eternity. Suddenly, I feel him grab my hand, pulling it to his mouth.

"Mick?"

"Yeah?"

"Is this the way most of your dates end?" I ask, curious but unsure if I really want to hear his answer. With a body like his, I can't imagine he leaves his dates to go to bed alone.

"Ava, I don't really date. I had a girlfriend in college, but it didn't work out. Since then, I've tried to avoid romantic entanglements."

"The iceman, huh?" I ask. I hear a snort from his side of the bed, then the room grows silent. Taking in his words, I consider what this means. He's referred to this as a third date. So, am I different? In the car, he said I was his *only girl*. What was he used to before me? Did he just sleep with the women he met? I need to stop overanalyzing things and try to relax.

"You're awfully quiet," he utters softly. "I'm a man, Ava. I'm sorry. I'm sure the way I've lived my life isn't attractive to someone as sweet as you are. But I'm careful, and I'm not out looking for someone new every night."

"Have you? Uh…" I can't get the words out.

"I haven't been with anyone since I asked you out, princess," he reassures me.

The silence returns as I take in his words. My body is feeling pulled in two different directions, torn between hot lust and concern for a possible future with this magnanimous man who admittedly doesn't do *entanglements*.

"Goodnight, baby. I had a great time with you tonight."

"Me too, Mick," I murmur back. Staring at the ceiling, my heartbeat is racing in my chest. This is crazy. "Mick?"

He rolls on his side, facing me. "Yeah?"

He's so incredibly handsome. Lying here naked in this bed with me. There's no ignoring it. I want him. I want him bad. I roll toward him, reaching out to stroke the dark stubble along his jaw. Dropping my hand to his chest, I stroke his pec and look into his molten brown eyes.

As if he's read what I'm thinking and feeling, he leans in to place a gentle kiss on my mouth. Yet, as I open my mouth for him, our tongues' connection ignites a fire between us. Suddenly, the kissing is explosive, occurring at a pace we can no longer control. He begins running his strong, muscular hands through my hair and around my back. Sliding my hands up and around his neck, I feel his palm inch from my waist to my belly. It gradually ascends my torso, under my shirt, until he grabs ahold of my breast, gripping it and stopping to tweak my nipple with his fingers.

"God, Ava. I've dreamt of this for so long. But I don't want to do anything you aren't ready for."

"I'm not sure if I'm ready for sex, Mick," I quickly return. I know it's a lie. My body is more than ready. I simply haven't allowed myself to consider how I'll handle seeing him in the office regularly if things don't work out. And honestly, I don't want to be another notch on his heavily indented bedpost.

"It's okay. Is it okay to kiss and touch you?" he asks, nibbling on my neck.

"Yes." Why do I suddenly feel disappointed he didn't try harder? My mind is completely at war with itself.

He slides his other hand under my shirt, both hands now squeezing at my breasts and tight nipples as he continues to kiss and nibble along my throat and collarbone. I'm so wet I don't know why I bothered to put those panties back on. I feel my shirt lift and watch as his head drops down to suckle from my left nipple, then move to the right. I'm acutely aware that the towel between us has shifted as I can feel his hard, heavy erection along my thigh. The pulsing in my sex grows more prominent. *Who am I kidding? There's no way I can sleep with this man and not give in to this temptation.*

"Ava," he groans against my skin as he licks my breast. Lifting his head, he looks down at me with raw hunger in his eyes before clamping down on my nipple and sliding his hand to the apex of my thighs. I hear him let out a low moan as he strokes my swollen flesh. Dipping his fingers into my folds, he brings them to his nose briefly before sliding them into his mouth. I'm momentarily unable to breathe. "Ava? Can I please taste this sweet pussy?"

Now I'm the one groaning as I roll onto my back and lift my hips, allowing him to remove my worthless underwear. He sits up long enough to pull my shirt overhead and then leans back on his heels.

"Fuck, Ava. You're the most beautiful thing I've ever seen."

Before his words have completely sunk in, he's lowered himself between my legs and nudged my opening with his nose. Using his fingers to stroke and spread me wide, I tremble as he blows warm air across my skin. Every nerve ending in my body feels electrified. This exquisite torture might break me. I've never been this ravenous for anyone.

"Your soft, pink pussy is even prettier than I imagined." I'm just about to beg him to touch me, lick me, fuck me, anything when all of a sudden I feel him drag his flat tongue from the base of my opening to my clit. Clamping my legs against his head, I consider there's nothing ladylike about my response to his devouring of me just as he begins teasing my sensitive bundle of nerves with the firm tip of his tongue. I can't contain the noises I'm making in response to his pleasurable assault. The sensation, the sounds of his voracious licking, the feel of his heavy muscular hand on my belly as it attempts to control the bucking of my hips. It's all too much. I reach overhead to grab the pillow to steady myself, feeling completely overwhelmed with sensation. As if this torrent of physical delight isn't enough, unexpectedly, his lips clamp down around my clit as he sucks.

"Oh, god, Mick."

My hands move to grab fistfuls of his now dry, soft hair as he continues to lick and suck while placing two thick fingers inside of me. As he curls them forward, I know I can't hold out much longer. My entire body begins to shake.

"That's it, princess, don't hold back." He glides his fingers in and out of me a little faster, returning his talented lips to my clit.

"Oh, god." My body is shaking with force. I've never felt a climax build like this. If it didn't feel so damn good, I'd be worried I was having a seizure. I fear my grip on his hair could cause bald spots when he's done, but I continue holding on with a death grip as my body careens over the edge. Still quaking at the force of the orgasm, my blood pulsating through my ears, I fight to catch my breath.

I feel Mick crawl up toward the head of the bed and open my eyes just as he bends to kiss me. "Fuck, you're beautiful when you come." I can taste myself on his lips and am overcome with the need to repay his gift.

"Mick?"

"Yeah, baby?"

"Can I?" I pause, unsure how to ask this. I've never spoken words like these to a man before. Usually, sex is merely a nonverbal physical connection until it's over. I actually had a man shush me once. I was so mortified I've tried to contain myself ever since, biting my lip if I feel the need to moan. But there's no keeping a lid on this fervor when Mick's bringing you to the brink.

"Can you what, Ava?"

Reaching down, I grab ahold of his hard cock and hear a hiss escape him. Whispering, my lips against his throat, I ask, "Can I suck your cock?"

"Holy fuck. Yes."

He starts to move away from me, so I quickly grab ahold of him, trying to gain his attention.

"What is it?" He looks perplexed.

"I want you to climb up here." Pulling myself up against the headboard, I motion for him to come closer.

He climbs up my body on all fours, straddling me. Once he's at my shoulders, he lifts his torso so he's lined up with my mouth and grabs ahold of the headboard.

Sliding my hands around his granite backside, I pull him into me. Again, I hear him grunt and moan as my mouth welcomes the head of his cock onto my tongue. Gliding my mouth down the length of him, I try to coax him to rock his pelvis into me. He appears to gladly accept the invitation, as he slowly undulates, releasing guttural groans of pleasure as he rocks into my awaiting mouth. I retract one of my hands from his rock-hard ass to cup his balls as he slides in and out. The musky scent of him, the feel of his heavy cock in my mouth, the vibration of his heavy groans above me are more than I can manage any longer. Overcome with need, I drop one hand to my throbbing sex in an attempt to soothe the ache.

Abruptly Michael stops and withdraws from my mouth while looking down at me, eyes hooded, arms braced on the wall overhead. "Do you need my cock, princess?"

Nodding gratefully, I reach up to stroke him once more. "Do you have a condom?" I ask, feeling almost desperate.

"If I don't, I'll build a fucking arc." I watch as he springs from the bed, heading toward the bathroom. "It's going to take more than a class five hurricane to stop this from happening." Returning within seconds, he climbs back over me and holds up a condom. Ripping open the packet with his teeth, he gingerly rolls the latex over his engorged length and lines himself up with my opening. He's not wasting any time.

I'm keenly aware I'm again trembling with need. I've never been this out of control with lust for anyone.

"You okay?" he asks, concerned.

"Yes. I just want you so much, Mick."

Nudging the head of his cock into me, he bends down to kiss me. The kiss deepens as he ruts further and further into me until he's fully seated. The sensation is out of this world. I've never felt so full. I don't know if it's his size or simply that it's Mick. Everything about this man is so much more than I've ever experienced before. More than I imagined I could experience with anyone.

I need a minute to absorb all of this pleasure. To appreciate this moment. My heart is racing. He feels so damn good.

"Fuck, Ava." He exhales. His groan adding to my delight. "Feeling you stretched around me. So wet and warm. Jesus." I feel him breathe against my ear as he leans on his forearms above me. "I knew you'd be incredible, but I can't get enough of your sweet pussy." He kisses my neck as he starts to slowly glide his length in and out of me with a deliberate and steady pace. I'm lost in the sounds of wet flesh and heavy exhales until we suddenly feel in synch, his breathing now matching mine.

"Oh, Mick. It's never... Oh, god." I clutch onto his backside, feeling my legs tighten around his hips as the friction against my clit builds to a crescendo. Our panting increases, both of us clutching the other in a desperate need for release.

"El," Mick growls out.

"Oh, god. Mick. I'm going to come," I practically shout into the room.

"Let it go. Let it go. I'm right behind you."

The pace is at a frantic pitch now. His hips bucking wildly into me. His fingertips claw into my hips as he pounds himself into my body, colliding against my clit with every delicious thrust. It's as if we're striking two branches together, waiting for the spark to ignite. Once, twice, three more times, I feel his hard cock slam into me. Then, with the next stab of his hard shaft into my quivering body, I feel the orgasm detonate.

"Micky!" My fingers clutch his skin as the tremors take over my body, and I ride the wave of ecstasy to its completion.

"Fuck, fuck." The pounding is now ferocious. "Fuckkk," he shouts above me, groaning out his release. I feel him bite into my shoulder as his body shakes, joining mine in aftershock after aftershock. The only sounds left are heavy exhales.

"Av." He pants out after a long moment of silence.

"Yeah," I respond, trying to regain control of my bodily functions.

"I have to tell you something," he utters, sounding concerned.

"Okay," I answer warily.

"When I dream about you. I call you Elsa." He buries his face in my hair and chuckles. "That's why I snorted earlier when you called me the iceman." Turning in my direction, his face appears to become a shade of pink I'm not used to seeing on a man. "I wanted to warn you in case I blurt it out by mistake."

Suddenly, I can't contain the hilarity of this situation. I'm shaking for an entirely different reason now, clutching my sides from fits of hysterical laughter.

Sitting upright, he looks at me, seemingly embarrassed. "What? Okay, it's not that funny."

"Mick." I try to stop cackling to finish my sentence. "You told me to let it go." I start giggling again. "You said, 'Let it Go, Let it Go,' to be specific." I'm laughing so hard I'm crying now. "The only thing better would've been if you'd started singing it."

"Oh. My. God. Now there's some dirty talk. That's what I get for having a sister eleven years younger. I blurt out lines from *Frozen* during sex." He throws his head back, joining me in uproarious guffaws. "Admit it. Olaf makes you hot." He continues to laugh between words. "You like his dirty talk," he teases. "Grab my butt," he says in an animated tone.

"Oh my god. That's what that was from?"

"What?"

"Your crazy texts. You told me to grab your butt, and that shoe size didn't matter to Anna."

Mick begins to hoot again before he clutches me to him. "Yep, I can do a girl's hair and quote sexy lines from a children's movie. I don't know how I'm still single."

We eventually settle down, giving in to sleep. My last thought before drifting off... *Please, God. Let me have the fairy tale ending with this man and not the frigid nightmare.*

CHAPTER FOURTEEN

Ava

We return home the following day, making quick time of the trip back to Hanover, despite a late start. Once the sun had broken through the drapes causing us to stir, Mick advised he wanted to get an early move on our journey to beat the traffic. He placed a breakfast order with room service for us while I showered and tried to keep my routine quick.

However, the plan for a quick getaway was unexpectedly derailed once I emerged from the bath, wrapped in a towel, looking for my T-shirt and panties. I may or may not have bent over in front of him a little longer than necessary while looking for my missing garments, and was gratified when Mick pounced on me. In my defense, I tried to remind him of our need to hit the road. But was thrilled when instead he gave in to temptation. Thank god there was another condom in his wallet. He assured me the delay was worth it, but I could tell he was anxious about the time as he continued to glance at the clock the entire trip home.

As we pull into the medical office park to retrieve my car, I feel the dread building. It's been the most amazing date of my life, and I hate seeing it come to an end. I know it's part of the newness of a relationship to want to spend more time with him, but I hate saying goodbye. Between laughing, sharing stories, and singing off-key to random songs on the radio… well, we got back to my car a little too quickly, if you ask me.

"I had an incredible time with you," he says, running the back of his hand along my cheek.

"I did too, Mick. Thank you for everything."

"I'll call you later," he adds with a chaste kiss. I wish it were more like the ones in the hotel room, but he seems to be in a hurry to go. He pulls me in for another hug before turning back to his car. Getting in, he drives off without a look back. Hmm. I haven't even opened my car door yet. This seems so unlike his usual behavior. My heart starts to squeeze, pangs of paranoia trying to take hold of the pleasant thoughts of the last day. Alarm bells are sounding in my head to *beware of another who's going to cut and run*. I'm sure I'm just fearful. There's no reason to be negative. I just had the best date ever.

Driving home, I look down at the baseball T-shirt Mick bought for me and can't help but smile at everything that transpired since getting in his car yesterday. It was an incredible evening with an incredible man. Not to mention the best sex I've ever had. Clutching the shirt to my chest, I just have to pray this guy will be different.

After another shower and finally finding some clean clothes, I set about my weekend list of chores to keep my mind busy. I know if I allow myself to go there, I'll start getting anxious about this new relationship instead of enjoying it. It's simply a habit, getting used to the letdown. But I want this to be different, so I need a different mindset. I'm thinking positive for a change. I deserve a man like Michael.

After doing a few loads of laundry and cleaning the kitchen and bath, I'm finding I'm becoming restless. I haven't visited my mother in a while, so decide that might be the best plan for the day. I'll get my groceries for the week after checking on her.

• • •

"Mom, you here?" I call out, hoping she isn't in bed. Her migraines have improved over the years with the use of multiple preventative medications, a few lifestyle modifications, and a new neurologist. She still has a lot of tough days and hasn't tried very hard to join a social circle, but it's better than I recall growing up.

"Ava, I thought I heard you. I was in the guest room packing up some old books to take to Goodwill."

"I don't know how you're able to read with your headaches. I can't handle the eye strain."

"Oh, I don't think I've read more than ten pages in any of them. Most I buy to have something to occupy my time in the waiting room for appointments. If I like it, I usually try to see if it's available as an audiobook. That subscription you gave me has been the best gift."

"I'm glad. I like having narrators read to me when I'm unable to do it myself." Laughing, I look down into the box she's carrying and notice we have similar taste in genre. I guess I get my love of romance books from her. At least she has book boyfriends to keep her company. Heck, no wonder she's not interested in meeting anyone. In my experience, they're the only men capable of giving you a happily ever after.

"Come, sit down. It's been a while since I've seen you. How've you been, dear?"

"I've been good, Mom. Work is a bit stressful. But for the most part, it's okay."

"Your boss still making you miserable?"

"Yes, but I try not to let him get to me. If it gets too bad, I'll start looking for something else. But I hope it doesn't come to that."

"So, what have you been doing with yourself lately? I feel like it's been ages since we've been able to sit and talk."

"I'm sorry, Mom. When I came by last Sunday, you were sleeping, so I didn't want to disturb you." Hesitating briefly, I decide to go all in. "I've actually started seeing someone."

"What?" My mother's face lights up at the comment. I never know whether to bring up my social life with her. I always feel so guilty for how isolated her life has become. I understand the impact of the headaches, but I just wish she could find a way to improve her quality of life. Enjoy spending time with people again. "Oh, tell me everything, Ava. You've been holding out on me."

"There's not much to tell. And it's all very new. He's been coming to my office for over a year now. I've always thought he was handsome but assumed he must be in a relationship. Then one day, out of the blue, he asked me to lunch. We've only had a few dates. But, Mom, I really like this guy. I'm so nervous it won't work out."

"Honey, any man would be lucky to have a girl as beautiful as you." I wince, knowing she believes my physical appearance is all I need to catch Mr. Right. If only that were true.

"Well, looks haven't gotten me too far with anyone else. And honestly, after spending time with him, I'm glad. I've never felt a connection to someone like I do with Michael. He's polite, funny, caring..." My mind wanders to last night and how he made me feel, in and out of the hotel room, and I can sense the flush creeping onto my cheeks.

"Well, I can see the effect he's having on you. I'm happy for you, Ava. You deserve to find a nice man who'll make you happy."

"Mom. It isn't too late for you to find someone. This new doctor seems to be finally helping. Sure the headaches are still there, but nothing like they were. Maybe you could join a church group or a book club?"

"Ava, I've been alone so long, it's almost uncomfortable to consider stepping outside my bubble." She looks at her entwined hands a moment before returning her gaze to mine. "I'll think about it. I'm actually considering volunteering at an animal shelter. I used to love having a pet growing up but could barely manage myself with these headaches. My goodness, you raised yourself." I grab her hand to assure her this isn't something she should perseverate on. "This way, I can spend time with the little guys without the fear I won't be able to care for them if the headaches keep me in bed all day."

"That's a great idea, Mom. I'm happy to go with you."

"Oh, you're so busy. I can manage. It's time I try to do a little more than grocery shopping and doctor's visits."

"Well, speaking of grocery shopping. I have to head there myself.

I'm hoping to meet Eve for brunch tomorrow, and Sunday is my usual day to get caught up on shopping."

"Well, you enjoy yourself tomorrow. And I want updates on this Michael. I hope I can meet him sometime soon."

Me too, Mom. Me too.

~

As I'm getting ready for bed, I hear my phone buzz with an incoming text.

Michael York
9:30 p.m.
Mick: I miss you.

9:33 p.m.
Ava: I miss you too.

Michael York
9:37 p.m.
Mick: That was the best game ever!

9:40 p.m.
Ava: Yeah. Goodnight (laughing emoji)

Michael York
9:47 p.m.
Mick: Goodnight, Elsa.

I lie in bed, replaying the prior evenings' events. The game was good. Who doesn't love a home team win? I had a great time getting to know Michael better, and it was cute seeing his excitement over teaching me the sport he loves so much. But the afterparty is the part I can't stop thinking about.

Is sex always like that for him? He's obviously a skilled lover who has a keen command of dirty talk. I giggle to myself. He at least seems open about his lifestyle. And I have to trust that he hasn't been interested in anyone else since asking me out. I try to reassure myself this handsome man isn't like the rest and lay my head down to sleep.

∼

"Hey, working girl." I greet Eve as she approaches the table at the Belleview café.

"Well, I don't know if you'd call it working when you're not getting paid. Just paying my dues until I can graduate, sit for my boards, and get my license like you. You been here long?"

"No. Just ordered two cups of coffee."

"Rough night?"

"No. One's for you, silly. Although, I admit I didn't sleep well."

"Oh no. Headache?"

"No. Potential heartache."

"What? What do you mean? Is it over already?"

"No. I shouldn't already be thinking negative. Just my bad track record talking. I had the best date ever Friday night, and the devil on my shoulder has been working overtime to convince me it's only a matter of time before he bolts."

"Oh, I get it, Av. I have the same trouble. Of course, *I'm* the one that gets in *my* way. I'm always finding some flaw, anything to dump and run before they do it to me. Tell me about your date. I haven't had a good one in so long." She sighs.

"Oh, Eve. It was incredible. He picked me up, and we drove to DC for a Washington Nationals game."

"Wow. That's different. I didn't realize you were that into baseball."

"I wasn't. Until Mick. He was so cute. He got really animated trying to explain the rules of the game and teach me the lingo."

"It sounds fun."

A server approaches with our coffees, and we quickly place our order. We've come to this regular brunch spot so long we don't even need to look at the menu.

"So, did anyone score besides the team?" she asks, waggling her brows.

"Maybe." My instant blush giving away my answer.

"Holy shit, Av. Why didn't you start with that? How was it? Is he everything you hoped?"

"And then some. I think that's why I'm nervous about this. I've never wanted anything to work out so much in my life, E. He's so hot. Between the wall of muscle, the panty-melting tats, the dirty talk, and well… let's just say, I don't think I'll ever find someone that good in bed again. Like, ever."

"Oh my god, Ava." Eve squeals. "I'm so happy for you."

"Yeah, me too. And he's not just a one-night stand. He told me I was his only girl. That he hadn't asked anyone else out since asking me for lunch that day. I know I'm getting ahead of myself, E, but I want this to work out so badly. I can't explain how good it feels. And not just the sex. I've never been so happy."

"Oh, honey. Try to relax and enjoy it. I know it's easier said than done. Look at me. I'm as single as they come. But you deserve this. You're beautiful, smart, caring. Those other guys knew the writing was on the wall with you. They'd never be good enough. They were smart enough to bow out early before you gave them the ax. This guy is different. I have a good feeling about it. You should have the whole package. The romance and the hot sex."

Looking up, our timing is again priceless as the server is standing at the end of our table holding our plates. But unlike 'fucking Edward,' she just giggles as she puts our food down directly in front of us. "Get it, girl."

~

It's Monday, and I haven't heard from Mick since our short text conversation Saturday evening. I spent a relaxing day Sunday at home after brunch with Eve. I made a light dinner, had a rare glass of wine, and went to bed early. I woke up this morning with a slight feeling of tension in my head and neck but no aura. I can manage this. This is nothing new for me. I'm sure part of it is knowing my weekend is over, and I have five more days of being at Dr. Stark's disposal to deal with.

I drive to work, curious about what the week will bring. Dr. Stark will be back from his trip. No telling what kind of mood he'll be in. Sadly, I must admit it has a direct impact on my work. Not only can his mood affect how much of a caseload he chooses to dump onto my plate, but his attitude affects my stress level and thus, my migraines.

∽

The week, unfortunately, becomes more taxing by the day. Dr. Stark has been in a particularly demanding mood, and the Monday morning mild tension headache has now, several days later, developed into a vice grip about my temples. There's still no aura, but the pain has not responded to my many attempts to treat it so far.

"Ava, I have a surprise for you." I lift my head from my desk to peer up into Joanie's sweet face. It's hard to make out in the dimly lit space, but she appears to be smiling as she carries a large bouquet. As she enters the office and places the gorgeous spray of flowers on my desk, she quietly pleads, "Ava, can I please read the card? I'm dying to know if they're from Michael."

Knowing looking at that little card is one more eye strain I could do without, I nod gratefully.

"Oh, Ava." I hear, looking back up to see her place her palm onto her chest. "It says, 'some people are worth melting for.'"

I smile at the *Frozen* reference and place my head back down. *Or perhaps I'm melting the iceman?* I need to call or text him thank you later. He'd called and text late last night, but I'd just gotten out of the shower, and my migraine medication had kicked in. There was no way I could focus on a conversation. And after the craziness with his texting under the influence of cold medication, I wasn't willing to tempt fate. I'll try to send him a message this evening if I can get control of this headache.

The stunning spray of all white flowers is so thoughtful. But, alas, the pungent aroma of the lilies is starting to make my nausea intensify. They're so beautiful, but the smell is overpowering.

"Joanie, do you think we could put the flowers out where more people can enjoy them?" I look up to see a disappointed expression cross her face, and I quickly interject. "I love them. And I'm so touched he sent them. But the smell of those lilies might push me over the edge. I don't think I have enough peppermint here to compete with them."

The instant relief on her face is evident. "Oh, of course, Ava. I didn't think about that. I'll move them for you, honey. I'll make sure they're somewhere I can see them all day and think about how sweet Michael was to send them to you. Oh, what I'd give to see the two of you together."

"Me too, Joanie," I mumble face down into the desk, praying for relief from the sensation of a tight band around my skull.

I finish out my day and start to pack up my things, anxious to get home and try to take some more powerful medication to relieve this ache when Dr. Stark approaches.

"Ava, I'm sorry for the late notice, but I need you to accompany me to a dinner lecture I'm giving tomorrow."

"Dr. Stark, I'm not sure I can make it. I've been fighting this migraine all week, and it isn't getting any better. I'm trying hard to not miss work, but I don't think I'm able to commit to anything outside of normal office hours."

"Well, I'm sorry you aren't feeling well. But it wasn't a request. This isn't optional. Dr. Morgan's PA, Justin, was supposed to attend. But he's out sick, so I need you to be there to work alongside the drug rep to ensure everything goes smoothly."

Let me get this straight. It's mandatory I go, but Justin can call out sick? *What. The. Hell?* "Dr. Stark, I'll try. But I really don't think—"

"There's no sense continuing this conversation, Ava. It's at 6:00 at Rivercity Chop House. I'll have Joanie move your afternoon appointments so you can head home to get ready around 4:00."

I look up to notice he's already exited my office. *Bastard.* There's no more pussyfooting around. I'm looking for another job. There's no way I can keep working for this asshole!

CHAPTER FIFTEEN

Mick

It's Sunday afternoon, and I'm visiting my mom, Rob, and Emmaleigh for dinner. I've admittedly not seen them nearly enough over the last few months. Grabbing a meal on Sundays had always been routine. A way to stay connected. However, between traveling, little league baseball practices two days a week, and games on Saturday, it's been a busy time of year.

"How've you been, Mick?" my mom asks, pulling me in for a big hug.

"I've been really good, Mom. Except for missing my team's little league game yesterday, I've had a great weekend."

Spinning on her heel, she gives me a look of concern. "Missed your game? That's not like you. Did something happen?"

"It's a long story, but I'd gone out of town for a game and got stuck in traffic."

"Well, your little league games are always in the morning or afternoon. When on earth was your out-of-town game?"

Realizing she's not going to drop this, I decide I might as well come clean. She knows me well enough to understand it had to be something big for me to not make my team's game. She's had to listen to me go on and on about how the parents and other coaches aren't invested in the boys more than a time or two. Taking a deep breath, I go all in. "I took my girl to her first Nationals game where they won spectacularly. We had a great time, but a storm rolled in." Reaching for a banana from the fruit basket sitting in the center of the table, I peel and try to look nonchalant as I continue. "I guess I should've paid more attention to the weather."

"Your girl, huh? Michael York, I haven't heard you refer to anyone as your girl in years. I thought you'd sworn off women after Paula," she states, appearing shocked. Shocked but undeniably happy.

"I did. But Ava just caught me off guard." Putting down the banana, I look up at her from my seat at the table. "Awe, Mom. She's just beautiful, inside and out. You'll love her. She's so sweet. I honestly feel like she's different. That I can trust her. I can't imagine she has a cheating bone in her body. I know I've got a bad track record… and it's only been a few dates, but… well, I think she's the one."

"Oh. My. God. Did you just say she's the one?" Emmaleigh shouts as she comes flying into the room. "I can't believe it! Mick's finally found *the one*. Are you going to marry her?" She claps her hands in excitement as only a teenage girl can. She's practically swooning. About that time, Bruno, their tiny dog, comes in and starts to skip and prance with Emmaleigh as if they're part of a traveling circus. *Good lord.*

"Calm down. We've only had a few dates, but I've known her for almost a year. And I can't explain it. I just have a really good feeling about us."

"Us," my mother and Emmaleigh squeal in unison.

"I can't wait to meet her! What does she look like? How old is she? Is she girly? Do you think she'll like me?"

"Oh, my god, Emmaleigh. Will you get ahold of yourself?" My mother encourages. "I'll have to pull out the hose and spray you down. You're a mess."

"Mom, I'm sixteen. I've been waiting for Mick to bring a girl home since I knew what dating meant. You can't blame me for being curious.

Plus, I'm practically an only child with our age gap. I can't wait to have a girl around here."

"Hey, what does that mean, squirt? I'm around."

"Oh, get over it. You know what I mean. Now spill. Please tell me a little more about her."

"Okay, okay. So she's my age. She's an only child, like you, apparently." I laugh. "She works as a physician assistant in an orthopedic practice I call on."

"What's she look like?" Emmaleigh pushes after dropping into the chair beside me, resting her chin in her hands. She's giddy. God. If this doesn't work out with Ava, this will crush her. *Me and her both.*

I start to chuckle. "Well, if you could imagine what Elsa would look like in real life, you've got a good picture of Ava."

"Elsa from *Frozen*. The movie?"

I nod, reaching back for my banana.

Emmaleigh squeals, springing from her seat, clapping and dancing as if I've just won the lottery. *Hell, maybe I have.*

"So, why did you have to miss your game yesterday?" Rob inquires, trying to get a word in edgewise. He knows I'd move heaven and earth to be at all of their games.

"The traffic was so bad coming out of that Nationals game, we ended up having to spend the night up there. The car barely inched forward a foot in an hour and a half. We got up in plenty of time the next morning but got delayed due to an accident." I don't need to tell him I accidentally shoved my dick back into my girl instead of getting on the road as I should have. Telling a little white lie seems like the better way to handle this story. "By the time I got home, changed, and made it to the field, they'd lost so bad they were basically glad to have the game over with. The other team was full of players that have played travel ball. They've got a lot of experience, and as much as he rubs me the wrong way, a really good coach."

I take another bite of banana. The smell of the burgers wafting into the kitchen from the grill as Rob comes in and out is making my stomach roar. "My team is so young. They're still learning. They'll get there. They're great kids and have a good attitude, but just need some direction. They're kind of a hot mess right now, but we'll work it out in practice."

We spend the rest of the evening chatting over burgers and grilled veggies, watching baseball highlights on Sports Center, and catching up on Emmaleigh's current boyfriend drama before I head home for the night. On the drive back to my place, I consider how it'd feel to have Ava there with me. I've never brought anyone home to spend time with my family but Paula. I have to admit, I'm excited about the chance to introduce her. I think they'll love her. I mean, who wouldn't?

As I park the car and walk inside my quiet apartment, I'm immediately aware the weekend has caught up with me. I'm grabbing a shower and heading for bed, happy to doze off to sleep with thoughts of my ice princess in my head.

∽

It's been a busy week, but it's finally Thursday, and I'm excited to stop by Central Orthopedics to see Ava today. I spent Monday and Wednesday evenings out of town, and Tuesdays are always committed to my little league team. I'd tried calling and texting her but hadn't heard back. I'm sure she's as busy returning to the hectic work week as I am. Looking at my watch, it's only noon. I know my appointment is at 12:30, but let's just call it like it is. I miss her.

"Hi, Michael. She should be in her office. Her last appointment of the day was canceled. You can go on back," Joanie advises.

"Thanks." I offer a big smile until I notice the large bouquet behind her desk. They look eerily similar to the ones I ordered online for Ava. But why would they be out here instead of in her office? Well, at least I know they arrived. As sweet as Ava is, I'm surprised she didn't call to thank me or at least send a quick text.

As I make my way down the hall, approaching her door, I notice it's only cracked a fraction, and the light appears to be off. *That's odd.* As I reach for the doorknob and start to lightly knock on the door, I see she's sitting at her desk with her head resting atop her crossed arms. I feel a pull in my chest, concerned she's not well. My first thought is to rush to her side to check on her, but the worry she may not feel well disappears quickly as I notice a smile cross her face and realize she's not alone. Taking a step back, my eyes refocus, and I watch as Dr. Stark's hands are massaging her shoulders briefly before he moves her hair from her ear and bends down near the crook of her neck.

"I've got to go, but I'll see you at dinner, doll."

What. The. Ever. Loving. Fuck?

CHAPTER SIXTEEN

Ava

"What are you doing?" I ask, flabbergasted at the realization this is Joseph Stark and not Mick. "Have you lost your mind?"

Looking up, I note Dr. Stark has his hands up as if he is being held at gunpoint.

"Calm down, Ava. I was just checking on you since Joanie said you hadn't felt well all week. I'm going to need to head out soon to get ready for this evening and needed to make sure you weren't going to let me down."

"Well, unlike Justin, who's allowed to take a sick day, it didn't sound as if I was afforded the same basic courtesy. And the next time you want to check on me, do it with your words and not your hands." I cross my arms across my chest in complete disgust. "I need you to know, Dr. Stark, the last few months have been very difficult for me. I come to work and do my job despite my chronic migraines, and you've made my work environment less than pleasant. I'll come to the lecture this evening and will be leaving immediately afterward. But I plan to actively start searching for new employment. I'll give you plenty of notice once I find something, but do not ask me to participate in anything else after hours." I huff. "And if I cannot make it to work because it's not safe for me to drive, I *will* call out sick for the day." I push myself from the desk and storm past the arrogant asshole toward the front office. *Where's Mick? He should be here by now.* Feeling unshed tears collect, I think to myself. *I need a hug.*

As I attempt to check with Joanie regarding Mick's whereabouts, I discover she's gone to lunch. My headache is so incredibly painful after my rant with Dr. Stark, the thought of food makes me want to hurl. I look at the schedule and realize I only have about twenty more minutes before my next patient arrives. I can leave at four to get ready for the abomination of a dinner lecture I've been forced to sit through. Thinking this through, I decide to call my mother.

"Hi, Ava. Is everything okay? You don't normally call me during business hours," my mother states as soon as she answers.

"Mom, I'm hurting really bad. I'm going to take another pain pill, but I'm not expecting it to work since the last eight I've tried haven't helped. I have to go to a dinner meeting tonight. If I manage to get through that and this headache is still bad, would you mind meeting me at my house? I think I might need to go to the emergency room and get a shot."

"Oh, baby. I'm so sorry. It must be bad for you to break down and ask for help. Of course, you just call me. Maybe you'll get lucky, and it'll break by then. But I'm here if you need me."

"Thanks, Mom." I hang up the call and fight to prevent the tears from flowing. That's the very last thing this headache needs. Plus, if they start, I'm not sure I'll be able to stop them in time for this dinner tonight.

∿

The rest of the afternoon moves along at a snail's pace. I feel like I can barely concentrate with the pressure in my skull. I feel like someone is trying to crack my head open with a nutcracker. I finish up my last few patients and immediately head for home. Once there, I take a long, hot shower and drink a large glass of water. I try taking a potent anti-inflammatory and a dissolvable nausea pill. Anything to help stave off the worst of this headache. I'm dressed, sitting on the edge of my bed, ready to go with twenty minutes to spare, when I notice my folded laundry sitting in my rattan basket next to the dresser. The Washington Nationals T-shirt proudly sitting on top. *Mick. What happened to him today?* I decide to shoot off a quick text before I leave.

5:25 p.m.
Ava: Hey, I miss you. I was looking forward to seeing you today.

Watching my phone screen for what feels like an hour, I realize it's actually only been about ten minutes. Nothing. Maybe he's busy. I decide to shoot him one more message before I go.

5:35 p.m.
Ava: I wanted to thank you for my beautiful flowers. I'm sorry I haven't been in touch. I haven't felt well. I'll explain when we talk next. I've got to run to a work dinner I'm dreading. Hopefully, we can catch up later.
5:35 p.m.
Ava: Message failed to send.

That's odd. I check my wi-fi and that my phone is working by calling my home number. I
copy my message and try to send it again.

5:41 p.m.
Ava: Message failed to send.

I just send an emoji this time, thinking the message was too long. Again, I receive the same
message. Suddenly, it hits me. I've been blocked.

CHAPTER SEVENTEEN

Mick

Is she fucking kidding me? *I miss you.* I'm done with this shit. I immediately block her number from my phone.

Once I'd bared witness to her two-timing behavior, I backed from the door like I'd been struck with a two-by-four. I could barely breathe. What the hell is wrong with this girl? And me, for thinking I'd found someone different than Paula.

Was this some kind of fucking game? Had she been looking for some kink on the side? Because I'm sure as hell Dr. Dick isn't giving her the orgasms I've given her. My blood felt like it was going to boil over at the sight of them. I had to get the hell out of there.

Driving straight home, I knew I'd have to visit the other clinics on the day's calendar tomorrow or the following week. I was too riled to continue to work. I'd had a history of being reliable, so I knew if I needed some impromptu time off, no one would question it. What I really wanted was a stiff drink. But I had the boys to coach tonight, so it'd have to wait until afterward.

Arriving home, I contacted the office and advised I haven't been feeling well and planned to take tomorrow off. I also tell a white lie and say I'll need the Thursday off, two weeks from now, to make an appointment. Boy, I seem to be telling a lot of these lately. All for what?

The office thanked me for calling and wished me a speedy recovery. Well, at least I won't have to see that shallow, lying Ava for a month or more. I decide to hit the gym and take a long shower before meeting the boys. Hopefully, their losing streak will finally come in handy and distract me from the gut punch I just took, watching the girl I thought could be *the one* with her boss.

"All right, boys. Gather round. We need to come up with a game plan. We have three weeks before we have to play the Devil Dogs again, and we need to be in top shape."

"Coach Mick. Did you get hit in the head? We got beat so bad last time I thought they stopped keeping score."

"Yeah, you must have known how ugly it was going to be. I wouldn't have shown either if my dad didn't make me get in the car."

"Boys, that was on me. I'm sorry. You're my priority from now on, I promise. Nothing short of a hospital visit will ever make me miss another game. I know that team is tough. And I'm not saying we can beat them, but we can certainly bring it better than we have in the past. We just need to take this seriously. For the next two weeks, we're going to do drills at the beginning of each practice, and then we'll play. For anyone who can come more often, we can meet on the fields over there..." I point to the tattered old baseball fields that remain in the distance after the newer ones were constructed. "I'll be here every evening I'm in town, including Sundays."

"I'm in, coach." I hear from the back of the group.

"Thanks, Tommy. I know a lot of it will depend on your parents' ability to get you here, but for anyone who can make it, I'm happy to work with you."

"You got it, coach." I hear a few additional players toss out.

Sure, I want to see these boys improve. Hell, I'd give anything to give Coach Dillon and the Devil Dogs a run for their money. But I have to admit, this is to keep me occupied so I don't have time to sulk over once again being two-timed by a beauty queen.

~

It's been three weeks, and I'm in no better mood than the day I walked in on Ava and her paramour. I was able to finish up early, given Central Orthopedics was no longer on my roster for the day, and so decide to drop by to visit my mother before Emmaleigh arrives home from school. I admit I need to decompress over recent events. And she's always been one to have my back.

"Hey, Mom," I greet as I walk into the kitchen, my mother standing at the stove.

"Oh no, what's wrong?" she asks, knowing me better than anyone. "You look terrible, Mick. Are you eating or just drinking? I'm making you a sandwich, and then I want to hear everything," she says, finger pointed at me like she did when I was twelve.

"I'm just having a rough few weeks. My boys have lost every game but one. The only reason they won that one was because half of the other team had been out sick. They had enough boys to play, but the way the poor kids kept running to and from the portapotty, odds were good they shouldn't have been there either." I reach back to massage my stiff neck, shaking my head at the recollection.

"And the travel is starting to get to me. It gets tiring in these hotel rooms all alone." I admit I've tried to return to my old routine, picking up women to while away the hours, but I'm just too bitter with the female race to enjoy their company right now.

"And what about your girl?" She eyes me knowingly. I can't put anything past her. I think I hear something behind me and turn to look over my shoulder, only to see Bruno scamper in. The chihuahua gives me a solemn look with his big brown eyes as if he's sending his condolences.

"Yeah, that didn't work out. It's my fault. I think I just got tired of all the different women and saw something there that wasn't. Hell, Mom. They're all the same. You think you know someone, just to find you had it all wrong."

"Mick. I feel like there's a big chunk of this story you're leaving out." She lays the sandwich, chips, and a glass of water in front of me and crosses her arms in indignation. I'm not sure I can even eat this.

I've had no appetite. At least, not for anything but beer or something harder.

"Ava seemed sweet, honest." I reach over to take a bite of the sandwich before continuing. "The office she works at is full of some real smug people. A lot of the providers I meet with treat me like I'm an inconvenience. Even some of the other physician assistants, not just the surgeons." I pop a salty chip into my mouth and follow it with a gulp of water. "But Ava was never like that. She actually went out of her way to set up a standing appointment with me, so I didn't sit idle in the waiting room each time I came to the office."

"Well, that sounds nice. She didn't have to do that, right?" My mother sits down at the table with me, bringing her coffee with her.

"She's like that with everyone, though. It isn't just me. But her boss, the surgeon she works with... he's the worst of all of them. So condescending. He's a real asshole. Anyway, we'd had a few dates. Nothing big, just lunch. Then I took her to the Nationals game recently, and things seemed like they were getting serious. Mom, I'm pretty sure I fell in love with her that night. But after we got back to town, things seemed different. I didn't hear from her, and then when I showed up at her office, I found her and her asshole boss together."

"What do you mean, together?"

"I went back to her office, and the door was cracked, the lights were off, and he was rubbing her shoulders and whispering in her ear." I notice my mother's expression is blank. "She was smiling, Mom. She liked it."

"Well, what did she say when you asked her about it?"

"I didn't." I crunch on another salty chip and then reach down to give one to Bruno. Not sure why salt always tastes so good when you don't have an appetite for anything else. Salt and beer.

"Mick. So, you just walked away and didn't say anything to her? Has she tried to call you?"

"Don't know. Blocked her number."

Slam!

I look up to see her coffee has spilled onto the table from where her hand has come down on it. "Michael York. You mean to tell me, a girl you thought you were in love with... a girl who you said could be *the one,* did something you didn't understand, but instead of confronting her about it, you block her number without letting her explain?"

"Yes, ma'am. She did text once. She sent me some phony-assed text about missing me. That's why I blocked her number. Why confront her? I did that with Paula and a hell of a lot of good that did me. Just made me feel like more of a chump." I take a long drink of water and quickly realize this conversation hasn't helped like I'd hoped it would. I reach down to hand Bruno another chip and realize he's left me too.

"Oh well, I have to go. I want to get in a good workout before I meet with the boys tonight. At least they're always there for me."

"Mick, you mark my words. You need to hear her out. Sure, she may be just like Paula. But what are the odds? And if she's as special as you thought she was, think how bad she's hurting right now, wondering why you left without saying goodbye. You aren't a kid anymore, Son. If nothing else, maybe she could shed a light on why it wouldn't have worked out between the two of you. It could help you grow."

"I don't need to grow, Mom. I didn't do anything wrong. My mistake was trusting another woman." I snap in a much sterner voice than I'm used to speaking to her. "I should've known I didn't stand a chance with someone like Ava. She's surrounded by successful surgeons who all make a ton of money. What could she want with me?"

"Mick. When your dad left us, I could've taken the same stance. I could've shut the world out and decided no man was ever worth trying again. If I'd done as you're suggesting, I wouldn't have found Rob, and we wouldn't have Emmaleigh. All I'm saying is life's too short not to take a chance. Sure, things don't always work out the way you want. But sometimes, they do. How will you ever know if you don't try?"

"I know you're right. I just need more time. I think the thing with Paula did such a number on me, I wasn't ready to handle being rejected again. Especially not by someone I let myself imagine forever with. I know good and well I'll never find another woman as close to perfect as Ava again."

"Well, I know it's tough when you look like that." My mother waves her hands from my feet to my head, smirking at me. "But some poor girl will take a chance on you." She comes in for a hug, making me smile a little. My biggest cheerleader.

"Thanks. I'll talk to you later." I head for the door and out to my car. As I approach my SUV, I notice Emmaleigh's car parked on the street. *That's odd. When did she get home?*

CHAPTER EIGHTEEN

Mick

"Hey, where are you? There's not going to be any sunlight left by the time you get here. We're waiting."

"Cool your jets, man. The game ran late. Sorry I'm keeping you and Otis."

"What on earth could have run late with your team? Did somebody wet their pants, and they had to delay the game?"

"Shut up. You know good and well that's not what happened."

"You're right. They'd just pull out their junk and pee on the grass." *He's not wrong.*

"No, believe it or not, they were tied up until the very end. Still lost, but a huge improvement."

"Well, hot damn. Get your ass here, and we can celebrate. Better yet, stop on the way and get us some cold beer so we can celebrate your loose cannons losing at the last second."

"Already did, smart ass. See you in ten."

For fuck's sake. Hanging up the call with my wisecracking best friend, I turn into the main entrance of the park. We'd been coming to Yorktown State Park for years to fish. There was something about the familiarity of it. Zach had another fishing spot he liked when it was just him and Otis. Somewhere he could sit for hours and go undisturbed. That's how he liked it. Although, he'd complained about noticing increased traffic there recently. He said, "My little slice of heaven is being invaded by a bunch of hippies." Apparently, one of the local community colleges had been offering an art class that focused on landscapes and the like, and word had gotten out about what a pretty spot he'd been enjoying all of these years.

He never seemed to catch much from that location. But honestly, I'm not sure that's his goal. He enjoys outdoor activities if a few of the guys are together, but when he's alone, I think he just sticks his pole in the ground and reads or reflects on the past.

As I come around the familiar curve lined with trees and a small area for campers to set up for the night, I spot Zach's old beat-up Ford pickup truck. Putting my car in park, I head to the back to grab my gear before setting out to look for him.

Making my way to our usual spot at the end of an old neglected pier, I spot Zach and Otis in the distance but am surprised to see another person with them. When he said, "We're waiting." I assumed he meant him and the mutt.

"It's about fucking time. We've been parched. Hand me a cold one, will ya?"

"Will it get me off your shit list if I say yes?" Looking to Zach's right, I take in a dark-haired male about my age sitting in a lawn chair about to cast his reel. He appears to be in similar shape to Zach, and I immediately deduce this must be one of his firehouse brothers.

"Hey, man. I'm Mick," I introduce, extending my arm. "Nice to meet ya."

"Likewise. I'm Trevor." As we shake, I receive confirmation regarding his occupation as a St. Florian cross firefighter emblem tattooed on his forearm comes into view.

"Take it you work with grandpa, here."

"He's not too bad. For an old guy."

"You plan on walking home?" Zach spits. "Where's that beer?"

Opening my chair and sitting down beside him, I unzip the cooler and hand both of the guys a fresh one. I'm glad fate intervened, and I stopped on the way here. There's no way my provisions would have been enough for three people without grabbing a few more.

As I pop the cap off of my beer, I notice Zach and Trevor clinking beer bottles together. "Did I miss something?"

"Nah. Trevor's already got one foot out the door. He's moving to North Carolina."

"Oh, yeah? What's there?"

"A new life," he answers flatly, taking a swig from the amber bottle.

I'm afraid to dig any deeper on this, so decide to focus on getting my line ready to cast.

"Trevor's ex did a number on him," Zach mutters under his breath. "You know how that goes."

"Man, that sucks. Had you guys been together long?"

"Couple of years. I thought she was the one, man. Dropped by the house one day to grab something. I'd been on shift all day and needed to get an assignment I was working on for a class I was taking. Guess since we work twenty-four-hour shifts, she didn't think there was a chance she'd get caught."

"Oh, fuck," I utter.

"Who knows how long it'd been going on. I went to work and never gave it a second thought that she'd be two-timing me. I should've known. Ashley's gorgeous. She had men coming on to her everywhere we went. I've learned the hard way. Only date down."

"What do you mean, date down?"

"She was a fucking ten, man. I'm not a bad-looking guy, but I'm not dating anyone above a seven ever again."

My eyes connect with Zach's. All guys seem to think their girl is hotter than she really is. *Well, except Ava.*

"Nah, man. This girl was a ten. You know those billboards you pass when you go downtown. The ones with the girl wearing the big ass rock on her finger for Carlson's Jewelry?"

"Yeah?"

"That's her."

"Holy shit." I guess she is a ten. "I'm sorry, Trevor. I know that has to suck."

"Yeah. I was completely in love with her. But her damn face is everywhere in this town. I can't get away from it. Every time I drive by that fucking billboard, I want to hurl something at the damn thing."

"Do you have family in North Carolina?"

"Nope. I grew up here."

"He got a job with the fire department there. He's going to be living the mountain life," Zach says, looking almost envious. "Sycamore Mountain. Has a nice ring to it."

"Well, I have a funny feeling that place is more suited to loners like you," Trevor adds. "I'm not looking to date again, but hell, I don't want to have to drive an hour to get some pus—"

"Ah, you got one, I say, tipping my beer toward Trevor's line."

Damn fish probably felt sorry for the loser. He probably threw himself on the hook all Hari-kari to make him feel better.

"What the fuck ever, Zach." As Trevor struggles to reel in his catch, I have to fight not falling off of my chair when the tiny spot fish that could fit in his hand breaks through the water. He'd been working so hard to pull the thing in I expected to see a largemouth bass on the other end.

"Awe, isn't he cute?" Zach chuckles. "Catch ten more, and you can serve it up on a cracker."

Trevor removes the sorry excuse for a fish and quickly tosses him back in the water.

"Sorry, man. About the girl. And the fish." I take another gulp of my beer and decide to join the He-Man Woman Haters Club. "If it's any consolation, I know how you feel. The only difference being, we'd only been going out for a little while. But I was all in, man. I thought this girl was it for me."

"Bitches, man. I'm not going down that road again. Zach here has it all figured out," Trevor says.

Looking over to my friend, I notice his stoic expression. It's now evident to me that Trevor is a newer acquaintance. Most anyone in fire, EMS, or the police in this area knows Zach's story. And there's not one who'd say Zach had it all figured out.

"You still haven't heard anything from her? I thought you had to see her at work," Zach asks.

"Well, I managed to get a pass on calling on their office for a bit. But I have to go next week, and I'm dreading it."

"She cheat too?" Trevor asks as he casts his line in a completely different direction than where it had been before.

"Yeah. With her boss. Wish I could say I'm surprised. She was every bit as beautiful as your ex. She didn't model or anything. Won a bunch of beauty pageants when she was younger to help pay for school." I'm not sure why I feel I'm betraying Ava to talk about her in this way? Fuck. She's the one that cheated on me. But it still feels wrong somehow. "Anyway, there might be something to your system."

I turn, and both Zach and Trevor are looking at me deadpan.

"Only dating down."

They both nod and return to watching their lines. Boy, the three of us are some sad lot. Zach's avoided women for years unless he needs a rare hookup. And the two of us youngbloods can't be more bitter. Yet, we're not young anymore. That's the thing. Zach has done the married life. He's made his choice to live this way. I'm pushing thirty. Do I really want to spend the rest of my life hanging out with bitter, lonely guys like this? I reach over to scratch Otis behind his ear. God, what I'd give for a dog. If I didn't have to travel so much, I'd at least have a loyal companion. But between life on the road and the frequent practices and games, it simply wouldn't be fair to the pup.

"Are you sure about what you saw?" Zach pushes. I'm surprised by his questioning. He tends to think the worst of all women.

"Come on, man. It was clear as day."

"Did you walk in on them?" he continues.

"Well, they weren't fucking or anything. The lights were off in her office, and he was massaging her shoulders and whispering in her ear."

"I know what you think you saw, Mick. But you went from telling me this girl walked on water to this. It just seems like a big leap."

"Well, I guess money and status talk. Plus, he's not a bad-looking guy. He's just a asshat. And not because he was with Ava. Hell, she's beautiful. Why not go after her? But I swear I thought he was married. And he's a real dick. I've never met a more condescending asshole."

Zach shakes his head, reeling his line in to change lures. "What're you going to do if you see her? Next week, I mean?"

"I don't know. I was thinking about going later in the day and just asking the receptionist if one of the docs could sign for me. I don't have to see her."

"It's never that easy, though. You just going to ignore the elephant in the room if you can't avoid seeing the girl?"

"Yep. I'm at work. I can't fucking quit. I'm the only rep in this area. I'd have to move or take on a different product line, making a hell of a lot less money. Shit. I've thought about it. But I don't see any way around it."

"Women," Trevor spits as he casts his line again.

~

Driving home, I feel different than I expected after spending time with Zach today. It was nothing against Trevor. I hadn't been fishing with Zach and Otis for weeks. Between almost squeaking out a win with the boys today and knowing I was finally meeting my best bud to hang out, I was optimistic I'd have a better outlook on the week ahead.

Instead, the three of us commiserating together about our shitty luck with women seemed to amplify my foul mood. That and none of us caught a goddamn thing. Well, unless you count Trevor's fish the size of a postage stamp.

What will I do if I see Ava next week? Sure, I probably should confront her. Tell her she only had to be an adult and let me down easy. I could take it. But I have no plans to see her outside of work ever again, and that isn't the type of conversation I need to risk having in her office.

I'll just be an adult about it. I'll show up extra early or super late and hope she's not there. Like the scaredy cat I am. If that doesn't work, I'll simply say I'm sorry things didn't work out, and I hope we can keep things professional.

As I continue the drive home, I look down at the empty cooler on the passenger seat, and it dawns on me I have nothing at the house to eat. I'm not in the mood for anything heavy, so I decide to stop at a local sushi restaurant and order a few things for takeout. Their food is fresh and fast. I'll just place the order once I arrive, and it should only be about fifteen minutes until it's ready.

Arriving at Fuji, I put the car in park and search on my phone for their number. I need to just add them to my contacts as often as I order from here. Ah, there it is. I place my order for miso soup, a salad, a spring roll, a Tiger roll, and a Dynamite roll. The memory of my encounter with the Naga pork curry dish quickly comes to mind, and I decide to change the Dynamite roll to something less risky. Not willing to chance that again anytime soon.

Scrolling through my phone, I check out a few posts on TikTok while I await my order. Time passes quickly as I watch one grown-assed adult after another making a video where it appears a pen they are using disappears into their nose. These are some of the most ridiculous videos I've ever seen on this social media app. *Why am I watching this?* Realizing it's probably been about fifteen minutes, I grab my keys and begin to open my car door when I spot one striking, tall blonde standing in front of the sports bar down the sidewalk from the Asian restaurant.

The guy she's with is clearly not Joseph Stark. But then again, if he's married, they probably can't be seen together out in public. This guy is tall and broad. He appears pretty muscular compared to Dr. Dick. Watching the two of them, they must be pretty familiar with one another. Their postures both appear quite relaxed. I watch as he leans in for a hug, giving her a quick peck on the cheek before turning and walking away. Hell, maybe he's gay. There's no way I could kiss her on the cheek and not slide over to devour her mouth. As I watch her walk to her car, I replay the many hot, sensual kisses we've shared. *How could she have kissed me like that and then want Stark? I don't get it.*

Hell, I need to just pull the bandaid off and get back out there. I'm out of town twice this week before heading to her office. If I can score while I'm in Salem, it'll make it easier to move on. Two can play this game.

CHAPTER NINETEEN

Ava

"Ava, I've got an add-on for you in room four."

Looking up from my stack of messages Joanie handed me as I walked in this morning, I don't see anyone at the door. But I know that was Dr. Stark's voice. Heck, he probably tossed out the statement walking by to his office without stopping. *Asshole.*

Serves me right for sifting through this stack, thinking I was going to find a note from Michael asking me to call him. That he was so sorry and couldn't wait to apologize. He'd been trapped under something heavy and was just extricated this morning. Or he had to go out of town on his usual business but ate a corn chip and ended up in the emergency room having an allergic reaction. *Whatever.* There's no point trying to make excuses for him. No matter what happened, I deserve better than being ghosted. We're not teenagers, for fuck's sake.

I'd managed to get myself out of the house and out of my funk when Carson called at the last minute asking if I wanted to meet at the Sport's Page for dinner. Not my usual choice for a meal, but once we arrived, and I realized he was meeting some of the guys from the police department, it all became clear. I was getting set up.

I know he meant well. And I had to give it to him for not saying *I told you so*. I'd tried to put the conversation we'd had about traveling salesman out of my head. But turns out, he was probably right on the money.

I'm not sure who Carson had in mind when he brought me to the sports bar. I recognized Eve's twin brothers, Tate and Tanner Manning, right away. The others, not so much. But I'm in no way ready to get back out there. While I appreciate his effort, I'll find my own dates. Although from now on, I'll rely on a more tried and true method for finding true love versus getting to know someone through your job for a year. I'll stick with Tinder. *Probably just as reliable.*

Grabbing my lab coat, I slide it on and head to room four. Collecting the patient's chart, I see they're here in follow up of a Boxer's fracture. He was seen in the emergency room last week, and a splint was placed to stabilize the broken bone. The most common cause of a Boxer's fracture is striking something with your fist, allowing the high-velocity impact to break the bone in the hand that extends from the patient's wrist to the base of their pinky. Knocking on the door before I step inside, I enter and abruptly stop. *Fucking Edward.*

I quickly look back down at the chart I'm holding to see his full name. "Hi, Mr. Seamen," I greet with an extended hand, trying to maintain my composure, both at his presence and his name. *No wonder he's always in a bad mood.* Realizing he's probably right-handed, and that is the hand currently immobilized with a splint, I drop my hand down by my side.

"You're a doctor?" Edward sneers.

"No. I'm a physician assistant. I see you're here to follow up on your broken hand," I add quickly, hoping I can keep this professional and quick.

"I was supposed to see a doctor."

"Oh, I'm sorry. When you call to make follow-up appointments, they're frequently with a midlevel like myself or a nurse practitioner. If you'd like to see one of the doctors before you leave—"

"No, I want to see a doctor today. Not you. You can run along and tell them if I can't see a physician, I'll go somewhere else."

"Yes, Mr. Seamen. I'll let them know." Turning on my heel, I open the door and make my way toward Dr. Stark's office. *Well, I didn't expect it to go quite that quickly.* I can't imagine *Fucking Edward* is actually upset about seeing a mid-level provider. We tend to have more time to spend with the patients than the surgeons who are frequently called away. I could've changed his splint into something more user-friendly that he could shower in and wasn't hot and itchy. Dr. Stark would've seen him before he left. This feels personal. I've worked here for years and have never had a patient refuse to be seen by me.

The tension in my shoulders builds as I approach Dr. Stark's office. I'm dreading this. Dr. Stark hates people who behave this way. If nothing more than it causing him to see another haughty, demanding patient, much too close to his own personality, he could've otherwise pawned on me.

I start to knock on Dr. Stark's door but stop once I see he's in his office with Dr. Lee. Both of their heads spring in my direction, so I drop my hand back to my side and advise Dr. Stark of the situation with *Fucking Edward. Boy, does that name suit him.*

"I tried to explain you'd be happy to see him before he left so that I could remove the splint, assess him, and apply a fabricated one, but he wouldn't have it."

Dr. Stark purses his lips together as he looks back at me, annoyed. "Fine. I'll be back, Sebastian. Let me go and do Ava's job for her."

What the fuck? Really?

"I'm sorry, Ava. What did you say this patient was here for?" the handsome surgeon interjects. There's an obvious bite in his tone after hearing Dr. Stark's derogatory statement.

"He has a Boxer's fracture. He was seen and diagnosed in the ER recently and sent here for a follow-up."

"Well, given I'm the only hand surgeon in the office today, why don't I go take a look at him, Joe?" Dr. Lee winks at me while Dr. Stark's back is still turned. "It's not Ava's fault the patient is being so demanding. You had a call to make. I'm happy to give him a thorough evaluation."

"Ah, sure, Sebastian. If you don't mind."

"Not at all." Dr. Lee takes Edward's chart from my hands, points that sexy dimple in my direction, then exits Dr. Stark's office heading to exam room four.

As I step into the hallway, Joanie approaches. "Ava, I wanted to let you know I was able to block off a few hours Friday afternoon so you could make your appointment. You know Dr. Stark always leaves on Friday after lunch. He won't have to know a thing."

I bite the inside of my cheek. I hate lying to her, but I couldn't tell her I needed the afternoon free for an interview with a competing orthopedic clinic for a job. *Damn Dr. Stark.* Except for him, I've really enjoyed all of the people here.

"Thank you. I'm sorry about the late notice."

"Aaaaaah!"

Joanie and I both jump simultaneously. "Oh my goodness. What was that?"

"Is that necessary?" I now recognize Edward's screeching voice and determine he really is getting a thorough evaluation. The door suddenly swings wide, and Dr. Lee exits.

"You can stop at the receptionist desk on your way out to make your next appointment. I'd personally ask for Ava, as she's our most gentle provider." Without another word, Dr. Lee casually strolls toward the front of the office and exits.

A few moments later, Edward is stomping out of the exam room toward the front of the clinic.

"Oh, that's probably my cue to get back there," Joanie says with a bit of a giggle.

I bite my lower lip at how differently this day is going than I first expected. *That Sebastian Lee is all right in my book. Not ever considering anything outside of the office with that playboy, but he's still all right with me.*

◊

The following days seem to drag. The office is stressful, with Dr. Stark barking at everyone. Nosey Joanie thinks there's trouble at home, but I bet that this is his norm. I can't for the life of me imagine any woman putting up with him for long. I don't care how much money he has.

"Ava, I need to see you in my office." *Speak of the devil.*

"You needed something, Dr. Stark?"

"Have a seat, Ava."

Not that I want to stay here any longer than necessary, but I do as requested, hoping we can get this over with, and I can get out of this office.

"We had a complaint about your care recently."

"What?"

"Yes. I'm afraid I'm going to have to put a notation in your personnel file. This won't bode well for your performance appraisal coming soon."

"But I don't recall having anyone I took care of upset—"

"Well, it's inconsequential whether you recall it or not. As you know, our patient feedback scores directly reflect the level of reimbursement from some insurers. We must receive top marks in patient experience from all of our patients."

He's lecturing me? How on earth could this man possibly get good feedback scores?

"As I've mentioned, your care is a direct reflection on me, as you are, in essence, an extension of my care. I should actually make two marks in your file, given we've had a conversation about your professionalism once already. But I'll let that one slide."

I glare back at him. That damn interview tomorrow cannot come fast enough.

"Well, I'm sorry this occurred, Dr. Stark. I have always tried to give the very highest level of care and treat all of the patients assigned to me as I would treat any member of my family. I'll try to place even more effort on the patient's experience in the future." Now, can I get the hell out of here before I fucking lose it?

"I appreciate that, Ava. It's my duty to bring these things to your attention."

Standing from my seat, I walk out the door without another word. I'll get fired before I can quit if I sit in there one more minute. I can feel the color rising on my face. My skin feels hot. I'm so ready to be done with this guy. Oh, if only he could leave instead of me. But this guy, pompous asshole or not, makes the company too much money for them to let him go because he's treating me like crap. So I might as well look elsewhere.

Once in my office, I reach for my purse. Grabbing my nausea pill and some ibuprofen, I reach for my bottle of water to swallow them down. As I place the bottle down on my desk, I notice the clock reads 1:00 p.m. Not only did I not realize the morning appointments had been running so late, but it's also thirty minutes past when Mick would've been here. *Hmm. Is he quitting too?* Good riddance. No matter. Maybe once I have that interview tomorrow, I can completely put thoughts of him behind me. *Unless he calls on them as well. Ugh.*

I walk over to Joanie to determine how much time I have before my next patient arrives, to see if I can run to the cafeteria quickly.

"Oh, you have time, dear. Go run and get you something."

"Hey, is Allison here?"

"Yes, I think I saw her in the breakroom."

"Thanks, Joanie."

Walking down the hall to the small room with a table covered in a cheap plastic tablecloth, a coffee pot, and a refrigerator, I see Allison placing a frozen meal into the microwave.

"Hey, Ava. How are you?"

"Uh, don't know, really. I got called on the carpet by Dr. Stark about a patient who complained about his care. He wouldn't tell me anything about what happened, just said I needed to try harder. I feel like I bend over backward for patients and him. Do you know anything about the situation?"

"Not really. Just some guy who said he was treated poorly during his visit. He said the provider was really aggressive, and he felt it was a personal issue. That he was being attacked."

"Allison. When have you ever known me to attack anyone? If I was going to lash out, it would be at Joseph Stark," I whisper.

"I agree. Mr. Seamen didn't provide specifics but was adamant he voice his concern about his displeasure with his care."

Fucking Edward. "Well, that clears things up. I didn't provide any care to him. He refused to let me evaluate and treat him because I wasn't a doctor. Dr. Lee took care of him." I wish I could share that little tidbit with Dr. Stark, but I knew he wouldn't care how this had occurred. He wouldn't care less that *Fucking Edward* just had a bone to pick with me—and Eve—and this was how he chose to do it.

"Would this be the guy yelling from the patient room that Joanie told me about?"

"That'd be the one."

"Well, I'm sorry you had to put up with him or Dr. Stark, Ava. Trust me, whatever Joe Stark gives me for your file will not be acknowledged."

"Thank you," I answer, rubbing the back of my neck. I honestly don't even want food anymore. I just want to lay down. Retreating to my office to lie still for a few minutes before submitting myself to any further torture, I drop into my chair, close my eyes, and rest my head on my desk. As I reopen them, I see the notation on my desktop calendar of Mick's scheduled visit. Looking at the clock, I realize he's not coming. Probably just as well. How would I have handled it if he did?

Thinking more seriously about the situation, I'm better off not seeing Michael. I might've lost it and been called back into Stark's office when my behavior wasn't deemed professional. And that would've been my third out. *If only Dr. Lee could fix Michael as he did* Fucking Edward.

But deep down, I know this isn't how I feel. Despite the way he's treated me, I strangely don't want to see any harm come to him. Not sure why. He's had no problem with walking away and taking my heart along for the ride. Sure, I'm angry. No one deserves to be treated this way. But I was falling in love with him. It's hard to wish ill will on someone you care about, even when you're mad.

I just have to channel all of this emotion into something constructive. To be an even stronger person. One who doesn't take any shit from anyone. The next man who wants a relationship with me is going to have to prove his worth!

CHAPTER TWENTY

Ava

Dropping my keys on the counter, I decide to take a long, hot shower. The sensation of scalding water pounding against my flesh might distract me from the constant feeling of my heart being torn to shreds. I'd thought about picking up Luigi's for dinner. Something pleasurable to distract me from this constant heartache, but I couldn't bear bumping into Michael.

Walking into my white marble bath, I remove my clothes and turn on the water. Turning to look in the mirror, I take in my reflection. Tilting my head, I briefly examine my profile. I'm a pretty girl. Probably a little too flat chested for most men, but I'm not that bad, I think cupping my breasts. *Oh, whatever.* I'm smart. I'm funny, kind. And there's no doubt after the other night, I'm good in bed.

What am I missing? I can feel my eyes fill with tears and walk swiftly to the shower before I succumb to this pity party. Lifting my head as I step into the spray, I give myself a much-needed pep talk. I'm changing the channel on these thoughts. I don't understand why men behave the way they do. But this is no reflection on me. I have friends, I'm dependable. I have a good job, even if Dr. Stark makes me crazy.

Most of my patients are happy with their care and seem to prefer seeing me to many of the physicians. I can tolerate him until I find something better.

Rinsing the shampoo from my hair, I apply a little body wash and try to give my shoulders a little massage. The tension appears to be a permanent part of my existence now. *Change the channel, Ava.*

Getting out of the shower, I quickly dry off and slide on my thick terry robe. I'm going for comfort tonight. However I can find it. Looking through the refrigerator, nothing grabs my attention. Shutting the door, I move to the freezer. Ah, Ben & Jerry's Chubby Hubby ice cream. My go-to ingredient for turning my mood around. Grabbing a spoon, I head to the couch. Curling my legs underneath me, I flip through the channels looking for anything that will distract me. Distract me from this gnawing in my chest.

The Bachelor pops onto the screen, and for a moment, it holds my attention. The couple is seated at a private oceanfront table near the beach. There are candles and flowers... snap out of it, Ava. There's also a camera crew, and the guy is probably flying to meet the next girl for a *romantic date* tomorrow. And if I'm not mistaken, these guys often hook up with multiple women on this show. Women who are looking to land him. Why would I want to land a guy who's sleeping with other women? Yuck! See. There's something to be positive about. You haven't stooped that low. You don't need to audition for a man.

I chew the inside of my lip, wondering if Michael has, in fact, moved on to sleeping with other women. I mean, I haven't heard a word from him in weeks, and he's blocked my calls. Why would I think he's holding out for me?

Now the ache in my chest has spread to my belly. Dropping the spoon into the almost empty pint of ice cream, I place it on the coffee table in disgust. Why did I have to go there?

I don't need him. He's a master manipulator. I'll give him that. Any man that can go to such extremes to get what he wants, just to walk away. I must be quite the prize. To have pulled out all the stops with Luigi and spent an incredible night at the Nationals game just so he could score. Heck, he probably planned the date to be out of town, knowing the forecast called for stormy weather. Isn't that the definition of a player?

Wrong channel, Ava.

Well, this evening went downhill quickly. Grabbing the remnants of my dinner, I deposit the carton in the trash, place my spoon in the sink, and decide to head to bed early.

"Hey, Mom. Just wanted to check in before I went to bed."

"Hi, Ava. It's not even nine o'clock. You have a headache, hun?"

"No. Just tired."

"No word from Michael?"

"No. I don't want to talk about him. You doing okay?"

"Yes. I'm going to the shelter on Saturday. I have to fill out some papers to volunteer and get a tour of the place. They said I could spend some time with the pups while I was there."

"Oh, Mom, that's fantastic. I'm so happy for you." This is the best news I've heard in ages.

"Why don't you come along? I know I need to do this on my own, but I wouldn't mind the company if you're free."

"Sure. I'll meet you there. Just text me what time."

"I will. Get some sleep, my beautiful girl. I love you."

"I love you too." Hanging up the call, I place the phone down on the nightstand and find some sleep clothes. I'm proud of my mother. This is a big step for her. As I slide into bed, I close my eyes and end my day with gratitude. Thankfulness for all the good things in my life. Other than my migraines, I'm in good health. My mother's health has improved beyond anything I could've hoped for. Now she's looking at volunteering. I have great friends, a nice home, and I'm gainfully employed. What more could I want?

Change the channel, Ava.

〜

Walking into the lobby of the Hanover area animal shelter, I see my mother standing at the counter speaking with a young woman. As I approach, I see she's holding a clipboard and dropping a pen into a cup on the counter.

"Hi, Mom."

"Oh, Ava. This is Janet. She's going to be showing us around." My mother returns the clipboard, and I smile in Janet's direction. Little dachshund earrings dangle from her lobes which have legs that appear to be walking when she moves. Janet is perfectly suited for this job.

"It's nice to meet you." I give my mother a brief hug and ensure she's included my contact information on the paperwork in the event she is feeling unwell and needs me to come to pick her up.

"Right this way, ladies. It's pretty crowded today." We trail along behind her down a bright yellow corridor that smells of old concrete and dog. As Janet opens a heavy metal door, we're instantly greeted with the animated barking of confined animals. "We have dogs and cats here, but we keep them separated. We're happy to have you assist in both areas. The animals benefit from walks and affection. You can help with feeding time and grooming. If there's a dog or cat that makes you nervous, you just let us know. We rarely have any issues with aggressive animals, but I want you to feel comfortable.

As I walk into the kenneled area behind my mother, I take in the rows of excited dogs. There are smaller dogs on top and larger dogs on the bottom. There are a variety of breeds present. Some with a beautiful dark, shiny coat, and others with spots. They all appear well cared for. Several look thin. A few sit back in the corner, a bit scared.

"I wasn't expecting so many," I utter.

"They're all so sweet," my mother states as she approaches a small, white tuft of fur with big brown eyes. "Is it okay to pet them?"

"Sure. Just let them smell your hand. Don't reach in unless they seem receptive," Janet advises before she walks down the corridor to grab a large container of food to distribute.

I let out a laugh, watching the tiny mutt practically lick my mom to death. "I think that one's a little too receptive."

"Oh, she just needs some love," my mom coos, her statement instantly causing a sharp, stabby sensation in my chest.

Observing these two, my introverted mother and this lonely,

extroverted dog, should make me smile. But it's bringing tears to my eyes. My eyes scan the room. All of these lonely creatures. Had they been cast away? Had they served their purpose until they were no longer convenient? My gaze lands on a small beagle mix that had fallen asleep with his head resting in his dog bowl. Had this one been here so long that the arrival of strangers wasn't exciting any longer? Had visitors coming and going just to leave them behind become commonplace?

Unable to stop them now, the tears begin to pour down my cheeks. Swatting at them as they tumble to the ground, I inwardly scold myself. *What is wrong with you, Ava? Are you seriously having a breakdown here?*

"Ava?"

I feel my mother pull me into her before I can make eye contact with her. I love her so. But I can't end up this way. Spending day after day alone, feeling discarded. But this is so much harder now that I know what I'm missing. Do I just move on and settle for someone who'll be good to me? Not worry about chemistry any longer? Because anything has to feel better than this.

"I'm sorry, Mom. I don't know what's come over me."

"Baby. I understand. It's okay."

"I just got my hopes up. With Michael. I thought he was different. He said and did all the right things." Pulling back, I brush back the tears with the back of my hand and dig deep for renewed resolve. "I'm so proud of you, Mom. For doing this. I know this is out of your comfort zone. I'm going to take a page from your playbook and work on me for a while."

"Ava. You're so strong and smart. It's his loss, you know that, right?"

"Yes, ma'am. That's one thing I'm certain of. It just hurts. I think I'd been burying my disappointment for too long. These sweet pups pushed me over the edge." I chuckle half-heartedly. "Are you okay here? I think I'm going to go home and put on a pot of tea, now that I've gotten that out of my system."

"Of course. I'm fine. Please give me a call later to let me know you're all right."

"I'm fine. I'm sorry to worry you. But I'll call you later." Giving her a quick hug and a kiss, I wave to Janet as I head for the front doors.

Walking through the parking lot to my car, I turn to take in the shelter once more before climbing inside. I say a silent prayer for a miracle. One where all of the animals inside find forever homes. Homes where they'll all feel loved.

Slipping into the driver's seat, I grasp the steering wheel and take a deep breath. I'm giving myself permission to have a good cry. I'm allowed this. But then I'm turning this page. I'm not going to allow Dr. Stark to continue to mistreat me. It may take a while to find a new job, but find one, I will. And until someone comes along who proves they're worthy, I'll focus on living my best life. It may make me a frigid bitch, but I'll decide who stays or goes from now on. I'm not giving any man that kind of power. This ice queen doesn't need a man to save her.

Being cold and alone never bothered me anyway.

CHAPTER TWENTY-ONE

Mick

It's late. Another day is done. They all seem to be running together. It's no different than before, but why do I feel so much more hollow now?

Get it together, Mick.

Grabbing a beer from the minibar of the hotel I'm staying in, I plop myself down on the bed and grab the remote. Sports Center. Now that's a reliable relationship.

Bzzz. Bzzz.

Zach Hunter
9:20 p.m.
Zach: Just checking on you. Give me a call this weekend after your game. I'm taking Otis to the cabin this weekend. Pack a bag and bring your sorry ass along.

I don't have it in me to respond. He wouldn't expect one anyway. How does he do it, day after day? Just him and his dog. I take a long pull from my beer, hoping this might be the sip that cools the burning sensation in my chest. I think I preferred the curry pork to this ache.

Might be nice to get away after the game. Even if only for one night.

Tilting back my amber bottle, I continue to flick through the channels until I give up and return to Sports Center, as I always do. My life's predictable. I snort, placing the nearly empty bottle on the nightstand.

Beer, baseball, a weekend trip to the mountains... who needs women?

I do, that's who. But not women. Just one woman. Her.

God, I miss her.

CHAPTER TWENTY-TWO

Mick

It's Thursday night. I should've gone by the Central Ortho office today, but I'm putting it off until tomorrow. I'm hoping I can somehow avoid Ava, but if not, I'll just have to deal with it. I can't lose my job over this. If I have to see her, I can spend the rest of the day with a stiff drink.

"Coach. Did you see that?" Billy yells from the hill.

"Yeah, bud, that was an awesome pitch. Keep it up, and we'll strike out that team on Saturday." I try to encourage, knowing there's about as much luck in that this season as there is of having someone like Ava back in my life.

"Hey, coach. Mom sent me with some cookies for the boys," Emmaleigh shouts from behind me as she walks to the pitcher's mound. There's about a ten-second delay before the boys realize what she's carrying. Once they've figured it out, poor Emmaleigh is bombarded by ten-year-olds. It's like watching piranhas attack a fresh piece of meat.

I walk over to my little sister and give her a big hug. "That was nice of her. Tell her we all said thank you." I direct toward the boys whose mouths are now full of chocolate chip and sugar cookies.

"Thank you," they all shout in unison.

"What's the occasion?" I ask.

"I don't know. I think she's feeling sorry for the underdog lately." She gives me a suspicious look with one brow cocked I can't quite decipher.

"Are you referring to the team or me?"

She just shrugs her shoulders, face appearing deadpan. "Whoever fits." She manages to swipe a treat from the plate before the vultures grab for seconds. Chomping into a still warm, gooey chocolate chip cookie, she asks, "Hey, can I borrow your phone? Mine died on the way here, and I forgot to bring my charger."

"Sure." Reaching into my back pocket, I hand her my phone and watch as she heads to the dugout. She's probably letting Mom know she almost lost a digit from their special delivery. I can't help but chuckle. If only those boys were that aggressive about the game. Wondering how I got so distracted I missed out on the cookies, I shake my head and return to my wayward ballers.

"Okay, line up. We're going to do some more drills."

"Ohhhh." They all groan. I really need to get these little cookie monsters into shape if we're ever going to win a game.

An hour later, the kids have all packed up their bat bags and are headed with their parents to their vehicles. We have little hope of winning our game on Saturday against Coach Dillon's team, but I guess there's always the chance this time his kids will all have strep throat instead of dysentery. If enough players don't show up, we could win by forfeit.

But our team's coming together. I honestly don't want them to win that way. I'd love to see their proud, jubilant faces when they shock themselves and everyone around them with their first real win. At least the kids seem to be open to learning and participating, and they're getting better day by day. Maybe I should bribe them. Mom makes a mean Rice Krispy treat.

"Hey, here's your phone. Thanks for letting me borrow it."

"No problem. You doing okay, Sis? I came to visit Mom the other day, and when I left, I saw your car out front. You didn't even come into the kitchen to say hello."

"Oh, I'm good. Sorry about that. A friend was having relationship trouble. Guess I got caught up in it. I really wanted to help them out. You know how it is." Again, she looks at me and shrugs as if it is no big deal, but after the way she was dancing and clapping over my finally meeting a special girl, I know these types of things are huge in her world. I forget what it's like to be a teenager. Every moment is so dramatic. But then again, I didn't have to deal with teenage angst and relationship drama because I was always with Paula. My teen torment didn't hit 'til I was twenty.

"Well, you're a good friend to try and help them through it. I hope they know that." I put one arm around her shoulders and pull her in for a side hug.

"Yeah, I think they do. We'll see." Emmaleigh's face appears downtrodden, serious.

"And I'm sorry I got your hopes up about meeting a girl, Em. Your big brother just doesn't have the relationship gene. I think Dad leaving must've done a bigger number on me than I thought. It can't all be about picking beautiful girls that end up leaving me hurt and disappointed." The statement takes me by surprise as I complete the sentence. It feels like an out-of-body experience, watching a conversation balloon in a cartoon or comic strip. How had I not considered this before? I'd blamed all of my worries about a committed relationship on Paula.

Feeling a reassuring squeeze from her, I know she's all too aware of the impact of his departure on my life. I'm grateful my mother and Rob are so strong. So Emmaleigh never has to suffer that rejection. It would've been hard enough watching my parents go their separate ways, but my father's walking out of my life completely had caused a larger impact than I'd allowed myself to examine before.

Needing to change the somber mood, I tickle her along her ribcage where I know she's sensitive, as only a big brother can. She checks me with her hip, laughs, and turns to head for her car. "Don't be a stranger, Mick. I miss you when you're not around."

"I know. I'm sorry, Em. I'll do better. Just had a lot on my plate lately." *And on my mind.* "Hey, tell Mom thanks for the cookies. Maybe next time, I might actually get one." I chuckle.

I watch her wave and walk ahead of me while I gather up the remaining things the boys have left. She's a good egg. The conversation sitting in the kitchen with my mom the other day quickly springs to mind. *If I'd done as you're suggesting, I wouldn't have found Rob, and we wouldn't have Emmaleigh.* I couldn't imagine life without that sassy kid. She means everything to me. Mom's right. Maybe one day, I'll need to try again. Just not any time soon.

Ava

It's officially been a month since I've seen or heard from Michael. I still can't believe how wrong I was about him. He honestly seemed so different. Genuine. After taking a chance on him, my way of life went from an acceptable reality of 'table for one' to utter heartbreak in an instant.

I thought my existence was fine before. Sure, nothing exciting. But I dated on occasion. My friends kept me in stitches. I enjoyed my job when I didn't want to stab Dr. Stark with my splinting sheers. Now all I can think about is what is missing.

In retrospect, I'm sure Michael is just like all the others. For whatever reason, I appear to be a challenge to some men. It's predictable, really. Once they've slept with me, it's over. For some, it lasts a while. We hang out with their friends or coworkers. Do the rounds of being seen together. But in my experiences, they're more subtle about the cut and run.

For most, their calls started to trail off, or they became busier. 'Sorry, can't make it. Something's come up.' Or the 'I've met someone' excuse or 'it just doesn't seem to be working out.' But I've never been completely ghosted before.

I can hear his voice mocking me. 'Do you want to get a hotel?' It was probably all planned from the get-go. And I fell for it. He was one master player, all right. And I don't mean the baseball variety.

But boy, did he use that game to his advantage. And I fell into it hook, line, and sinker. Teaching me everything about the sport he loved. It had endeared me to him. Trying so hard to bring me into his world. I should've known once he dropped the dirty talk, it was all part of his master plan. It was just setting the stage for his end game.

Maybe this is the universe's way of telling me I really do need to get another job. I've been looking, but orthopedic physician assistant jobs don't appear to be that plentiful. I could transition to a different field of medicine, like the emergency room. But I'm good at orthopedics. It makes me angry to think I need to look for another job because of a man. No, two men. One I *knew* was an asshole but thought I could tolerate so that I could continue working at a job I otherwise enjoyed. However, the other completely broadsided me. It's still beyond comprehension that things had gone so wrong with him. Hell, I used to look forward to seeing him for those precious moments every few weeks.

The night of the dinner lecture had been about as bad as it could get. The stress from realizing my messages to Mick were now being blocked combined with the oh-so, enjoyable company of Joseph Stark intensified my already present headache. It became an unrelenting migraine of epic proportion about two-thirds of the way through the evening.

My mother quickly met me at the restaurant after my S.O.S. and drove me to the ER for treatment before taking me home. It was a long evening. The emergency room was full, and we had to wait in the waiting room for several hours before being placed in a room. But even without working in medicine, knowing my headache was miserable but not a life threat like a stroke or a heart attack reminded me I was waiting behind people who needed care sooner than I did. I tried to encourage my mother and hold back my tears, as I know that logic is hard to wrap your head around when the child you love is suffering.

Once I was evaluated and an intravenous line was placed to provide medication and fluids, things started to ease quickly. Yet, as the pain medication kicked in, I realized the crying was from the pain in my heart, not my head. How had I let this guy infiltrate my soul to this degree? I thought I was better about protecting myself after all of these years. I guess being human has its limitations.

I managed to get through the following day and then slept most of the weekend. I've had moderate headaches three days out of the week since that time, but nothing as bad as that Thursday. I'm making getting back to meditation and yoga a big priority. *I just need to keep my eyes peeled on the front of the class from now on.*

Looking down at my salad, I pick at my lunch. My mind goes back to the Caesar salad speed date I'd had with Michael in this office when we had our first kiss. God. Despite all that's happened, it makes me a little mad that I still miss him. I can't eat. My heart hurts. The man I was falling in love with apparently only wanted one thing. Well, he got it, and just like all the rest, he's gone in search of something better. What had the iceman said? No entanglements. I guess he tried to warn me. Even if a lot of it in hindsight seems like double talk.

Dropping my head in my hands, I pray for a miracle. A new job, my migraines to give me a break, and some type of magic memory serum that would erase the thoughts of Mick from my mind.

Bzzz. Bzzz.

Michael York
12:55 p.m.
Mick: I'm sorry. Really sorry. Can we talk?

CHAPTER TWENTY-THREE

Ava

I pull up to the little league field, wondering if I'm early. I've been a hot mess ever since receiving that text from Michael.

Michael York
12:55 p.m.
Mick: I'm sorry. Really sorry. Can we talk?

Recalling the feeling of my heart racing and my limbs trembling as I read the short line over and over, I lie my head back against the headrest and try to take a few calming breaths. I don't know why I'm so nervous? I did nothing wrong. I'm certainly not going to beg for him to try again or accept some lame excuse for the way he treated me. Wiping my hands atop my slacks, I continue my internal dialogue. *He's the one who should be nervous.*

I'm glad I held back after receiving that text and didn't blast him for all I was feeling since being so rejected. He was equally as short and to the point, asking if we could meet here to talk. At least I could put an end to all of the questions.

After lamenting about recent events one too many times, I decide to get out and stretch my legs. Walking around to the back of my vehicle, I bend and stretch my back and quads after assuring there's still no sight of Michael's car. Hopefully, it'll help the butterflies in my stomach to walk around a bit.

I convinced myself to come here if nothing more than to take one more thing off of my plate at work. Meeting with him outside of the office will allow me to address this and put it behind us, so there isn't another unprofessional occurrence at my job. While I'm still terribly hurt by the way he ended things, we do have to work together. It'll at least give me some closure, so it won't be so hard to handle his visits.

Knowing full well this was a convenient excuse, as I was anxious to see him if nothing more than to see if the electricity between us was all in my head. I couldn't have imagined that. Could I? Just to see his facial expression and to try and get a read on him when he had nothing to hide behind. No phone screens, just us.

I'd told Joanie I had an appointment today, so I'd need to leave the office at lunch. Up until my interview recently, I've rarely taken time off during the workday. However, as I'm on the hunt for gainful employment elsewhere, it shouldn't matter anyway.

Continuing to pace up and down the small grassy area in front of my car, I see a small blue Honda Accord pull into the parking lot and turn toward my car. Hmm, that's odd. Beyond the fact this isn't a large silver Ford Explorer, I notice the driver is clearly not Mick. Maybe they came here to take a walk on their lunch break.

A beautiful dark-haired teen exits her car and walks in my direction. "Hi. Are you Ava?"

"Yes." Stunned and immediately curious by this change of events, I take her in. She's fit, about five foot six, with long dark hair and deep brown eyes. She's very pretty. Her skin is radiant with little makeup, and her eyes appear bright and hopeful. She does seem a bit timid as she stops in front of me. I relax my stance as I try to continue our conversation without coming off as rude. It's not her fault I'm anxiously awaiting an uncomfortable conversation with my most recent player. But how does this girl know my name? "I'm sorry, have we met?"

"No. Please forgive me for the ruse. I was the one who text you. Not my brother. I overheard him talking to my mom the other day, and I knew I had to do something. Is it okay if we sit and talk for a minute?" I watch as she points to the dugout. Nodding, I follow her. Still trying to absorb everything she's just said, I try to remain calm until she can explain what she overheard. And why she's here and not him.

"I'm Emmaleigh, by the way," she adds.

"I figured as much. Your brother adores you." Giving her a small smile, I like being able to put a face to the stories. Even if it has to be under these painful circumstances. "He bought us matching baseball shirts," I blurt before I can think better of it. The immediate reminder of my loss practically slaps me in the face, making me wince.

Sitting down on the bench, Emmaleigh rotates toward me. "The other day, I came home from school and saw Mick's car in the drive. I was so excited because I don't get to see him as often as I used to. Between my busy social calendar and his traveling and little league… well, it's just not like it used to be. Anyway, the last time he'd been at the house, he'd gone on and on about this special girl he'd met, and I was almost giddy thinking he'd brought her, well, you, home for a visit. I practically ran to the door to see."

Watching this vivacious teenage girl describe this makes me sad it couldn't have happened the way she imagined. I bite my lip, trying to prevent my emotions from joining this story hour.

"But instead of meeting you, I managed to come to the hallway just outside of the kitchen as my mom slammed her hand down on the table and began lecturing Mick for the way he'd walked away from you without talking to you about it. She was so upset with him." She stops momentarily as if replaying the scene in her mind. "I can't remember her ever yelling at him. He was so unlike the other teen boys I knew when we were growing up. He's always been respectful, kind. He's helped me, so she didn't have so much on her plate. Never went to parties. Instead, he stayed at home with me and my mom and dad. It was a bit jarring seeing her scold him." Emmaleigh reaches for a large splintered piece of wood that's separated from the rest of the bench we're seated on.

Suddenly, she seems so young, like a child who's had to cancel her birthday party on account of being ill. "When he said you two were over, I was so heartbroken for him. I'd never seen him so happy. All of us... so happy he was finally getting a shot at a happily ever after. He'd been strong for so long after losing baseball. And that stuff with Paula." She wipes away a stray tear, and suddenly, my heart feels like this fragmented piece of lumber where we're sitting. Sometimes you can't see past your own grief to know how much the people around you are hurting.

"I don't know how much Mick told you, but he's been burned terribly before. So terribly, you're the first girl he's dated since Paula."

I look at her with a blank stare, trying to put these pieces together.

She takes a decidedly deep breath before diving into what I assume is the painful truth behind Michael's absence. "Mick dated the same girl all through high school and into college. I don't know anything about her because I was too young at that point to remember such things. I get most of my intel from Mom." She giggles. "But the awful wench tore his heart out. When he lost his baseball scholarship because of his shoulder, she left him for one of his teammates. The worst part, he found out by accident. He stumbled on them together. They'd been posting pics on Facebook and Insta as a couple behind his back. Like it was too much trouble to be bothered to tell him."

My hand flies to my chest as if needing the pressure to soothe the worsening crevice there by this news. My poor, beautiful man.

"When he confronted her about it, she acted like it was no big deal. Paula and Michael had been together for five years, and yet he said she simply shrugged it off like it was no big deal to her that she'd moved on." Emmaleigh used her fingers to make air quotes as she sneered the words, 'no big deal.' "She acted like he was the person in the wrong for having the nerve to ask her about it."

Covering my mouth with my hand in an attempt to stifle the gasp, I'm utterly shocked that any woman could treat him this way. Despite what he'd done to me, my heart aches for him. *Or at least the man I thought he was.*

"So, when he came to your office, and you were with your boss..." She stops speaking and looks at me inquisitively.

"When I was with my boss, what?" I ask slowly and deliberately. What did she mean?

"You know… getting it on with your boss—"

"What?" I blurt out, jumping from my seat on the hard wooden bench before I can control my reaction. "I'd never do anything like that with him. Like, ever! If he was the last man on the planet. That guy's a sleaze." I must look like I've been stung by a hornet. My whole face feels hot, and I'm sure it's bright red.

"I knew it! I knew there had to be a mistake," Emmaleigh says, clapping her hands together.

"What do you mean?" I prod, still trying to calm myself after such a ludicrous accusation. "What on earth would make him think something like that?"

"He told my mom he came to your office and the lights were off, and you two were together."

I sit back down momentarily, wracking my brain, trying to recall what events could've transpired to make him think for a second that I would've… "Oh. My. God. The day of the dinner." I look to Emmaleigh, who's watching me with bated breath.

"I suffer from terrible migraines, Emmaleigh. I've had them since I was your age, actually. My overbearing boss's behavior doesn't help. The added stress and all. Anyway, I had a brutal one that day. I often take an Excedrin or a nondrowsy prescription, turn the lights off, and lay my head down during my lunch break to get through the rest of the day when they get bad. That day, I recall expecting your brother to arrive. When I felt someone massaging my shoulders, I assumed it was him. Until I heard my horrid boss's voice in my ear." Jumping back up, I feel the need to pace as I shake my head at the memory of that discovery. "I almost ripped his arm off and beat him with it."

Emmaleigh watches me silently, allowing me to get it all out. Plopping back down on the seat, I drop my head into my hands. "I remember wondering what happened to Michael that day. I'd hoped seeing him would make the whole situation a little more bearable. But then he didn't show, and I never heard from him again." Voicing this recollection aloud causes a large knot to form in my throat. *I will not cry in front of his sister.*

"That has to be it," Emmaleigh agrees. "I'm sure all of this is a terrible misunderstanding."

"I thought I'd told Michael about my migraines, but thinking back... I'm not sure it ever came up." These debilitating headaches have become such a predictable part of my life, I guess I just assume everyone knows. But I don't typically share this with men I'm seeing right away, for fear of being cast aside like my mother.

Feeling Emmaleigh's soft hand on my forearm, her gentle voice carefully interrupts my thoughts. "Ava. I know what he did was wrong. Mick should've talked to you. But he was so hurt by Paula he assumed you were doing the same. Plus, he's a boy. They're stupid."

A small chuckle escapes. It feels good to laugh about something for a change. And she's so right. *They are stupid.*

"Could you please forgive him and give him another chance?"

"Oh, Emmaleigh. I'd give anything to have Michael back. I think the world of your brother. But what makes you think he'd want another chance with me?"

"Ava. He said you were the one." Again with the air quotes. "I never thought after everything Paula did, he'd ever let anyone in again. He's never brought anyone home since her. Plus..."

"Plus, what," I ask hopefully.

"From what Mom tells me, he never said Paula was the one. Only you."

I feel my eyes fill with tears. It's getting harder to contain these emotions. This poor tortured soul. How both of us have hurt because of what he thought he saw. *Stupid boy.* Turning away, I again stand to my full height. Blinking rapidly with my back to her, I try to regain my composure and push on.

"I want this to work. I do. But Michael needs to understand that if there's a chance to turn this situation around, I'll never allow him to behave like this again. Hurt or not, his behavior is unacceptable." I pace a minute before turning to her.

I watch as this staunch advocator for her brother tilts her head down in a short nod of understanding.

"Emmaleigh, even if I thought this was a good idea, considering trying a relationship with a grown man who wouldn't have a conversation with me before walking away, what do I do? He's blocked my number. He won't talk to me."

"Well, I'm glad you asked. I think I have a plan."

CHAPTER TWENTY-FOUR

Mick

Tossing back another beer while sitting in this overcrowded bar, I'm already regretting my decision to come here. My usual hotel was sold out tonight, so I had to move to Christiansburg, Virginia. This is a big college town. Home to Virginia Tech and their award-winning Hokie football team. Now that summer's here, I'd expected the bar wouldn't be crowded. But I've been proven wrong.

"Hey, you want another?" The bartender nods toward my empty glass.

"Sure, why not?" Hell. I can walk to the hotel, and I've got nowhere to be until tomorrow. I'm not usually one for tying one on alone, but maybe if I can't score tonight, the bed won't seem so cold and empty if I'm seeing double when I get back.

"Hey, this seat taken?"

My head tilts up to see a pretty redhead with big green eyes sliding onto the stool next to me before I can utter a word to indicate the contrary. "No, it's all yours." She appears young. Maybe she attends college here?

"What can I get you, Tilly?" the bartender asks as he slides a napkin in her direction. Guess she's at least twenty-one.

"A cosmo and his number."

Caught off guard at this brazen young woman's comment, I gaze back over to see her grinning at me as she retrieves something from her purse. *Hell, she was talking about me.*

"Tilly, is it?"

"Yeah. My mother was psycho. Who names a beautiful baby girl Matilda? I've been going by Tilly since I could talk. Gotta light?"

I notice the cigarette between her outstretched fingers and recoil. Smoking is not a quality I can usually get past. And if she's lighting up the moment she's sat down, I suspect she's not the type to limit it to my absence. "No, sorry."

"You're new here."

"Not really. New to the bar, maybe. But I've been to this town plenty."

Reaching for my glass of pale ale, I suddenly feel her hand skating over the tattoo on my left arm.

"It's nice. You got any others?" Again with the coy smile.

"Maybe." She's cute. A little more forward than I like. But, just get your rocks off for the night, Mick. You never have to come back to this bar. "How 'bout you?"

I barely finish my sentence before I notice Tilly's on her feet, pulling the plunging V neck of her shirt down, exposing her tits with a poorly drawn tattoo that travels across both of her breasts that reads, Worth the Wait.

"Tilly, here's your drink. Stop flashing your tits at everyone," the bartender, who's obviously been privy to her antics in the past, interrupts. "And you know you can't light up in here."

Tilly gives the bartender a glare before continuing. "So, if you've been to this town plenty. Where are you from?"

"Near Richmond. Just here for the night on business."

Tilly takes a long sip of her drink, and as she places it on the bar top, she scoots her chair closer to mine. "Well, it just so happens I'm free for the night."

Her aggressiveness coupled with the flashing of her classy tattoo has me thinking even just one night is one too many with this girl. My decision is barely made before I see a striking brunette glide through the door to the bar. A familiar striking brunette. As our eyes meet, she saunters over and sits on the vacant stool to my right.

"Hey, Mick."

I'm suddenly filled with rage. I should've made for the door once Tilly's boobs came out, but this has closed the lid on this evening.

"Oh, come on. Don't be rude. It's not like you."

"No, that's more your speed, Paula."

"Speaking of rude…" I hear off to my left. Tilly's leaning over the bar to get a better glimpse of my ex-girlfriend. Great. Can't think of a worse place I could be right now. Watching my kids lose another game in the last inning or a root canal might be preferred options.

"Where's Brett?" I ask, irritated and just intoxicated enough not to give a shit what comes out of my mouth right now.

"What? Oh, we didn't last six months. I'm sorry for that, Mick. You were always the better man. We'd just been together so long, and I needed to live a little. You were so serious, driven."

Turning on my stool, I look at her deadpan. "I understand we were still young and finding our way, Paula. But it was the way you did it. We were friends before we were together. I deserved a little more than that." Feeling a little self-conscious at having this conversation in a public place after all of these years, I turn to see Tilly watching us both while popping beer nuts into her mouth like she's got front row seats for the latest thriller.

"You're right, Micky. I've had a lot of regrets about the way we handled that."

"We?" I practically shout. "Not we, you. I could've sucker-punched Brett in the face in the fucking library where I found the two of you. But I waited until we could speak privately, and you acted like I was the unreasonable one in the situation."

"I guess I meant more to you than I thought. If you're that torn up about it after all these years." Again with that fucking shrug of the shoulders. Jesus. She's so infuriating. What did I ever see in her besides a pretty shell? "Well, it's water under the bridge now."

"Can I get you something?" the bartender asks.

"I'll have what he's having," she answers playfully, pointing to my pale ale.

"Well, I'm having the check," I interrupt.

"Oh, come on. Let's bury the hatchet. I'm only in town for the night, visiting my friend Laurel. It'd be nice to put this behind us, move on with a clean slate."

Is this girl for real? I attempt to calm my anger, which has probably been fanned by alcohol, and the realization I'm not going to be getting over my snow queen with a quick lay tonight. Getting up from my stool, I throw five twenty-dollar bills on the bar. "This should cover my tab, sir." I direct to the bartender, who's standing out of harm's way, drying off high ball glasses. "Please take care of Tilly's drink and keep the rest for yourself. Paula's never needed me. Why start now?" I start to make a clean getaway to the door just as I hear her retort.

"I would've loved to see you fight over me in that library, Mick. Sucker-punch my ass. You had one working arm. He would've made you more of a laughing stock than you already were."

Not looking back, I head for the hotel. Suddenly, a cold and empty bed doesn't sound so bad.

∽

It's Saturday, and I'm trying to get my shit together before our game. I've had two cups of coffee and tried to eat a bagel, and I'm still not centered. I admit I haven't slept well in days. I'd like to say it was because of the run-in with Paula, but if anything, that unpleasant interaction had made things clearer. Once we split, I realized it was the humiliation and anger over how the relationship ended that had left me reeling. I wasn't pining for her.

I'd finally called on Central Orthopedics and was initially relieved when I discovered Ava wasn't there. But this relief quickly morphed into a dull, lingering ache in my chest. As if someone had reached inside and stolen a piece of it. I miss her. She meant more to me in the few short months we'd grown close than Paula ever had.

Joanie had been sweet. Telling me how much she and Ava had missed me. I'm sure she was just being polite. I guess Ava and her boss have been able to keep their office romance on the down-low. Stealthy of them, given Joanie appears to be quite the busy body.

I pull up to the ball field and notice most of the boys have beaten me here. No sleep or not, these boys deserve better than this. This is a big game for them. The Devil Dogs are the team we've been training to beat. I need to get my head out of my ass.

Sliding out of the car, I pull my equipment from the trunk before heading to the field. I notice the boys are crowded around someone at the pitcher's mound and wonder if my mother and little sister have been bribing them to win with sweet treats. As I get closer, I spot a platinum-haired stunner, and my mouth goes dry. She's handing out water bottles and other swag from the Ortho clinic. My instant response is to go to her, my heart hammering in my chest at the sight of her. God, she looks beautiful. Then clarity hits me like a sledgehammer. I've had enough run-ins with the women who've done me wrong this week. I don't have any patience for this today.

"What're you doing here?" I practically growl at her.

"Hi, Mick. I talked to Dr. Morgan, and we've decided to sponsor your team."

"No one asked you," I grumble.

"Well, we thought it was a cause worth promoting. Good luck with your game, boys. I'll be rooting for you!" She claps jubilantly as if we just got back from the Nationals game this morning, and everything between us is fine. The boys all jump excitedly, waving their T-shirts, water bottles, and misters.

"I think you should leave," I spit, unable to hide my anger.

"We need to talk, Mick. Don't make a scene in front of the boys," she scolds. "I'll talk to you after the game." With that, she whirls away from me, walking swiftly toward an open folding chair. *What the fuck? Is she staying for the game? Like I need that right now.* I've barely recovered from Ava being here when my nemesis approaches.

"Hello, York." The smug bastard reaches out his hand.

There's no point avoiding it, I have to shake it if I'm going to set a good example for my kids. "Dillon."

"Was nice of the beauty queen to get your boys looking like a real team. She belong to you?"

Suddenly, I feel my chest swell as steam builds in my ears. I feel like I could go off. I *wish* she belonged to me. But like hell if I'll let him know otherwise. "What's it to you, Dillon? Don't you have your pick of women? Every time you come to a game, there's some new tart waiting over in the wings. Or are you entertaining some of the team moms?"

"Hit a nerve, did I? Just trying to see if she'd be interested in spending time with a coach whose team knows one end of the bat from the other."

If this guy goes anywhere near Ava, I'll fucking kill him.

We're interrupted as the baseball referee for the game approaches. Good timing. The visiting team is always first at-bat, so we dispense with any required business and head back to our respective dugouts.

"Coach, did you see all the cool stuff? We look like real players."

"I did. Did you say thank you?"

"Yes!" they all chime in together. I've never seen these boys so excited.

"Okay, now that you look like real players, let's show them we can win like real players."

"Yes!" they again cheer.

"We've been working hard. Don't think about who you're playing. Just give it your all. I've seen you at practice. You can do this."

"Hey, coach. We got this. Tommy brought us some good luck on the way here."

"Oh, yeah," I pipe in.

"Yeah. A bird pooped on him when he was in the parking lot. You know, like that Giants' pitcher who threw his best game ever. Same thing. We got this!"

"Yeah!" they yell, now all jumping up and down.

Looking over at Tommy, I notice his head's a little damp but don't see anything resembling bird shit.

"The pretty lady used about ten bottles of water from the trunk of her car to help get it out," Joel says, pointing toward Ava, who's sitting in her folding chair watching us, I'm sure unable to hear what we're saying from this distance. A smile breaks out on my face before I can catch myself. What the hell? *I don't know what she's pulling, but get your head together, Mick.*

The game starts, and we manage to get through the first inning without the Devil Dog's putting up any runs. No real shock, we take two turns at bat without a single hit, but at least the other team only accumulates one run on the scoreboard.

Corey Dillon is a good coach. Sure, he acts like he's coaching an Olympic team instead of little league baseball, but he consistently has teams that perform well. They're typically well behaved, and beyond their facial expressions, none of them gloat over their wins. He's lucky to have a bunch of kids who've been able to play their whole lives. They train at expensive summer camps to be winners. Not like this team of rag-tag players who only today got anything resembling real uniforms.

Thinking of their excitement over the matching T-shirts again makes me think of Ava. Looking over toward the stands, I see her clapping and cheering as the next player gets up to bat. My mind drifts to the seats of National Field stadium, where I tried to teach her the rules of the game. How eager she was to learn. How could I have been so off about her? *And why is she here?* My irritation again rises, and I return my focus to the game.

An hour and a half later, our boys win two to one. I'm almost as shocked by this turn of events as I am that Ava is sitting in a folding chair watching it all happen. Turning my head to see her expression, I notice one Corey Dillon standing at her chair. The hair on my nape rises. *What the fuck?*

"Come on, boys, line up," I bark. I'm not looking to tame their excitement over the surprise win, but protocol says you line up after every game and shake the other team's hands as a show of sportsmanship. Fuck, I've been waiting all season for this. To the victor belongs the spoils. And shaking hands with the other team after a stunning win, well, we're taking it.

We bump fists or elbows with the assorted players and coaches until Corey and I meet at the end of the lineup.

"Nice job, York. Honestly, didn't think your kids had it in ya."

"Well, we had a good luck charm."

I watch as Corey looks over his shoulder at Ava and have to pull my arms into my sides so I don't rip his head off of his neck. I'm sure she's every bit the good luck charm he thinks she is. Whether she's an A-class liar or not. But he doesn't need to know that. "Yeah, I meant Tommy. Some bird took a shit on him in the parking lot before the game started."

"Ha, like Anthony DeSclafani? I didn't think you had it in you to play dirty." He laughs.

"We're nothing if not classy."

"So, the blonde?" He tilts his head in Ava's direction.

"Is taken," I bark, making things abundantly clear. It might be Joseph Stark that has her and not me, but we don't have time for that discussion right now.

Corey lifts his arms up in surrender. "There's plenty of other fish in the sea."

"Yeah, well, go catch one of them."

Coach Dillon turns and heads toward his team, who are gathering their belongings in stunned silence while my guys are acting like they just won the world series instead of the only legitimate game all season.

As the boys run to their parents, prideful smiles crossing their faces as they greet each other, I look toward Ava, who's headed in my direction.

"Congratulations," she states, smiling jubilantly at me.

"What do you want, Ava?" I can't even enjoy this surprise victory because I'm overwhelmed at the sight of her.

"We need to talk," she says, reaching out her hand to mine.

Jerking it away from her, I sneer, "What on earth about?"

"I need to tell you that you're wrong. You're wrong, and I love you."

CHAPTER TWENTY-FIVE

Ava

He's so angry. And hurt. As much as I've been hurting, I try to remind myself how awful this had to be for him. To see what he did and instantly think the worst. Because the worst had already been done to him, and so it's what he expects. I try to reassure myself of this, so his anger won't derail me from my mission.

"Mick, your incredibly sweet sister text me from your phone. She overheard you talking to your mom about how we weren't seeing each other any longer and knew how badly you were hurting, even if you didn't want to admit it. She wanted to do something to help." I stop to take a breath, feeling my voice quivering with nerves. "She sent a text, asking if I'd meet her, pretending to be you." I again pause, stopping to take another breath, waiting to see if he'll join me in this conversation. When he doesn't, I proceed.

"Emmaleigh told me what you saw in the office. It wasn't what you think. I suffer from horrendous migraines. I have for years. My mother turned to pills, became depressed, and spent much of my youth bedridden. I refuse to let that happen, and so I've pushed through and continue to work as best I can. That day was awful. The headache was so bad I ended up in the ER that night." I again stop momentarily, taking in his blank expression. Why is this so much harder than I expected? Why can't he reach out and make this a little easier? Please, just say something. *Crickets... I can practically hear crickets.*

"Anyway, I often take a pill, turn off the lights, and spend my lunch break with my head down. When I felt hands on my shoulders, I thought that you'd come in when my eyes were closed, only to find Dr. Stark. I thought it was you, Mick."

I watch his face closely for any hint of understanding, but there's nothing. He just stands speechless, looking at me.

"He was making me attend a stupid dinner lecture he was giving with one of the drug reps, and the stress of that made my headache worse. I barely made it through the PowerPoint presentation before my mother had to come to get me and take me to the emergency room. I told him I'm going to find another job because I can't stand working for him anymore." I wring my hands, wishing this was a two-person conversation versus feeling like I'm throwing myself at the mercy of the court. *I didn't do anything wrong. So why does it feel like I'm the guilty party? He should have talked to me.*

"Emmaleigh told me about Paula. About how she hurt you. I'm so sorry, Mick. Please know, I'd never hurt you that way." I look at his handsome, rugged face. Imploring him to speak, trying not to cry as I stare into his dark brown eyes. "I've been so miserable, wondering why you left without a word," I manage to squeak out, praying these tears will stay back. Lord, give me strength. I want him back, but he has to answer to this. I refuse to let him think I'm weak and begging for him to come back, just because I'm opening the door for this conversation to finally happen.

"Mick?" *God, please say something.*

"You really love me?" he asks as if in disbelief.

Yes, you stupid boy. After all of that. Was that all he heard? *Did he stop listening after those three words came out?* "Yes. I've been heartsick without you." I can't stop the tears from falling now, darn it. But I've been brave long enough.

Suddenly, he pulls me into his strong, sweaty body and clutches me to him like I'm his life preserver in a class five hurricane.

Standing in the middle of this deserted little league baseball field for what feels like an hour, we just hold one another. There's no place else I'd rather be. His arms feel so good around me. He smells so good, covered in sweat and surrender. My heart feels as if someone's placed a bandaid over the hole that was previously there. We have a long way to go to feel restored, but this is the most comfort I've felt in weeks.

Mick pulls back and looks down into my swollen tear-filled eyes. Cupping my cheeks as if making a declaration, he finally opens up to me. "Ava, I'm so, so sorry. I never meant to hurt you. I felt so betrayed and couldn't see beyond my anger. God, I've been horrible to you." Pulling me back into him, stroking my hair as if verifying this is real, I feel him rest his chin on the top of my head. "I don't deserve it, but could you ever forgive me?"

Now it's my turn to stay silent. I need to tell him exactly how I'm feeling. That as much as I care for him, I cannot allow any man to treat me this way again.

As the silence stretches on longer than is comfortable, he withdraws from our embrace to peer down at me in earnest. Swiping my tears with his thumbs, he proceeds to lay gentle kisses on my cheeks.

"I forgive you, Mick. You were just hurt. I'm so thankful your sister could see that."

As if in relief, he squeezes me in his tight embrace, continuing to kiss my temple. "I promise to make it up to you, Ava. I'm going to make this right."

That's my cue. Standing taller, I take a few steps back and notice a look of concern dot his features. "Yes, you will." I continue to step away from him, knowing I could cave if I don't have some distance between us.

Taking a calming breath, I begin just as I practiced at home. "Michael York, you're a grown man. I understand you've been hurt, but you had no right to walk away without a conversation. The thought this relationship could've been ended because you couldn't grow a pair… couldn't man up and talk to me." My tears start to tumble again. As he takes a step toward me, I hold up my hand.

"I'm done letting men treat me like I'm disposable. That I'm not worthy of them once they've slept with me."

"Av—" Again, I hold up my hand.

"Hurt me like that once, shame on you. But if I let you hurt me like that twice, shame on me. This will be the only time miscommunication will derail us. If you *ever* withhold anything from me in the future, it's game over."

"You're right. I understand, Ava. I'm sorry."

"Well, you're not the only one who's been hurt before, Mick. But I was willing to go all in. To trust you." Stopping to take a cleansing breath, whispering to my heart to calm down, I begin again.

"The night I received those crazy texts from you, I worried you were texting the wrong girl. You'd never acted that way with me before. I decided to call you and clear the air, rather than play games and wonder all night about what was happening. But when I called you, the situation wasn't any clearer. There was no way of knowing your ridiculous texts and near silence on the phone line were from taking cold medicine. I could've chosen to believe you were drunk and not alone. But I decided to believe you. Believe in the man I was coming to know and care about."

Mick hangs his head, the reality of the situation starting to become a little clearer. I don't want to shame him. But he needs to see this can never happen again.

"I need thirty days. Thirty days for you to think about everything that's happened between us. I deserve a man who's mature enough to come to me when there's a problem. Who'll talk to me. Who'll show me how much I mean to him. That I never need to doubt the type of relationship we have. I'm serious, Mick. I don't hand my heart to anyone lightly."

"I understand, Ava. I can do that." He begins to step toward me again, and once more, I have to back away and lift my hand to clarify.

"I won't see you over the next thirty days. When I do, I need to know you're all in."

"But, Els— Ava, please. I've been miserable without you." Sincerity shines through his dark, pleading eyes.

"I have been too, Mick. But I was the one left questioning what the hell went wrong. Wondering what I possibly could've done to deserve being ghosted like that. I'm not willing to chance enduring that again. So, if this is going to work between us, I need you to take some time and think about this. About us. Consider whether you're able to commit. We need this space."

He looks like a player who scored a big hit just to have it ruled a foul. Unable to stand so far away when he's hurting, I come closer and grab his hand in mine. "It's different choosing to be apart because you're trying to work on giving the very best part of you to the person you care about." Giving him a loving glance, I trace the pad of my finger along his strong jaw, hoping he can see how much he truly means to me. "It's much different than being apart because the other person quit on you."

His shoulders slump in defeat. "Ava, I'm sorry. You're right. You deserve so much better than me."

"No, I deserve better behavior from you. But it's you I want, Mick. Fix it."

"Shit. This is going to fucking kill me. Giving you space after all of this when all I want is to be with you. But I'll do it if it's what you want."

"No, it's what we need. Mick. This isn't some game to me. I'm twenty-seven. I want to settle down one day. If you aren't ready for romantic entanglements, then acknowledge that and walk away. I need to know when these thirty days are over, we want the same things. More than that, I need to know you'll fight for us." Self-consciously, I pull back and wring my hands together. Worried this might be too much, and he'll just say see ya. We hadn't dated that long to be giving him such an ultimatum. "One day, I'm going to make a mistake… do or say something I shouldn't. I need to know you won't abandon me but try to work it out."

"I wish you could just believe me. How committed I am. I swear. I'm never letting you go again, princess."

"I believe you feel that way. And I'm over the moon about it." I beam up at him, so thankful this has gone as well as I could've hoped. "Listen, I'm not looking for a ring. It's not a sentence you have to serve to prove something to me. I just deserve better from you. I understand why you left. You've been hurt before. Accept it and put it behind you. Not everyone who cares about you will betray you. Look at Emmaleigh. And me."

Michael swipes his hand through his unruly dark hair and appears to massage the back of his neck. I can see the seriousness of the conversation causing him to stop and think. Moments later, his expression changes. "What if I see you out?" he asks with a mischievous smirk.

"What do you mean?"

"Well, can I see you at the office when I drop by? If we're both at Luigi's, can I see you?"

"I'm not going to go out of my way to avoid you, but I don't think this is going to be a problem. I haven't seen you in weeks. I just want to feel comforted you've given this serious consideration."

"When do these thirty days start?"

"Today."

"Couldn't they start tomorrow?"

"Why?"

Mick scoops me into his arms, twirling me around. Looking about the field, I realize we're completely alone. He bends to drop me onto my feet, placing a chaste kiss on my lips. "Come home with me, Elsa."

I shake my head in response, for fear my mouth will deceive me with a big, fat yes.

"Well, can I at least kiss you before the thirty days begin?"

This could be dangerous. There's nothing I want more than to be back in his arms, enjoying the best kisses, caresses, dirty talking, and all the hot loving I can get. But I need to make sure he knows I'm serious. *Be strong, Ava! Be strong and kiss the hell out of this delicious man, so he remembers what he's missing.*

"One, then I'm heading out."

Mick looks back at me with sadness. His sorrow is almost enough to crumble my determination. But I can't. He needs to see who he's dealing with and know there won't be a next time.

Coming closer, that melancholy expression making me weak, he forcefully grabs my face with his strong fingers and devours me. There's a fierceness that's different than the lust-filled kisses at the larger ballfield. These are pleading. His tongue dances with mine, making me want more. His hands grip my hair, tilting my head to open deeper for him as if he'll swallow me whole. Little does he know, he's already done just that.

～

The next few days are torture. Trusting I'm doing the right thing. What if he returned home, had a stiff drink, and thought, *hell no*. It's the chance I have to take.

I have to admit, seeing how he reacted after I laid all of my cards out was pretty reassuring. The crushing ache of rejection is gone. I merely miss him. Now I just have to keep my self-doubt at bay.

"Ava, Michael's here," Joanie's voice lilts from the hallway.

What? It's only been a few days. Looking at my calendar, I realize it's Thursday. His day. I hadn't contemplated his being here this soon after seeing him at the ballfield and giving him my thirty-day request.

"Um, okay, Joanie," I reply, feeling a little flustered.

Before I can stand from my desk, Joanie enters the room with a huge grin on her face.

"What?" I can't help laughing at her expression.

"I need to know what's going on. I'm thrilled he's back. But he brought you a huge vase of flowers and said he's not supposed to see you. He asked if I could have you sign his form, and he'd be on his way. Then all of a sudden, he looked worried about something and asked if you didn't like the flowers he gave you last time. I told him about the lilies and how they affected you."

I sit dumbfounded, listening to this. Why would he tell Joanie he's not supposed to see me? Is he really trying to stick to the rules, or is this a ruse to get her on board to help break me down? "Well?"

"Well, what?"

"Is he still out there?" I laugh, feeling like I'm speaking to a child.

"Oh, no."

What? "Well, where are the flowers? Was there a card?"

"They're gone too. But here's his form." *What? He didn't even leave the flowers?*

Immediately feeling disappointed, I stare down at it. Knowing I did this to myself, I sign his form and hand it back to her. Suddenly, my eyes light up as a thought comes to mind. "Joanie, how's he getting this signed form back if he's left."

"Oh, he's coming back. He just went back to the florist to get you a different bouquet." She hoots. "I was afraid he'd hurt himself the way he darted out that door yelling, *'I'll be back,'* like the Terminator."

"Oh my gosh." I giggle. "He didn't have to do that."

"Sure he did. Make him work for it, beautiful girl." Joanie gives me the thumbs up and walks away.

Slumping into my chair, I can't fight the huge grin plastered on my face. *He does care. I think we just might be okay.*

∽

It's been a few days since I've heard from Mick. This self-imposed sentence is making me miss him even more. How am I possibly going to survive thirty days? Looking at the gorgeous flowers sitting on my dining room table, I put my teacup in the dishwasher and giggle. Mick had gone back to the florist and asked for a large bouquet with little to no scent. They were a variety of white flowers with a bright red bow tied around the vase, like something you'd expect to see at Christmas. The card he attached was so sweet. "True love can thaw a frozen heart. That's what you're doing for me."

Heading to my bed, I curl up under the covers and revel in how my world has turned around.

Bzzz. Bzzz.

Michael York
9:10 p.m.
Mick: I know I'm breaking the rules. But I couldn't help it. I miss you. I hope you liked these flowers a little better. Please don't be afraid to tell me things too. xoxo

Knowing I shouldn't but wanting to give him some reply, I send a short text before drifting off for the night.

Ava: I love them. And you. xoxo

~

It's been a week since Mick was here. I have to admit, I'm missing him even more than I anticipated. *Maybe I should've said we could have one night together first instead of one kiss.* Look at the bright side, Ava. He's back and seems to be trying hard. The flowers were beautiful, and the fact he took such great pains to make sure they were unscented says a lot. And the unexpected text was nice too.

The workday is nearly done. I can't wait to get home. Having spent the first three hours of my day in the emergency room and the OR assisting Dr. Stark before the whirlwind afternoon of clinic patients, I'm exhausted. Surprisingly, my headaches have been more manageable. It's nice to rush home to a hot soak in the tub, a good book, and leftover lasagna from Luigi's instead of pain pills and a big cup of peppermint tea.

Knock. Knock.

Looking up, I notice Allison standing in the doorway. "Hi."

"Hi, Ava. You have any big plans tonight?"

"As a matter of fact, I plan to take a hot soak with a book boyfriend." I laugh. "Why, what are you up—" Before I can complete the sentence, Joanie is now standing beside Allison with a very curious grin on her face. "Okay, what's up?"

"You got a delivery," Allison says, bringing her arm from around her back to display a beautifully wrapped rectangular box with a small gift card on top.

"Ava, please open it. We're dying here."

"Who delivered this?" I ask, biting down on my lower lip as I reach for the delightful gift.

"We've been sworn to secrecy," they say in unison with their right hands up as if they're being sworn into court.

Shaking my head, I carefully remove the card.

My dear sweet Elsa,

I wanted to show you I'm serious about this. About us.
Mick

"Can we read it? Or is it too personal?" Joanie asks.

"Is it from Michael?" Allison chimes in as if there's any doubt.

Handing the card to the two nosey nellies, I painstakingly remove the gift wrap to reveal an expensive box of chocolates from the Godiva store in town. Lifting the dark brown lid covered in an ornate gold script, I find uniquely different chocolate delights inside. I savor the decadent aroma of the luscious candies. Yet before I can turn the box to offer a treat to my friends, I notice another envelope attached to the inside lid. Removing the white envelope, I carefully slide out a photograph. The delicious torso I immediately recognize. He's wearing only a pair of oversized pale blue boxer shorts with Olaf in various poses all over them. Flipping over the picture, I read the note.

Got an extra-large pair to hold the big balls I'm growing.

I'm going to man up, Elsa. Just for you. Xoxo

"Oh, my god," I hoot.

"What?" they both squeal.

"Okay, I don't think he'll care if I show you just once." I turn the picture around so they can see, explaining I'd told him if he wanted to be with me, he'd need to grow a pair. Surprised that Joanie's so quiet, I worry I've crossed the line of professionalism. "I'm sorry, Joanie. This isn't—"

"No. I just feel guilty thinking the things I'm thinking about your soon-to-be husband."

Allison bends over in fits of laughter, and I soon join her.

"He's young enough to be my son, but he's got that V that makes women crazy." Joanie starts to fan herself. "I think I'm having a hot flash."

"Oh, lord." I quickly slide my photo back into the envelope for safekeeping. Well, until I can get home. This night is getting better and better. Now I have gourmet chocolates to add to my bathtub party and Mick's six-pack to keep by my bed. I'm not risking this smoke show accidentally ending up joining me in the tub.

. . .

Soaking in my tub, belly full of Luigi's finest pasta, I'm practically giddy. If someone had told me two weeks ago that I'd be eating gourmet bonbons, reveling in Mick's attempts to woo me, I'd have said they were crazy. Reaching for my glass of Pinot Grigio, I take a cool fruity sip. I don't know if I set the temperature of this bath too hot or if it's the replay of that picture of Michael in his Olaf boxers that's doing it.

Placing my glass down by my cell phone, an audiobook playing that I now have no interest in, I lay my head back and sigh. I miss him so. It's going to be a long few weeks without him, but knowing a healthy, long-term relationship awaits is what's getting me through.

Running my fingers over my breasts and down my belly, I remember how ravenous he'd been for me. For the first time, I feel like a man was really hungry for me, not just my body. Picturing him above me, his muscular chorded arms, his taut rippled abs, is causing my nipples to pebble despite the overheated water. The picture from earlier, in his oversized Olaf boxers, has me thinking.

Reaching for my phone, I click on my contacts and find Mick's name. *I really should say thank you.*

CHAPTER TWENTY-SIX

Mick

It's only been a week. One long-ass god damned week. How am I supposed to make it three more? I know, I know. I need to be grateful I have another chance with Ava at all. And she's right. I need to think hard about how I'm going to handle any sign of miscommunication or betrayal in the future. Because there's no doubt, she's it for me. I have to get this right. How I'm lucky enough to still have her in my life is a miracle.

Last week when I went striding into the Central Ortho clinic, just hoping I'd accidentally get to see Ava's shining smile, I felt like the luckiest man alive. Who cares if I had to run all the way back to the florist to get a special bouquet of fragrance-free flowers. Cygnature Blooms was so accommodating. I'll never go anywhere else. And I plan to keep them in business. My girl deserves it.

Joanie near about wet herself when I walked in with those flowers. I know she's been pulling for us. I guess that's why I figured I had it in the bag when I asked her to help me devise a plan. A few other nods to *Frozen* that might get my snow queen's heart to thaw for me a little more. Of course, she was more than happy to become my accomplice. I think she may have recruited the office manager as well. The more, the merrier.

Walking into my bedroom, I place my phone on the nightstand and pull off my shirt. Dropping it onto the end of the bed, I notice those crazy extra-large boxers with the Olaf characters imprinted all over them. I had to position myself just right when I took that photograph so she could tell they were a size my balls were going to grow into but not look like a sleeping bag for the family jewels.

After brushing my teeth and putting everything into my travel kit so I'll be prepared to hit the road to southwest Virginia tomorrow, I climb into bed. Lying back, I try to picture Ava's face when she opened my card. I bet her cheeks turned cherry red. And hopefully, because she liked what she saw and not because I embarrassed her.

Bzzz. Bzzz.

Ava Kennedy
9:42 p.m.
Ava: Thank you. They're heavenly.

Immediately located below the text is an image. An image of Ava soaking in the tub. She's taken the shot at an angle from above, so I can see from her neck down to the water line. There's a glass of wine and a couple of gourmet chocolates to her right. But being the man I am, I zoom in on the picture. I can just barely make out the firm pink tips of her nipples underneath the opaque shimmer of soap suds. Her platinum locks are draped down her chest, cascading around her beautiful tits. Fuck, they're heavenly, all right. *Oh, the little witch. She's trying to kill me.*

Reaching down, I fist my hard shaft with force. I'm fucking hard every night thinking of her, and now I have a real visual to focus on as I jerk myself off. Sliding my hand up and down my needy cock, I rock my hand to the tip to spread the fluid that's already collecting there as I picture my sweet Ava. Her body is the stuff of fantasies. Lithe soft limbs, long wavy blonde hair to grab, and the sweetest tits. They're just as I like. Perky, not quite a handful, with dusky firm nipples that beg to be sucked. Remembering our night together, I grip my dick and tug a little more aggressively, spreading my legs as I feel my climax building. Oh, the sight of her wrapping those supple lips around the head of my cock, coaxing me to fuck her face. It was the best night of my life.

Cupping my balls with my left hand, I give them a tug as my right hand is pulling firmly against my steely erection. I can still see my gorgeous girl trying to swallow me whole as I jerk harder and harder still. I'm right there. Spreading my legs a little wider, I envision her doing the same as she's lying beneath me, mouth full of my heavy cock as she attempts to ease the ache in her sweet pussy with her fingers.

"Oh, shit." Rope after rope of sticky spunk splatters onto my chest and belly as I empty to thoughts of Ava with her hand bringing her to climax in the bath.

Holy hell. If I keep this up for three more weeks, my dick will be too raw to do its job.

⌒

The following week is my scheduled return to Central Ortho. I contacted Joanie ahead of time to get a headcount on lunch. Ordering from a popular local deli, I delivered lunch to the office. I may or may not have picked a small dessert item just for Ava.

Hoping I'd get to see her for a few short moments, I brought the lunch tray into their breakroom and approached Joanie.

"Hey, Joanie. Sandwiches, chips, and drinks are all set up. You got the card for me?"

"I do." She giggles before reaching into her overstuffed purse. What on earth do women put in there? "Here it is." She laughs once more.

Opening what appears to be a Christmas card, adorned with an ice blue background and multiple glittery snowflakes on the front, the inside is blank. Only Joanie's script is present reading:

Ava, we belong together.
      We practically finish each other's sandwiches.
      xoxo, Michael

Handing it back to her, I chuckle. "I think you're having a little too much fun with this."

"That I am. But this is like starring in a romance novel. You have to get the girl if there's going to be an HEA."

"A what?"

"A happily ever after."

Shaking my head at this meddlesome fairy godmother, I decide to press my luck. "I've got this form I need signed. Do you think Ava's available?"

"I thought you weren't supposed to see each other," she scolds. "Besides. You just got your form signed last week when you were here." *Busted.*

"Come on, Joanie. It'll only be for a minute." *Hell, I deserve a minute. After today, I have two more weeks of this shit. I just want a sniff of her peppermint hair. Is that a lot to ask?*

"I'll be right back," Joanie says warily as she heads down the hall.

Pacing about the small reception area, a few people come and go through the back office doorway I don't recognize. One is decidedly a surgeon. He just has that commanding presence as he saunters by. And a little too attractive if I do say so myself.

"I heard you needed a signature," a deep voice interrupts my inner dialogue.

Turning, I take in the man in question. Dr. Sebastian Lee imprinted on his starched white lab coat. "Yes, sir. I do." My reply is jumpy, likely revealing my disappointment. He signs my form quickly and returns it, looking me straight in the eye.

"She's making you work for it, huh?"

"What?"

"Ava's a good girl. You're lucky to have that one."

"I'm not sure I follow. She asked you to sign my form. How lucky is that?"

He turns his head to look over his shoulder, and I follow his line of sight to one gorgeous blue-eyed blonde who's leaning out of her office doorway, smiling in our direction. My fucking heart flips at the sight of her. *What the hell, man. Get a grip. I need to not look like a sap in front of Dr. GQ here, but I can't wipe the damn goofy smile off of my face.*

"As I said," he says, strolling past me toward the breakroom. Looking back toward my beauty, I discover she's gone. *Dammit.*

∼

I've just grabbed a beer from the fridge and plopped down on my couch to watch some Sports Center when my phone buzzes. Hopping up from my seat, I grab my cell from the kitchen counter. Praying it's Ava, I'm let down when I see a number I don't recognize.

"Hello?"

"Hey, is this Michael?"

"Yes."

"Hey, it's Trevor. We met recently fishing with Zach."

"Oh, yeah. I remember. What's up? Is he okay?" I'm certain I didn't give Trevor my number. Not that I mind him calling, but it just never crossed my mind with him planning to leave for North Carolina.

"He's fine. I called him and asked for your number. I hope that's okay."

"Sure. What's up, Trevor?" The background noise is loud, similar to what you'd expect in a bar.

"I called because he told me you'd gotten back together with your girl. Ava, right?"

"We aren't officially together. But I think things are heading in that direction. Why?" This is an odd time to have a relationship chat.

"Zach told me you were pretty stoked about having another shot with her. I was shocked the old curmudgeon was happy for you. He's so down on relationships. But after he told me what you said she looked like, I figured maybe that was it. He wanted to see one of us with a hot chick," he practically yells over the background noise.

This is nuts. Is there a point to this conversation? Maybe Trevor is drunk and losing it after getting dumped by his supermodel ex. "Trev—"

"Well, I think she's here. And she's with a guy I wouldn't want my girl anywhere near."

What the fuck? My back stiffens, and my arm hairs stand on end at this unexpected piece of intel. "What do you mean?"

"There's a guy here a lot of the fellas from the fire department recognize. I've never met him, but I know he's a real player. When I asked who the hot blonde was with him, they said her name was Ava. That she worked as a PA at St. Luke's. Apparently, a few of the guys are friends with her friend, Eve. All I know is I'd get down here if I were you."

"Where are you?"

"The club at 25th and Main."

"I'll be there in twenty. Thanks, man."

"Don't mention it."

Hanging up the call, I grab my keys and head for the door. As I approach my car, I try to cool my jets. If I go down there half-cocked and make a scene, I'll ruin the very thing I'm trying to repair here. But there's no way I can stay home now and not obsess about this. I know Trevor was trying to do me a favor, but I hope I don't lose my shit and push her away in the process.

I take the drive to the club as carefully as I can. Thank God I didn't drink that beer. I'm probably going to need a stiff one once I get there.

Pulling up to the curb down the street from the club, I park and try to calm my breathing as I head for the door. I'll just look for Trevor and act like I was supposed to be here all the time. It's not that I don't trust her. But Trevor's description of the jackass she's with has me on edge. I don't want anyone pulling any fast moves on my girl.

Handing a ten-dollar bill to the door attendant, I get the customary hand stamp and head inside. It doesn't take long after I arrive to locate a group of men who look like they could each star on American Ninja Warrior. Or a firefighter calendar.

"Michael, over here." Trevor summons me to the end of the group closest to the bar. "Let me get you a drink."

"Yeah, just one. Probably should keep my wits about me."

As if sensing my next question, Trevor pivots and points his beer bottle in the direction of a corner booth. Seated there are my strong-willed snow queen, another attractive female, and a built-looking guy with a nearly bald head. He's attractive and has a relaxed way about him. There's no domineering presence. He's not leaning in, appearing to put the moves on her. Upon further inspection, he resembles the guy Ava was with in front of Fuji's the other evening.

"Here you go," Trevor says, handing me a cold one.

"How long have you guys been here?"

"Not too long, about an hour. Ava and the guy were here before us. Her friend, Eve, came with her brothers, Tate and Tanner." Trevor points to two identical appearing men before taking a pull from his amber bottle.

Casually peering toward Ava's table, attempting to conceal my presence, I note this player she's with seems to be spending more time checking out Eve than my girl. Shifting my stance, I notice Ava is wearing a short little black number. Her skirt barely covers the top of her creamy thighs as she sits in the booth. Despite her tall height, she's wearing fuck hot black stilettos that make her legs look even shapelier. If that's possible.

Feeling myself growing hard at the sight of her, I realize I need to make a decision. I'm either going to trust her and walk away or end up doing something that could cost me everything. What I really want to do is go over and tell him whatever he's thinking, it's fucking not happening.

I'm unable to focus on a thing Trevor is saying, my mind distracting me as I go to war with myself. *Just go over there and act like it's a total coincidence you're here. You're likely to get arrested if he says anything you don't like, and you knock his lights out.*

Suddenly, baldy stands up and walks over to Ava. Taking a sip of my beer, I watch as he leans down to whisper something in her ear. As he stands to his full height, she starts to converse with Eve, and he walks away. My curiosity is killing me. *Lord, please don't let me fuck this up.*

"I'm going over," I tell Trevor.

Looking toward the table, he replies, "You sure? Want me to keep an eye out in case he comes back?"

"No. I've got it. I won't stay long." Just go over and get a feel for the situation. Make sure she knows what's at stake. Then leave. I take another long sip of my beer and then place it on the bar before heading in Ava's direction. Placing my hands in my pockets to calm the fuck down, I walk over slowly and deliberately.

Ava

"Ava, why the hell didn't you tell me your cousin was hot as shit?"

"Don't really think of him like that." I shrug.

Eve's giving me a deadpan stare. "Hello. It's me. Haven't gotten any for months, and holy hell in a handbasket, I bet that guy could—"

"I honestly don't want that mental imagery, thank you." I giggle at Eve. "Besides, your brothers would kill you if you hooked up with Carson. He's got a reputation. Heck, he's picked up girls when he's been out to dinner with me."

"Well, I'm not looking to marry the—" Eve stops her sentence short, causing me to look up from my gin and tonic to see what's happened.

My eyes widen as I see Mick standing at our table, hands in his pockets, short sleeve black shirt revealing the delicious ink on his chorded arms. Before I can address him, he sits down beside me, wrapping one arm over my shoulders. I want to protest. He's supposed to be giving me space while he makes sure he can have a healthy, committed relationship. But my body starts to tremble at his nearness.

He curls his body into me, and I feel his warm hand land on my upper thigh. Glancing over at Eve, who's wearing the biggest shit-eating grin I've ever seen, I try to keep my cool. I'm supposed to be calling the shots here. Not him. I try to ignore him. Act like his presence in no way affects me. Lifting my glass to my lips, I notice his warm hand is now skating up my thigh and under my skirt. With this move, I have to bite the inside of my cheek to keep from squealing. I can't give away how many times I've yearned to feel his strong fingers there, stroking me again.

My stare returns to Eve, who is lifting her martini glass to her mouth. As she sips, her smile resembles a Cheshire cat. I nearly gasp as his fingers graze my clit.

"How's my girl?" he moans in my ear. What is he doing here anyway? "You being a good girl for me, Ava?" Unsure what this game is he's playing, I just keep my stare fixed on Eve, who I notice is peering about the bar. Probably looking for Carson. Abruptly, I feel my panties move to the side as he slides his finger through my folds. A moan almost escapes as he glides it back and forth through my wetness, teasing my clit with each stroke. Lifting my glass to my mouth, I bite down on the skinny plastic red cocktail straw to prevent groaning.

"Sorry about that, ladies." I see Carson slide onto the seat across from me just as Mick withdraws his finger. The table is completely silent. Everyone staring at Mick. This is so awkward. Just as I think I should introduce him to everyone, he lifts his hand from under the table and starts to draw circles in the condensation of my cocktail glass.

Looking across the table, I notice Carson and Eve having their own silent conversation with one another. Except, unlike Mick's new language, all four of their hands are clearly visible on top of the table. My eyes flick to Mick, who's concentrating on his water painting as if he's the star of a private art gallery showing. Inspecting the drawing more closely, I notice he's drawn three circles on top of each other with stick figure arms.

Biting into the flesh of my lower lip to prevent laughing, I try to make eye contact, acknowledging his primitive Olaf artwork just as he lifts his finger into his mouth. The same finger, I'm certain, that was teasing my clit moments ago.

A little gasp escapes before I can stop it, attracting the attention of my table mates. My attempt to collect myself is thwarted as he stands, nods, and walks away. *Holy shit.*

"Ava. Was that?"

"Michael."

"Oh. My. God." Eve exclaims, throwing her hand over her mouth. "That was hot as fuck."

"What? What'd I miss?" Carson inquires.

"Nothing," we blurt simultaneously.

"I'm impressed, Ava. You've got some restraint. I'd be all over that like fleas on a hound dog."

Looking toward the door, I watch as Mick casually strides away, much in the way he approached, hands in his pockets, looking like he doesn't have a care in the world. Reaching the exit, he turns, gives me a wink, and walks away. "Restraint or ridiculous." *Why on earth am I sitting here with these two when I could be getting some with Mr. I'm too sexy to speak but can get you off in minutes?* How am I going to make it two more weeks? Then it dawns on me. That picture I sent him in response to his. This was payback.

CHAPTER TWENTY-SEVEN

Ava

Flipping through the patient messages I've received from Joanie, I'm struggling to do basic tasks. I can't concentrate. This mission of making sure Mick knew how important it was to me he communicate his concerns rather than run is starting to backfire. I couldn't stop thinking about him all weekend. It was torture.

I spent the weekend replaying his spontaneous visit to our table. Just seeing him up close after the weeks of missing him since our talk at the ballfield had my heart thumping. But when he sat down next to me. The warmth of him, his sexy tattooed arm draped over my shoulder. His always intoxicating manly scent. The devilish way he moved right in and seduced me, despite my friend sitting across the table watching it all unfold.

I'm not an exhibitionist. I admit it. I thought I was as vanilla as they come until the night I slept with Mick. We didn't do anything that outlandish, but since being with him… well, I don't think my inhibitions are the same. He makes me feel safe. Any other man touching me in that way, I would've slapped him and laughed when Carson tore him limb from limb. But with Mick, I just wanted more.

I'm not sure I would've stopped him if he slid his finger all the way inside me and—

"Ava. Good morning. I'm going to have a busy week. I have a few unavoidable appointments outside the office and will need your help getting caught up. I'd appreciate your help."

Looking to the door as Dr. Stark breaks my lusty thoughts, I have to replay what he's just said. That almost sounded like a concerted effort to be polite. He's never *appreciated* anything I've done before. "Sure, Dr. Stark. However, I can help."

"Thank you. I've got a lot to contend with, and knowing you've got my back will make things easier for me."

Holy hell. Is he feeling all right? He's never been this professional. Or thankful. "My clinic calendar is as full as ever, but since it's Monday, I can work with Joanie to move things around a little if needed. Just let me know how I can help."

"Thank you. Joanie already has my appointment calendar, so I'll ask her to get with you. I'm leaving for a meeting in about an hour. I'll touch base with you this afternoon or tomorrow." He gives me a rather glum half-smile and walks away.

After sifting through my messages a final time and contacting the patients regarding their inquiries, I finally give in to my curiosity and go in search of Joanie before seeing my first patient of the day. Dr. Stark should be long gone by now.

"Joanie. I hate to be one for gossip, but what's going on with Stark? He was actually nice to me just now."

"Don't get used to it." She sniggers. "I'm not one hundred percent sure, but my gut tells me there's trouble in paradise."

"What do you mean?"

"Well, most of his appointments appear to be with a lawyer." Joanie grimaces.

"Oh, god. Like trouble at work or at home?"

"My guess is at home because Allison's trap is bigger than mine. If there was something legal brewing here with him, I would've heard about that by now."

Biting my lip, I actually feel a bit sorry for the guy. Don't know why after the way he's continually treated me. But I hate to hear of anyone having a relationship end if they could've otherwise repaired things. "Well, just let me know how I have to adjust things. It's going to be tough adding too much more to my caseload."

"I managed to get his call shifts covered. So that was a big stressor. And Sebastian is here on Friday morning for a couple of surgical cases. He told me he could come up and see a few of Dr. Stark's patients that afternoon. He's a tireless flirt and has probably slept with half the women on staff at this hospital, but underneath, I think there's a softie," she says right before her eyes spring wide.

"What?"

"Maybe he's into older women, and he's making a play for me."

"Oh, Joanie. If that's true, you don't need some arrogant playboy."

"Why not? I could use him for sex just the same as he does."

It takes everything in me not to laugh. I can't tell if she's serious. "I need to go see Ms. Baxter. I'll catch up with you and your wild flights of fancy later." I giggle.

"Uh, Ava. Do you have a second?" Joanie asks, peeking her head into my open doorway.

"I think so. What's going on now? Has Jason Momoa called and wants to take you to lunch?"

"I wish," she blurts as I follow her down the hallway to her desk.

"Oh my gosh. What's this?" There's a large wicker basket full of spa essentials, relaxing candles, oils, lotions, and bath salts. The aroma is mild but smells fresh and clean as I lean forward to take a luxurious whiff.

"Open the card, Ava. You know who it's from."

My cheeks hurt from the strain of the excited smile I'm wearing as I delicately open the envelope.

Dearest Elsa,
    I hope you enjoy the Big Summer Spa Blow Out.
    To relax you when my hands can't do the trick.
    xoxo, Mick

An immediate burst of heat floods my already sore face. I'm not sure how he was planning to use his hands to relax me, but I vote for finishing what he started the other night.

"What's it say?"

I hesitate to give it to her. Thinking maybe I should just read it. But there's nothing overtly risqué about this note. Handing it over, I watch her light up as she reads it. Yet she doesn't seem surprised. *Hmm. All of these items are delivered to work. Is she somehow in on this?*

"Ava Kennedy. If you don't put that poor guy out of his misery soon."

"It's only two more weeks." If I keep telling myself that, maybe it won't seem so long.

～

By the week's end, things have taken a complete 180-degree turn. The kindness Dr. Stark displayed Monday is long gone. The week has been a bear. I've developed one of the worst migraines ever. Initially, it felt like a typical headache, brought on by too much work. But as Dr. Stark has become even worse than his former rude-assed self, this migraine has moved into unrelenting torture chamber mode.

"I don't care what she wants, that's never going to happen!" *Slam!* Sounds like things are getting worse by the minute down the hall. My money is on Joanie's prediction. I think things are going south in the Stark household.

There are only a few more patients to see before I can head home. I'm sure after that phone call, I'll probably be the only provider left seeing patients, as I'm sure he's already stormed off. Grabbing my lab coat, I slide it on and lift my chin. I can do this. Only a few more and then I can head home and take something strong before I curl into bed.

Arriving home, I put on a pot of herbal tea and open a peppermint candy to drop inside once it's hot. I have no appetite for food but decide to pop some bread into the toaster. I didn't eat any lunch, and sometimes the nausea is made worse with not having anything in my stomach with my pain medication.

Preparing a small cup of chicken soup, I reach for my dry toast, flick off the kitchen light, and sit at the kitchen island. I can't manage cooking in the dark, but any bright light intensifies this awful feeling. Massaging my temples briefly, I gingerly take a sip of soup. Once I've managed to eat a little something, I can take a pain pill and sip my tea. That, and a long soak, will hopefully abate this vice-like grip on my head.

It's so lonely here. When you live with chronic pain, you don't always notice. You're too uncomfortable to care about anything but the hug of the blankets around you. But knowing there's someone out there that cares about me is pulling at my heart. If only this could work out.

He now knows about the migraines, but I need to be careful how I let him in. Everything about this relationship is so new. I believe, deep down, Mick's a handsome, sexy man with the heart of a giant. If anyone would stand by me and help when I'm not well, I think it could be him. Yet my father couldn't do it. Any man could snap if their patience was tested beyond their limit.

Taking a few sips of peppermint tea, I drop my head in my hands.

Ding. Dong.

What on earth? Who'd be coming by here at this hour? I frequently order items on Amazon, but I wouldn't think they'd be delivering at 8:00 p.m. Glad I hadn't already gotten in the bath.

Heading for the door, I hear what sounds like music playing. Carefully cracking the door in case there is some nutjob, I peek outside. Holy crow. That's *my* nutjob.

Standing in the center of my meager yard is one hot as hell ex-ballplayer wearing a long black trench coat, gloves, a scarf, and a hat. It's got to be almost eighty degrees outside. He has his arms held up over his head, holding a Bluetooth speaker in both hands like a scene from the eighties John Cusack rom-com, *Say Anything*. I notice there are three baseballs stacked on top of each other on the ground beside him with sticks extending from the sides like makeshift arms. It's honestly hard to wrap my head around what I'm seeing. Probably would be even without this horrific headache. But suddenly, the chorus of the song playing on the Bluetooth rings out about wanting to build a snowman, and it's all becoming clearer.

Oh. My. God. He's lost it. Looking closer still, I see a pile of something white beside him. What is that? It appears to be some type of *snow*? I can't help myself any longer. I step out onto the porch and strain to look at it, still coming up short.

Mick continues to hold the Bluetooth, not making eye contact with me like one of those human statue street artists in Times Square. As I look down at the mountain of white flakes, I dip my finger in.

"Potatoes."

Laughing. "What?"

"They're potatoes. Couldn't find any snow," he whispers, still looking ahead like someone else is watching this ridiculous show besides me.

Standing up, I turn to face him when something catches my eye. A little farther behind where he's standing, there are more *potatoes*.

I love you, Elsa.

Unable to contain the gasp, my hand flies to my mouth as Mick's gaze finally turns to me. Walking over to him, I curl my arms around his waist and bury my face in his solid chest. Tears flooding his shirt.

Mick's position changes as he slides the speaker into his coat pocket, music still on repeat, and he wraps his steely arms around me.

"This doesn't change anything. You still have a week to go," I utter into his chest.

"Fuck, that doesn't give me time off for good behavior?" He chuckles.

"I don't know if I'd call torturing me in front of my best friend last week *good behavior*."

"It was good for me."

"How did you know where I live?"

"A little birdy told me."

I knew it. "A little Joanie?" I laugh.

Looking up at his brilliantly beautiful smile, I can't help myself. Pushing up onto my tiptoes, I plant a chaste kiss on his big lips and sigh.

"I'm so in love with you, Michael York. This thirty days is not just about you. I have things I'm working on while we're apart too. I'm desperate for this to work between us. I've never felt like this with anyone."

"I know, baby. I feel the same way. But what could you possibly have to work on? You're perfect."

"Hardly. I need to come clean about these migraines. It might be more than you're willing to take on. I have them a lot. Like, A LOT. I try to manage as best I can so I don't live feeling like I'm doped up on pain pills all the time, but I'm struggling."

"Babe, you know I'd be there for you, right? We can manage this. You just haven't had me there to help before."

"I know. And you're probably right. But emotionally, I'm working on my fears about it. My dad left my mom because he couldn't take it anymore. And when he left her, he left me. The domino effect could be big."

"Nothing personal, but your dad's a toad. It's one thing if he and your mom split. You'll never really know if it was just the migraines or if there was more to it. But no man walks away on their kid. I've been there. I'd never do that to my child."

Snuggling in deeper, I take a deep inhale, hoping I can remember his scent long after he's gone. "It's only one more week, Mick. I love that you did this for me. I actually have a pretty wicked headache now. I was about to get in the tub when you arrived."

When my statement is met with silence, I look up to see one brow cocked at me. "I could help with that."

"Even you and your raw sex appeal can't break through this migraine. Sorry. I'll put you to the test some other night."

"Okay, Els." He leans down to place a tender kiss on my temple. "Climb into your bath. I'll go home and jackoff to your picture, imagining I'm in there with you."

My mouth flies open, instantly remembering the naughty bathtub photo I sent in retaliation for the Olaf boxer tease.

"Trust me. That photo is going to cause me to have blisters on my hands. And my poor dick."

"Oh, god." Shoving him away from me, as I attempt to walk back up the stairs, he pulls me into him for one last steamy kiss before saying goodbye.

"Mint. My sweet girl always smells and tastes like mint."

"It's for the nausea. But you're right. I think I'm addicted to them. They're everywhere."

Mick pats me on the behind as I turn for the stairs. "One week, Elsa. Then you're mine."

Reaching the top of the steps, I turn to him for one last glance before heading to the bath. *Trust me, Mick. I'm already yours.*

Mick

This last week was a little rough. I decide to show Ava how much I respect her decision for this thirty-day think session by giving us both some space. Having told her how I feel about her and holding her in my arms for a few short moments has helped.

She's so brave. Dealing with the headaches and facing the world with no one the wiser. I would've had no idea how bad things have been. Then to know your father left your mother for the very same reason. No wonder she wants to make sure I'm all in. Especially after the way I abandoned her. *Fuck. Just like he did.*

Our conversation had hit a chord with me. In all the years I'd been angry about Paula's betrayal, I never considered the impact of my dad's departure on my romantic life. The thought had briefly crossed my mind at the ballfield, talking to Emmaleigh. But until the other night, I hadn't allowed myself to go there. His walking away without looking back had a huge impact on me.

I never wanted my mother to see how much it affected me. She had enough to worry with. I'd cry myself to sleep when I was young but make sure to hide my hurt when she was around. I've never had close relationships with anyone but my immediate family and Zach. In hindsight, my relationship with Paula was only skin-deep. She was pretty and didn't seem terribly clingy or needy. I think I knew I didn't have it in me to give that to someone who could potentially walk out on me.

Even my friendships are superficial. Zach has always felt more like a big brother. Maybe because I think of him like family, I've allowed myself to let him in more. I know Mom and Emmaleigh would never betray me. As hard as I try, I still keep some distance with Rob. But my stepdad has been more of a father to me than mine ever was. I need to work on that. Let him in more.

I know we only dated a very short while before I ghosted Ava. But I think I was courting her each and every time I visited her office. She just didn't know it. I've been falling for her for over a year. And there's no fighting the way I feel about her. Telling her I love her was completely different than sharing that with my family or Paula. When I'm with Ava, I want to shout it from the rooftops. There's a feeling of being home when we're together.

Part of this newfound feeling of love is making me overprotective. It's not possessive, like the feeling I had when Trevor told me she was at the club with a man. And I know she doesn't need me to be this way. She's taken care of herself long before I came along. But I want to look out for her. Make sure she's safe.

I'd approached Joanie during a visit to the office, sharing my concerns about Dr. Stark's inappropriate behavior with Ava. I don't want my girl to have any extra stress knowing I've talked to the office staff about this, so I've tried to keep this between Joanie and myself. I know Allison's there if I need to include her, but it's not my place. Yet.

Dr. Stark's unpleasant, unprofessional treatment of Ava is bad enough, but the touching and getting into her personal space has to stop. I asked Joanie to pay a little more attention to the activities in the office moving forward and text me if anything's happening that's causing Ava to struggle more than necessary. It's not lost on me that Joanie's no fan of Joseph Stark, so I think I can count on her.

Lying back against the pillows of my bed in the Hampton Inn in Salem, Virginia, I decide to do some research. Opening my laptop, I begin to look into chronic migraines, therapies, preventative treatment. Anything I can do to help Ava. Once this next week passes, I'll ask her to include me when she's feeling bad. Let me know how I can help. I need her to know I'm not going anywhere.

∽

Coming out of my last clinic visit before lunch, I decide to grab a bite to eat before calling on the next office.

Bzzz. Bzzz.

"Hello?"

"Michael?"

"Yes."

"It's Joanie. At Central Orthopedics."

Sitting taller in my seat, I feel my heart rate pick up. "Of course, Joanie. Is everything okay?"

"I'm not sure. Poor Ava's been suffering from this headache for almost a week. But this one seems different. She honestly should've called out sick, but Dr. Stark has been on a tear lately, and I don't think she wanted to invite that wrath, so she just pushed through. But I'm worried about her."

Fuck. "Joanie, I'll cancel my next appointment, but it'll probably take me three hours to get back there. What time does the office close for the day?"

"We're usually wrapped up by 4:30, but Dr. Stark's been piling a lot on Ava lately with his frequent absences from the office. Between you, me, and the lamp post, I think he's going through a divorce."

Shit. That won't bode well for Ava either. Not only will he be a bear to be around, he already didn't have any boundaries with touching her when he was married. What will he be like now? "Joanie, I'm on the way. I'll be there as soon as I can."

"Be careful, Michael. It won't help Ava if you get yourself into an accident."

She's right. I need to keep that at the forefront of my mind as I head back so I don't get arrested or killed trying to drive back like a bat out of hell.

～

"Hey, Joanie. Where is she?" I blurt as I approach the window in the orthopedic office waiting room.

"Come on through, Mick. She's in her office. I'm glad you made it okay."

Practically sprinting down the hallway, my heart in my throat at how I'll find her, I hear someone shouting as I get closer to the door.

"I told you to never touch me again. That's it. I've been working nonstop for you for weeks to get your patients seen with you gone all the time. I haven't dared call out sick. And now you have the nerve to come in here when my head's down and touch me again? And you don't have to bother threatening my job! I'll quit before working another day here with you!"

That's it. I see red. Any logic is lost in this moment as I come around the desk, grabbing Stark by the collar and throwing him up against the wall. Bearing my forearm into his throat, it's all I can do not to snap it like a twig.

"Mick, don't," Ava pleads. "He's not worth you getting into any trouble."

"I don't give a fuck. You've already touched her once and gotten away with it."

Dr. Dick remains silent, his eyes demonstrating the terror he's feeling. He better be fucking scared.

"Mick," Ava again pleads from behind me.

"I don't know how you live with yourself. She works her ass off for you, and not only do you constantly treat her like shit, but you have the nerve to put your fucking hands on her."

Suddenly, I hear a gasp behind me that sounds as if it's coming from Joanie. Whirling around, I notice Dr. Lee's holding Ava, who's apparently collapsed in his arms. *What the hell?*

"Ava!" I yell.

CHAPTER TWENTY-EIGHT

Mick

"I'll call the ER and let them know you're coming," Dr. Lee says as he carefully transfers her frail body over to me. I think he can tell arguing about who's going to carry her down there will fall on deaf ears.

"I've got the door, Mick. Do you know how to get to the emergency room from here?" Joanie cries out.

"Yes."

"I'll meet you down there as soon as I can close things up here."

"You go ahead, Joanie. I've got this," Allison interrupts.

I run for the elevator, afraid my nerves will make it impossible to handle three floors of the stairwell carefully. I don't dare want to drop her. Trevor and Zach, I'm not. I don't know how they do this every day. As I get to the doors, a kind soul sees me coming and thrusts his hand in between them as they're closing to allow us entrance.

"Is she okay?"

"I don't know. She passed out," I answer. What I want to scream is, 'Does she fucking look okay?' How is this happening? Please could something teleport us to the ER so I know she's all right? *You're scaring the shit out of me, Els.*

The doors open as we hit the first floor and someone holding a wheelchair offers it to us. I think I can get there faster if I carry her, not having to worry about Ava flopping over in the chair. "I think I'm faster on foot, thanks."

I traverse the corridors of the first floor until I find the familiar hallway leading to the ER. "You're going to be okay, Els. I've got you. I'm sorry I upset you, baby."

Fuck. Please. She has to be okay.

"Over here, sir," the kind emergency room receptionist greets, pulling me immediately into a triage room to lie Ava on the stretcher. Multiple people descend on us, and I feel like I tell the story of what happened and how she's been dealing with this migraine about twenty times.

After vital signs are obtained and they've gotten an EKG, they move her into an ER room and ask if I can remain seated in the waiting room for a bit so they can get her undressed, draw some lab work, and place an IV.

"Of course. Do whatever you have to do. But can I see her when you're done?"

Sensing the panic in my voice, the nurse, Meghan it says on her badge, reassures me that she'll bring me right back as soon as they get Ava settled.

Pacing about the waiting room like a father to be, I run my hand through my hair and keep repeating silent prayers that she'll be okay.

"Michael."

Looking up, I see Joanie's puffy eyes greeting me.

"Is she okay?"

"I don't know. She was still out when I came out here to let them do their thing." She grabs my arm, trying to comfort me. "This is my fault. If I'd gotten my temper under control, she wouldn't be in this state."

"Michael, this isn't on you. That's why I called you. She hasn't looked well for days. I'm worried something's wrong."

Unable to help it, I pull Joanie in for a hug. Both of us trying to find comfort wherever we can. "I'm probably going to have to deal with Stark after this. He doesn't strike me as someone who'll let something like this go easily. I just snapped, Joanie. The thought of that guy making her upset was bad enough. But he put his fucking hands on her."

"I know, Michael. We can't worry about that right now. You'll have the full support of Dr. Lee, Allison, and myself. Don't you worry. If it comes to that, we'll be sure to set the record straight."

"I'm sorry, I didn't catch your name before," nurse Meghan interrupts. "You can come on back now."

"It's Michael. Thank you." Looking to Joanie, she pats me on the arm.

"Go, go. Just update me when you can. I'll be here praying for her."

Giving Joanie's hand a squeeze, I turn back to the nurse. I can't hide my panic any longer.

"Is she any better?"

"I'm afraid she's still not responding. We're going to give her some pain medicine and see if that helps. But the sedating effect may keep her groggy for a whole different reason if she receives some relief."

"I understand. I'm just worried. She was completely lucid when I was with her, but her coworker said she'd really been suffering from this last migraine for a week. She usually gets sick with them and probably hasn't eaten much. Then add stress..." *The stress I brought when I wouldn't listen to her and practically murdered her boss.* "If she doesn't come around soon, you might want to talk to Joanie, her coworker. She said this had seemed different than her usual migraines. I don't know if she could shed any more light on it."

"Thanks. I'll let Dr. Grant know. He'll be taking care of her."

"Thank you." She ushers me into the emergency department, walking me to Ava's room. Coming to her bedside, I sit and hold her hand, taking in her pained face. I remember the first time I saw that asshole touching her, and the light had been off. Jumping up, I quickly flick the switch, keeping the door cracked to allow minimal light to enter the space.

Rubbing her soft hand in mine, I lift it to my lips. "Please wake up for me, baby. This is killing me. I'll always be here when you need me. I promise. I just hate seeing you like this."

The only response is the constant chirping of the monitors. Her breathing appears normal, a light rise and fall of her chest under the unattractive, oversized hospital gown. God, I hope that pain medicine kicks in quickly.

Bending down by her temple, her soft blonde hair tickling my nose, I place a soft kiss on the shell of her ear. "We're going to get you better, Ava. I love you." As I lean back up, it dawns on me her mother would want to know she's here. I have no idea how to reach her, but maybe Joanie can help figure it out.

Springing from the edge of the bed, I open the door and notice someone familiar. Walking over to the counter, I see a nametag hanging from her lab coat. "Hi, are you Ava's friend, Eve?"

"Yes. Oh, I didn't recognize you at first. Are you her Michael?"

God, why does that feel so fucking good? *Her* Michael. "Yes. She passed out in her office, and I brought her here. I don't know if it's her migraines or something else. But I wanted to try and get in touch with her mother."

Eve's hand flies to her mouth in shock. "Oh my gosh. I had no idea she was here. I've been running all over the ER today. We've been so busy. Is she in there?" She points behind me to room seven.

"Yes."

Eve flies around me, gently opening the door and immediately sitting down on the bed beside my princess.

"Ava, honey. I'm so sorry. I'm right here. And Michael's right here. We've got you." Eve gently strokes her cheek, and I feel a lump in my throat. My whole life is lying on that stretcher. I'm going to marry that girl.

"Eve. Do you know how we can get in touch with Ava's mother?"

"Oh, yes. I've got her number. I'll call her. Can you tell me what happened?" I repeat the story, again, and tell her about what Joanie had shared about her headache seeming different. She reassured me she'd talk to Joanie and pass anything along to Dr. Grant that could be helpful."

Knock. Knock.

Twisting to see who's arrived, a young male in light blue scrubs enters the room.

"Come on in, Corey. She's all set." I look at Eve inquisitively. "He's here to take her to CT. They'll get some pictures of her head to make sure there's nothing concerning going on. It's standard practice with someone who passes out."

"Oh," I say as my shoulders relax a tad. "I'm going to update her friend in the waiting room. Can I come back once she returns?"

"Of course. I'll come and find you." Eve tries to give me a reassuring look, but I know we're equally scared.

Walking down the hall, I see Dr. Lee approach. "How's she doing?"

"The same. They just took her to CT."

"Oh, I'm sorry to hear that."

"Dr. Lee, I'm sorry I lost control in there. That guy—"

"You don't even need to finish that sentence. Joseph Stark is a self-righteous asshole. I can be an arrogant bastard, but nothing like that guy. You just focus on Ava. Don't worry about him."

"Thank you," I add, still dropping my head in remorse. "I'm just going to update Joanie and let her know I'll call her later so she can go home."

Dr. Lee gives me a swat on the arm and strides away. That guy's okay in my book.

~

"Hi. I'm Donovan Grant," a voice from behind me says. I think I may have fallen asleep in this chair in this dimly lit room, waiting for word on Ava's condition.

Standing, I reach out my hand. "Thank you for taking care of her. Have you got the results of her CT?"

"Yes. Please, have a seat," he responds, pointing to the chair beside me. Dr. Grant grabs a stool and pulls it up next to me. "This doesn't appear to be a migraine. Well, at least, not entirely. Her CT scan shows sphenoid sinusitis. Unlike most sinus infections, this one appears severe. Her white blood cell count is elevated, and she hasn't responded to the pain medications usually given for a migraine."

"I work in medical sales, but it's mainly orthopedic. So I apologize if I'm not following you. I thought with a sinus infection you'd be congested or have symptoms of a head cold."

"With most sinus infections, that's true. But not always. She most likely only had a headache. Given her history, she wouldn't have had reason to suspect something different was occurring unless she started running a fever or the more common symptoms of a sinus infection developed."

Looking back at Ava, I'm not sure what to make of this. There's no tumor. She's not having a stroke. So this is good, right? "So, you just give her some antibiotics, and she gets better?"

"I hope so. We have to do a lumbar puncture to ensure this has not reached her brain."

"Shit."

"It's very uncommon, but severe sinus infections of this type have the potential to cause infections of the brain, infections of the facial bones or the base of the skull, as well as abscesses or clots. I don't have any reason to believe any of those is happening, but it's my job to rule them out."

"I understand. Thank you. What's involved with a lumbar puncture?"

"It's a spinal tap. We numb up a spot along her spine and insert a needle so we can withdraw fluid to test for the presence of bacteria."

Wincing at the thought of this, I understand they're doing what's necessary. "Do you have any idea when she might start coming around?"

"It's hard to say. Between her history of migraines and this, we just have to give her medications and see what happens. We're going to prepare to get her procedure done very soon. I've ordered high-dose antibiotics and steroids, and hopefully, she'll start turning around. Someone will come and get you when we're finished so you can be with her."

"Thank you. I appreciate you updating me. I'll let her mother know once she arrives." I give Ava one last kiss on the cheek and tell her I'll be waiting for her before stepping out. As I make my way to the front of the ER, I see Eve standing with who I assume is Ava's mother. They have similar features, but her mother's eyes are dark, and her hair is shoulder length.

"Michael, this is Carolyn. Carolyn, this is Ava's—"

Before Eve can finish introductions, Carolyn has launched herself at me. She's so small. At least five or six inches shorter than her daughter. Her tiny body is wracked with sobs. Looking at Eve, I see the fear is in her eyes as well. She just has to put on a brave front. Like me.

"Is there somewhere we can go? Besides the waiting room?"

"Oh, yes. There's the consult room. Follow me."

"Let's go somewhere quiet, okay?" I tell Carolyn, keeping my arm draped around her. It dawns on me that Ava's probably all she's got. We walk down the corridor to a small room with a couch, a chair, and an end table with tissues and a Bible. I'm assuming this is where they take family members who are awaiting the news of a critical loved one. How'd we end up here? She seemed fine a week ago.

Sitting down carefully, I pull her into my side and stroke her back. "Your Ava is strong. The toughest girl I've ever known. She's going to pull through this, Carolyn. I know it. They think they've identified the problem and are getting her the correct medicines."

She sits quietly next to me, her sobs quieting.

"Plus, fate had it that Eve was on duty today. She's in great hands."

"Thank you, Michael. I'm so thankful she has you." She suddenly grows quiet. "Michael, may I be blunt?"

Hell. This doesn't sound promising. "Of course."

"Living with chronic pain is debilitating. I've dealt with it my entire life. It's harder still when the cause is invisible to those around you. No one truly understands what you're dealing with. I'm sure it isn't easy to be in a relationship with someone with chronic headaches. I couldn't be the wife Greg deserved. For me, I chose not to enter into another relationship. I didn't want to put anyone else through that. But Ava's made of tougher stuff than her old mom. She's achieved so much."

I watch as she reaches for a tissue, dabbing at her swollen face. This poor woman. How isolating her life must have been.

"Ava told me about the last thirty days. I think it was a wise thing to do. Particularly if you two are getting serious. You need to know what you're walking into. It's best to leave now if you don't think you can handle this. I'd hate to see her destroyed if you left once you'd created a family together."

Turning toward her, I wait for her sad eyes to meet mine. "Mrs. Kennedy. I've known your daughter only through work over the last year. And we haven't dated long. But I've never felt this way for anyone. There's nothing that could make me want to walk away from her. Nothing."

Carolyn reaches around my chest and pulls me back in for another hug. I'm relieved we can provide some support for one another. And hopefully, when this is behind us, she can meet Mom, Emmaleigh, and Rob. Maybe after all of these years, she'll try to take a chance on building a relationship. Become part of my family. If I can do it, I bet she can too.

CHAPTER TWENTY-NINE

Mick

Beep. Beep. Beep.

The steady pace of the monitors, the darkened room, and the stressful day have caught up with me. I managed to send Carolyn home an hour ago and returned to wait for more information in this uncomfortable chair in Ava's room. I feel like I spend most of my days in these God-awful chairs.

"Hi." I hear a faint squeak and turn back to the door. There's no one there, and the door is still shut, all but for the tiniest sliver of light that glimmers underneath. *Hell, I'm hearing things.*

As I reposition in my seat, I glance up to see a pair of ice-blue eyes staring back at me. Rushing to her side, I blurt, "Ava, baby. You're awake."

"What happened?" She looks down at the monitors and intravenous lines attached to her body before looking back at me.

"I think when I lost my temper, it must've been more stress than you could handle. You passed out. At first, we thought this had to be one hell of a migraine, but the doctor thinks you have a pretty severe sinus infection. Do you remember anything?"

"Like what?"

"I wasn't sure if you might've been aware of things happening but too groggy from the pain and the medication to open your eyes. I mean, they even did a spinal tap."

"What? No. I don't remember anything."

Thank fuck for that. "They'd given you a ton of medicine, so you probably were sedated. You had a CT scan first that showed the sinus infection, but they needed to make sure it didn't make it to your brain."

"Good lord. I had the sniffles some last week, but nothing that felt like a sinus infection. Did the lumbar puncture turn out okay?"

"Yes, it did," Dr. Grant says as he walks into the room. "Hi, Ava. I haven't seen you in months."

"I know. I don't make it down here often. Especially not on the evening shift."

"Well, we'll try to make sure your visits are for professional reasons from now on. I'm glad to report the lumbar puncture looks good. And despite your elevated white count, you haven't spiked a fever, so I'm optimistic with antibiotics, pain medication, and steroids, you'll be feeling human again real soon."

Feeling like I can relax for the first time since Joanie's call, I let out a relieved exhale and grab ahold of Ava's hand. "What happens next?" I ask Dr. Grant.

"Ava will be moved to the inpatient floor once the hospitalist comes by to see her and writes admission orders. How's your pain?"

"It's okay."

"Ava, don't be brave anymore. Tell them if you're hurting," I beg.

"It's about a five on a scale of one to ten."

"That means it's probably an eight for everyone else on the planet," I tell Dr. Grant.

"I get it. I'll get her a little more medicine and check in again before you go upstairs."

"Thank you, Donovan. I really appreciate it."

"Just get better, okay." Donovan steps out of the room, carefully pulling the door closed behind him.

"Oh, gosh," Ava says, attempting to sit up in bed.

"What's the matter? Are you going to be sick?"

"No. I need to call my mom. If she or Carson have tried to reach me, they'll be worried sick when I don't answer."

No sooner has she finished her sentence before the door opens and the player from the nightclub enters. Except he's dressed in a police uniform. "Ava, you okay?"

"I'm better now. It's nothing serious. Just a bad sinus infection."

Nothing serious? "Ava, stop acting like this is nothing. This could've been very serious. You need to let them help you."

"Okay, Michael." She pats my hand, trying to reassure me. "Carson, this is Michael. My—"

"Boyfriend." Standing from my chair, I reach out a hand.

"Carson's my cousin," Ava continues. *Cousin. Hmm. This must be the guy Luigi was goading me about. Glad I didn't jump the gun on that too.*

"Yeah? Well, you might have to fight Carolyn for him, Av. She's completely in love." He laughs.

"What?" Ava giggles. The sound healing places in my soul that have taken quite the beating today.

"Yeah. Apparently, he and your mom spent some time together today while you were getting tests performed, and she couldn't stop going on about him." Carson looks directly at me. "Thanks, man. I haven't heard my aunt that happy in years. But if you ever hurt Ava—"

"It'll never happen again. I swear." I return my attention to my girl. "I'm going to step out and call Joanie, okay?" Bending down, I kiss her on the forehead. "If they'll let you have something to eat, do you want me to get you anything?"

"No, Mick. I'm good."

I give her a little glare, knowing this stubborn girl probably won't ask for anything, and decide to pick something up close by.

After updating Joanie and telling her I'll text her with Ava's room number when I have it, I grab some chicken noodle soup from the deli around the corner and give them ten dollars to bring back every mint they have left in their jar by the register.

Returning to the emergency room, I find Ava's already been moved upstairs. *Hell. How long was I gone?*

Rushing up to her room, the nurse advises visiting hours are over. I give her the best puppy dog eyes I can muster and ask if I can just have a few minutes to say goodnight.

"Sure. How am I supposed to turn down that look?"

"Thank you!" I call as I walk swiftly toward Ava's room. Knocking lightly before opening the door, I feel instant relief when her dazzling eyes meet mine. *Hell, I'm going to be the next one needing medical help. She takes my damn breath away.* Coming to her side, I bend to kiss her and place her soup, roll, and bottle of water on her bedside table.

"I can only stay a minute. The nurse said visiting hours are over, and you need some rest. Please tell them if you're hurting. It kills me to think you're in pain, knowing they can do something to help you."

"I will, Mick. I just hate the way those medicines make me feel. Plus, I don't want to get accustomed to them. I've managed a long time without needing to use narcotics."

"I know. But once in a while, if you need them—" My sentence is interrupted by her soft hand on mine. I shouldn't push. But in my defense, I'm still learning how to help her through this. And it's hard watching the people you love in pain.

"I'll check on you in the morning." Leaning down, I kiss the corners of her mouth. "Thank you for not sending me away."

"Why would I send you away?"

"The thirty days doesn't end for two more days." I laugh.

"I'm letting you off for time served." She grins.

"Oh, I got you something."

"What?" She looks about the room.

"I left the stinky flowers in the car."

"Haha. What did you get me?" She laughs.

"Hold out your hands." I watch as she closes her eyes and extends her hands, palms up, awaiting her gift. I pull the plastic canister full of mints from the deli out of the second to-go bag and drop it into her hands with a thud.

"Oh, my gosh. I wasn't—" Her eyes spring open, and she looks at the mints, stunned. "What did you do? Did you steal this from the restaurant?"

"No. I paid for them, fair and square." *Overpaid actually.*

She lifts the metal lid, reaches in for a fluffy white and red mint, tears open the plastic, and pops it into her mouth. Her eyes close, and she lets out a delicious sigh.

"You're killing me, Ava."

Her beautiful eyes connect with mine, and the most radiant look shines through her pain. We're going to be okay. I know it.

~

Walking toward Ava's room, I have a bouquet of scentless flowers and her mother on my arm. I need to end these thirty days much better than the way I started it. Ava's been here for four days, and things are looking much brighter. Her mother had only briefly visited once before, as she was worried Ava wouldn't rest if she stayed. I'm hoping there will be word of her discharge soon.

Knock. Knock.

Carolyn gently opens the door to ensure her daughter isn't sleeping. As we peek inside, we find a bright smile on Ava's face.

"Oh my gosh, you're both here. And flowers."

"Aren't they lovely, Ava? And he found a place that can prepare ones with only a mild fragrance." I watch as she bends to kiss her daughter on the cheek and whispers loud enough anyone in the hallway could hear. "This one's a keeper."

"Yes. Carson told me you approved."

"Oh, the little tattletale." She laughs.

I place her vase of flowers on the windowsill and come over to kiss her. "How's my girl? You look better than I've seen you in weeks. I didn't realize how fighting these headaches day in and day out could put such a strain on you."

"Yeah. I think I've slept better here than I have in months. All those drugs."

"Well, you needed it," I acknowledge, squeezing her hand.

"You're right."

"Any updates on when you get to come home?" Carolyn asks.

"Yes, they say tomorrow morning. The repeat head CT I had this morning looked better. Isn't that great?"

"It is." Carolyn claps. "I hope you plan to take some time off of work, Ava."

"Yes, ma'am. I do. I just haven't had a chance to talk to Allison yet."

"Ava, I hope it's okay I say this. But if Stark's still working there, I don't know how I feel about you going back. He's a menace."

"I can't quit without another job, Mick."

"You can. Stay with me until you find something." I can see Carolyn beaming at her daughter from my periphery. "I know it's not ideal, but neither is working with that asshole."

"I've had an interview with another clinic. I planned to quit once things started getting worse. Maybe I should reach out and see if they've made a hiring decision yet. I was pretty optimistic about it."

"You'll do no such thing," a voice says from behind me. Allison enters the room, walks over to Ava's side, and gives her a quick peck on the cheek. "Joseph Stark no longer works with Central Orthopedics. Between multiple employees documenting harassment in the workplace, and Dr. Lee issuing a formal statement that he may retract his offer to cover call at our hospital if something isn't done about Stark, we felt the answer was clear. I'm just sorry I didn't have enough documentation to do it before it got so bad."

Moving my attention from Allison to Ava, the relief is evident. Her shoulders are more relaxed. There's a lift to her smile that's genuine. It's a prayer answered, that's for sure.

"Thank you, Allison. I was just so worried about her having to return to that... well, negative environment. She works too hard to have to deal with such unprofessional behavior."

"You're absolutely right. And as fate has it, a replacement is already waiting in the wings."

"Really? Already?" Ava asks, seeming stunned.

"It's going to take a while for hospital credentialing to go through, but we have an orthopedic surgeon from another facility who'd like to move to St. Luke's."

"He's already with Central Ortho?" Ava asks.

"Yes. I'm not at liberty to divulge details yet. But I can safely say you shouldn't have any issues if he comes on board."

"Well, I'd say there's a lot to celebrate." Ava's mom claps again. She and Ava exchange loving glances, and it warms my heart. I can't wait to have both of them over to the house to meet my family. I know I might be moving fast, but that damn thirty-day sentence is over. Fuck going slow.

Ava

It's odd having so much downtime. Sure, my weekends aren't typically over-scheduled. I tend to do most of my housekeeping and grocery shopping during this time. But this…

Sitting on the couch with Mick, my legs in his lap, rubbing my feet as we watch baseball on ESPN, I feel like I'm in a dream. Who would've imagined how different things could be in a span of a few short weeks?

Since being discharged from the hospital a few days ago, Mick has barely left my side. He still has to be out of town two days a week, but he feels comfortable knowing my mother drops in and makes sure to send text updates to let him know I'm not overdoing it. Yes, she sends him texts. Maybe Carson was right. I might need to watch her.

Looking about my small space, I have to laugh at the number of flowers here. They aren't all from Mick. But when word caught on about the special floral shop Mick had found that created bouquets of minimally fragrant flowers, Eve, Carson, and the office had each sent a different one. The newest bunch was an all-white bouquet of Star of Bethlehem. They're just stunning. Tuesday Palmer, a floral designer at Cygnature Blooms, made the delivery personally. She said she'd had such fun creating different sprays of flowers with little to no scent, she wanted to meet the recipient. I guess it's not a common request.

"Babe? I need to talk to you about something."

Wow, this sounds ominous. "Sure, what?"

"Are you sure you're doing all you can with your migraines? To prevent them, I mean. Maybe you should try a different neurologist. Just to get another opinion."

"You know, it's funny you say that. Dr. Lee mentioned I should consider seeing a friend of his."

His brow arches and he gives me a deadpan stare.

"What?"

"I'm wondering what kind of friend he's sending you to. If he looks anything like Dr. Lee…"

"He referred me to Kendal Kramer. *She's* a neuropsychiatrist who specializes in holistic medicine."

"Ah." He smiles, seeming relieved more about the gender of the physician than her scope of practice. "Not a bad idea. I'll support whatever plan you come up with, but we've got to get them under better control."

"I've been managing for years, Mick."

"Maybe you can live with the way you've been managing them, but I can't. I can't watch you continue to suffer like this if there's anything else that can be done."

Reaching for his hand, I grab it and give it a squeeze. "I love you, Mick."

He pulls my fingertips to his lips and gives them a sweet peck.

Using my foot to teasingly rub my toes over his semihard cock, I give him a come-hither look.

"Ava," he scolds.

"What? Come on. I'll be fine," I plead.

"It's too soon. And you forget. I've seen you come. It's the most erotic show in town but too powerful to risk the effect it will have on you until you're better."

For fuck's sake. I'm starting to think this is payback for the thirty-day rule.

Hopping up from the couch, I head toward the pantry. "I'm making some popcorn. You want anything while I'm up?"

"Yeah, will you grab me a beer?"

I grab a frosty amber bottle from the fridge, pop the top, and then pour my microwave popcorn into a bowl before returning to him and the game. As I come around the couch, I notice he's been texting someone, but immediately hides the phone as I sit down.

"So, who's that?"

"Who's what?"

"On the phone?" I ask, popping a kernel into my mouth.

"It's my friend, Zach. He's just giving me shit for not being around. I'll have to introduce you. He's kind of a loner, but he's a good guy."

"Ah, does he work with you?"

"No, we grew up next door to one another. He's quite a few years older than I am. Works at the fire department. I think of him more like a brother than a friend, really."

"That's nice. I can't wait to meet him. I hope you aren't missing out on seeing him because you're babysitting me."

"I'm not babysitting you. I want to be here. I waited thirty fucking days to see you."

Looking down at my popcorn bowl, I begin to hatch a plan. Snuggling up beside Mick, I pick up several kernels and place them in my napkin. Twisting the napkin into the shape of a cone, I flick my tongue out to grab a piece. I repeat the action several more times, thinking he must really be into the game.

"You're fucking killing me, Ava."

I have to bite down on my lip so as not to laugh.

"I could do something to take care of that," I say, flicking another popcorn kernel with my tongue.

"Ava."

Flick.

"Ava," he says a little more sternly now.

"Come on, Mick, it's just oral. *On you.*"

A loud groan rumbles from his chest. "If I remember right, last time you did that for me, you were practically begging me to fuck you."

"I was not!" *Well, maybe I was.*

Cupping my face in his strong hands, he kisses me sensually and then rests his forehead on mine. "Princess, there's nothing I'd like better than to see your pretty lips stretched around my dick right now. But, until it's safe for me to fill that sweet little snatch with my cock, we wait."

"Ughhh," I groan loudly. God, his dirty talk does something to me. "I'm starting to think you don't want me anymore." Flick.

"Shit. If I keep pounding one off to your bathtub picture, my dick's going to fall off. Trust me, when it's safe to go all in, you're getting it good." Mick reaches into my popcorn bowl, then mimics my action from his hand, flicking his talented tongue out to capture a kernel.

"Uhhh," I whine.

"We just need to be sure your head is cleared for takeoff. I can't promise you'll be able to walk or sit after I'm done with you, but at least your brain will be okay."

CHAPTER THIRTY

Mick

It's been a few weeks since Ava came home. And except for watching her like a hawk for fear she'll overdo it, things have been good. I've never lived with a woman. Paula and I had been living in dorms on campus when we moved out of our respective family homes. I honestly never thought I'd enjoy sharing my space with a woman. But I've never felt so at home as I do when I'm with Ava.

I know I need to slow my roll, so I don't scare her that I'm moving too fast. But after everything that happened with her recently, on top of our breakup and thirty-day separation, I don't want to be apart from her any more than I have to. I'm already out of town two days a week.

We've managed to spend alternate Sundays with our families. We've enjoyed one weekend making dinner with Carolyn, and this past Sunday, we had a cookout with my mom, Rob, and Emmaleigh. My family was over the moon spending time with Ava. Especially Em. She deemed the two of them instant besties. And Ava was so patient with her. My sister can be a little over the top. It was good to see, as my mom had said Em hadn't been feeling well recently. I chalked it up to girl stuff that I wanted to hear nothing about. I mean, she certainly seemed fine Sunday.

"Hey, old man. I've been waiting for you for like an hour. The boys had to keep me company so I wouldn't realize how much of my time you're wasting."

"Oh, whatever. I had to run back to the house to get the keys. I thought they were on my keychain, but I must have put them back." Zach extends the worn leather keychain to me and gives me a knowing swat on the shoulder.

"Trevor was introducing me to your newest recruit, Alex."

"Yeah, I think he'll make it."

"Hey, I'm standing right here," Alex bellows.

"You rookies are all the same. Think you know everything. You keep your eyes and ears open and your trap shut, and I think you'll do okay."

"Oh, good grief," Alex grunts. Trevor just laughs with the look of a guy who's been in Alex's shoes before.

"You taking your girl to Zach's cabin," Trevor asks.

"That's the plan. She's getting a little stir crazy in the house. But she has one more weekend before she returns to work. I thought a getaway to the mountains would do her good. Speaking of mountains, when do you head to Sycamore?"

"Two weeks. It was good meeting you, man. You need to come and visit. Zach said he'll come."

"Hell, if Zach goes to see you in mountain country, he might not come back."

"Nobody'd miss me," Zach says with a little too much seriousness in his tone.

"That's some bull, and you know it. You better get your ass back here," I say, smacking his arm. "Thanks for these."

"The place better not reek of sex the next time I'm up there."

I stretch out my hand, offering to return the keys. 'Cause hell if I'm promising that.

~

"Oh, Mick. I'm so excited about this getaway with you. I'm feeling so much better and was growing tired of the inside of the house."

"Well, once you see this place, you may want to turn back. It's pretty rustic."

"It'll be perfect."

Holding Ava's hand as we make our way toward the cabin, it feels reminiscent of our drive to the Nationals game. Except without the jitters. Thinking back on that day, I was so nervous. It was easy being with her. No forced conversation or awkwardness. But it was so new. We've been through so much since then. Good and bad.

"I love this area," Ava says, pointing out toward a pond with a small mountain as its backdrop. "I haven't been out here much."

"Yeah, it's gorgeous but pretty remote. Zach and I usually fish near Lake Anna, about an hour away from your place. There's also a place in Yorktown we like to go to. But his cabin is northwest of Lake Anna. There's a small lake nearby and some hiking. But that's it, really."

"He comes out here all alone?"

"Zach does just about everything alone. Sometimes he brings Otis. That's why I asked if you had spare sheets."

Ava gives me a look of shock. "Wow. I didn't realize Zach was gay. Not that it matters, but I just kept picturing a grumpy loner who was built like a lumberjack."

"Haha. Your description is right on target. But he's straight as an arrow. Otis is his dog. He probably sleeps with him." I chuckle. Pulling her sweet hand to my lips, I give her a peck and a wink as we continue the drive through God's country. There's nothing but pastures, hay bales, roadside farm stands, and old houses that look as if they should be condemned intermingled between large plots of land with gorgeous plantation houses and bright red barns.

Resting my hand on Ava's upper thigh, I try not to let my mind wander too much to what awaits us. She's feeling better, and I plan to make up for lost time. There's still too far left in our journey to get a hard-on now. And I don't want to finally get my hands on her on the side of a dirt road.

"Hey, can I ask you something?" I can't believe I'm doing this.

"Of course. You can always ask me anything."

"Is it okay I'm spending so much time at your house? I know I really didn't give you a choice. I was so fucking worried about you. Being there kept me from going crazy."

"I've loved having you with me, Mick. I'm just sorry it had to be like that. You've been so sweet taking care of me and bringing my mom into your world. It's meant everything to me."

Giving her hand a reassuring squeeze, I decide to push on. "I'm only home part of the week. And I spend a lot of the time I'm in town at work or with my team. At least until baseball is over. But is it too soon to talk about moving in together?"

A spectacular smile takes over Ava's face, giving me instant relief over approaching her with this. "You know. If we hadn't gone through those thirty days, I'd probably say it was too soon. But we took time to examine our commitment. And we've been hurt enough before I don't think either of us would enter into a living arrangement if we weren't sure. I mean, *I've* never lived with anyone before."

"I never wanted to live with anyone, until you." I again kiss her hand because I'm driving and don't want to wreck the car to respond how I'd prefer. Plus, every minute we're still moving northwest is that much closer to giving her all of the affection I want.

"Let's see how the weekend goes. But I'm excited about the possibility of it, Mick."

"Me too. I can finally get a dog." I guffaw.

Ava punches me in the arm, giggling. "Oh, I see now. And here I thought you just wanted easy access to my body."

"Well, there's that. I'm playing, Els. I love everything about coming home to you. Making it permanent would be even better. Knowing I'm coming home to you when I'm on the road." I shake my head. "I'm joking about the dog. Although, I have always wanted one."

"Oh, we could get a cute little pup—"

"No! There will be no cute fluffy pups. I've waited my whole damn life for a dog. Never had one growing up because my mom had a hard enough time keeping up with me. You want cute, go hang out with Bruno."

Ava laughs. She doesn't look the least bit offended I won't hear her out on a pocket pup. "What kind of dog do you want?"

"I don't know. A shepherd or a retriever of some sort. A manly dog."

Ava covers her mouth as her belly laugh takes over. "A manly dog."

"Yeah, a dog I can take to the lake. Not some ankle biter."

"Okay. Maybe my mom can keep an eye out for you. Did I tell you she's been volunteering at the Hanover dog shelter?"

"No. That's great." I spot a familiar cluster of rocks and natural wildflowers at the edge of the road next to a dirt-lined drive and point. "I think we're here." Ava immediately sits up taller in her seat, peering out the window. There's excitement in the air. Hope she still has that once she sees this old shack. Putting my hand back onto her thigh, willing to risk whatever happens at this point, my heart stops when my little finger grazes her warm skin. Suddenly, it dawns on me. Is she not wearing any panties? Has this little tart ridden next to me the whole way here without any damn panties on?

As we travel the bumpy lane, I can just barely make out the dark wood of the cabin in the distance. Sliding my hand a little further up her thigh, I stretch my index finger over her mound just as we pull up in the circular drive. "Fuck, Ava. You're killing me, princess."

The little minx slowly turns in my direction with a devilish glint in her eye. "I can't believe it took until now for you to figure it out."

That's it. I practically drag her across the center console until she's on top of me. Reaching for the seat adjustment, I push the driver's seat back as far as it can go and pull her legs on either side of me. Holding her hips, I grind the growing erection in my jeans into her bare pussy. "Kiss me, Els."

Ava plants her sweet mouth on mine, pulling at my hair as she undulates on top of me. Moving one hand under her skirt, I tease her now wet, swollen flesh briefly before pulling back to taste her. As our eyes connect, there's a hunger there that could almost mimic mine. Almost.

"I need you, Mick." She groans, leaning her head against my shoulder while she continues to ride me as if I were naked and buried inside her. I know the rational thing would be to stop and take her inside the cabin. But that house feels a mile away.

Instead, I lift her shirt and pull her lacy bra down, exposing her tits and firm pink nipples. "Sweet, Jesus." Diving in, I lick and suck one sweet peak and then the other.

"Can I touch you, Mick? I want to touch you."

"Baby, if you pull my dick out, it's game over. And I don't think I can lift us up enough to grab a condom from my wallet." She groans above me, and I chuckle. "We should probably get inside."

Ava quickly whirls her head in both directions as if trying to see if I'm referring to something or someone out here we need to shield ourselves from.

"There's no one here, baby. I just can't take care of you how I'd like in this car."

"Oh." She giggles.

Opening the door, I carefully attempt to twist so she can exit the car without falling. As she does so, the scent of sex in the air makes my rock-hard cock even harder. I've barely gotten both feet out of the vehicle before she turns to me with that same ravenous, almost desperate look in her eyes. *Fuck it.* I run to the back of the car, swing the hatch open, and grab the wool blanket I keep in case of emergencies. *Well, this is a fucking emergency.*

Unfurling it onto the patch of grass adjacent to the drive, I reach for Ava and pull her down onto the hunter-green wool blanket. Positioning her beneath me, I lift her skirt. "Ah, there's my girl."

"Oh, god." She laughs.

With one long swipe of the flat of my tongue, I'm immediately starved for her. The taste of her arousal on her soft, swollen pink folds is making me insane. I eat, suck, and finger her until I can't take her cries of ecstasy any longer and reach for my wallet before unzipping my pants.

Placing the wallet by my side, I slide my pants down and grab ahold of my needy dick. Giving it a few strokes, I sit down and decide to remove my shirt and pants entirely. Climbing over Ava, I remove her top. Her tiny little skirt isn't a hindrance. As I reposition myself, I decide to have another taste now that I'm comfortable and have easier access to the condom when I'm ready. "God, I've missed this pussy." I return to devouring her, alternating teasing flicks of my tongue to her clit and her wet center.

"Oh, Mick." She groans.

"You like, Els?"

"No."

"No?" Looking up, stunned by her answer, I find she's staring down at me. I hadn't even realized I'd been fisting my cock with my right hand while I leaned on my left forearm to eat her.

"I've never seen anything so hot in my life." She pants.

"You like watching me?"

"It's the only porn I'll ever need."

Chuckling, I sit up and give her a little front-row seat to her favorite porn star before reaching for a condom. She immediately starts to touch herself. If I don't get that condom on quick, I won't need it at all. I'm about to come all over my hand at the sight of her. Beautiful, platinum hair fanned all over the blanket, hungry ice blue eyes watching me as she teases her clit with the pads of her fingers. "You're killing me, Ava."

Making quick work of the condom, I crawl over her and slide myself in with one thrust.

I literally have to stop momentarily to catch my breath. The feel of her. Knowing she loves me. That she's mine after all we've been through. I need to come before I start crying like a baby.

Ava digs her nails into my ass, and I know she's as close as I am. Unable to go slow, I lift her hips and begin to steadily pound her into the ground. The carnal noises we're making out in the open adding to my heightened arousal.

"Mick," she yells. There's no holding back now. My balls draw up at the sound of her cries, and I buck wildly into her.

"Give it to me, Els. All of it. I'm going to come so hard."

She lets out another cry before I feel her body tense around me, detonating my climax. I hold myself deep, emptying into her, both of us shuddering under the intensity of this long-awaited union.

As our panting slows, I turn my head to the side to take in a calming breath of fresh air. Covered in sweat, my heart rate still thrumming in my chest, I start to laugh.

"What's so funny?" she asks.

"Fifty feet. We couldn't make it fifty fucking feet."

Ava turns her head in my direction as I point at the front door. "I can't believe we made it the whole drive here." She giggles, her golden locks stuck to her damp forehead.

"If I'd had any idea you didn't have panties on, we wouldn't have," I snap back, slapping her butt cheek. "Now, get your pretty little ass up off of the ground so I can fuck you properly in a bed."

We spend the rest of our weekend taking leisurely strolls, reading, and cooking together. Well, and fucking like rabbits. *Sorry, Zach. Maybe it'll smell like a musty old cabin fit for man and beast by the time you make it back here.*

Walking in from the car, I find Ava lying face down on the couch. *What the hell?* Dropping the extra bottles of water I'd retrieved, I run to her side. "Ava, honey. What's wrong? Are you okay?"

"Hmmm."

"Baby, is it your head?"

"No. I'm so tired I can barely move," she says into the couch, never turning her head.

"Oh, for fuck's sake. I thought you were hurt."

"I am hurt. I could barely walk to the bathroom. I think you broke me in half."

I almost laugh before I consider she could be right. "Shit. Did I hurt you?"

Finally turning her head in my direction, wrinkles from the couch embedded into her sweet pale face, she answers, "In only the best possible way. I've just never had sex for this many hours in a row. Can we take a nap?"

Chuckling, I say, "Yes, scoot over."

"No. You over there." With her eyes remaining closed, I follow her outstretched finger toward the bed.

"What? You won't let me nap with you?"

"You're the reason I need a nap. Have we gotten more than four hours sleep since we got here?"

"I'll keep my hands to myself."

Ava finally opens one eye, mocking me with her sarcastic expression.

"I promise. I'm sorry. Are you sore?"

"Only a little. I'm just exhausted. I went from not doing much of anything since being in the hospital to feeling like I just qualified for an Olympic medal in cabin sex."

"Well, you deserve the gold for front yard sex." I laugh. "Come here." Sliding my arms underneath her, I carry her over and lie her in the bed. Sliding behind her, I wrap my arms around her waist. Nuzzling her neck with my nose, I already know I'm going to get stiff. "So, if I get hard, just ignore me. I won't pounce on you again. But I can't help it. You make me crazy, Els. Now get some rest." I kiss the nape of her neck, feeling like the luckiest bastard on earth. "Because there's no way we're going back home without having you one more time. And the backyard seems a little lonely."

CHAPTER THIRTY-ONE

Ava

"Ava, honey. It's so good to see you," Joanie greets as soon as I walk through the door. "It hasn't been the same here without you."

"Oh, thank you. I've missed you guys terribly. Especially knowing I wasn't coming back to Stark."

"Yes, I have to say it's been pleasant here for a number of reasons. Thanks to his absence."

"A number, huh?" Noticing a glint in Joanie's eye, I realize her expression has altered a bit and follow her gaze over my shoulder.

"Dr. Barnes. You haven't met Ava yet. She's the physician assistant we've gone on about."

Holy crap. This man is sinfully good-looking. If I wasn't so in love with Michael, I might actually have a hard time focusing on my work. Let's just hope he's as pleasant to work with as he is to look at.

"Nice to meet you, Ava. I've heard great things. I'm glad you're feeling better." Jeez, those green eyes are mesmerizing. And he's nice, too.

"Yes. Much better. Thank you. Have you been here long?"

"No, today's my first official day. I'm only seeing patients in the office until my credentialling goes through at the hospital. I'll have to postpone any surgeries or arrange to have them done at Mary Immaculate if it doesn't come through soon."

"Oh, you must work with Dr. Lee," I blurt. I watch as his almost overly joyful expression changes to a scowl.

"Yes. He's a colleague there." *Hmm. Feels like these two handsome orthopedists don't get along.* Maybe they aren't used to sharing the spotlight. "Well, I better get back to it. Maybe we can meet over coffee later and talk about the best way to approach our schedule in the future."

I give him a blank stare. "I don't understand."

"Well, I think we should look at how the OR schedules tend to run, the call schedule… figure out how to divide and conquer."

Is he for real? He wants my opinion. "I'd love that, Dr. Barnes."

"Nick. Please call me Nick."

"Nick." I feel my cheeks blush at the familiarity. I would've never been asked this of my prior condescending supervising physician. I'm in awe at my luck in receiving such a kind man to work with. That this is Dr. Stark's replacement. And the fact he looks like he belongs on the cover of GQ isn't bad either. But I'm so in love with Mick, nothing could tempt me away.

Bzzz. Bzzz.

Retrieving my phone from my lab coat pocket, it appears Michael's telepathy has kicked in. He must have felt me thinking about him.

Michael York
9:10 a.m.
Mick: Hi, pretty girl. I miss you already.

This guy.

"Well, I know who that's from." Joanie laughs.

Smiling back at her in confirmation, I look back down at my cell. Before I can reply, a new text pops onto the screen.

Michael York
9:12 a.m.

Mick: I found us a house.

What? Oh, lord. I think we're going to have to have a long talk when I get home.

9:15 a.m.
Ava: Hey. First day back with the new boss. Can we talk later? It's going to be a busy day.

Michael York
9:19 a.m.
Mick: Of course. I'll see you tonight.

～

Arriving home, I find the first day back at work has exhausted me. It's different than the tension brought on by working with Dr. Stark day in and day out. This just feels like I'm getting used to spending a full day back on my feet after being hospitalized. That infection really did a number on me.

I'm barely in the door twenty minutes when I hear a knock. As the door swings open, I see my handsome man standing there with another bouquet of gorgeous flowers with the identifiable Cygnature Blooms logo hanging from the ribbon.

"Mick, you didn't have to get me these."

"I wanted to." He leans in to kiss me on the corner of my mouth. "There's my girl." Tilting in again, he now kisses the other corner of my mouth. "I've missed you today." He places a chaste kiss on my lips before standing straight with a loving smile. "It's a special day. After the way you looked in the hospital that day, there was a part of me that worried you might never be well enough to return to work." The dramatic shift on his striking face from smiling to somber takes my breath away. I never considered how difficult this was for him. How awful it had to have been for him in those early moments.

Stepping out onto the porch, I wrap my arms around his neck and bury my face in his chest. "I'm so sorry, Mick. I didn't realize how hard that must've been for you."

"I was scared, Av," he practically whispers.

Reaching for his dark curls, I run my fingers through his hair and look deep into his eyes. "I love you. Thank you for taking such good care of me. Do you want to come in?"

"Yes."

As Mick enters the space and drops his keys on the kitchen island, I come over and take his hand, pulling him toward the couch.

"Come, sit. We need to talk." As I plop comfortably into the corner of the couch, I notice Mick remains standing, still holding onto my outstretched arm.

"I don't like the way this sounds, Ava."

"Mick, it's not bad. I just need to clear the air. What's up with the 'I found us a house' text?"

"Oh, that. After we talked this past weekend, I went online and was shocked to find the perfect house with a yard."

"But, Mick, I like my house. I have a yard. It's not big, but it's big enough if and when we finally get a dog. You're gone two nights a week. We don't need anything bigger right now. Do you not like it here?"

"I love your place. And I guess there's enough room. I was just thinking down the road."

"What do you mean?"

"Well, kids and stuff."

My mouth drops open at this statement. Not sure why, but this was the last thing I was expecting him to say.

"Okay, you know how you were worried I might think moving in together was rushing it? That didn't worry me. But this kinda does," I say softly. Biting my lower lip, I worry I've hurt his feelings.

"You don't want to have babies with me?"

My hand literally flies to my chest, the combination of his hurt voice and his concerned countenance making my heart ache. "No, Mick. I'd love to have babies with you. One day. Just not now. You're my forever. I know that. But all of these things take adjusting to. And my headaches aren't going away. I have an appointment with Dr.

Kramer, the neuropsychiatrist. I'm hoping she can shine a light on some ways I haven't considered to get them under better control. But it's going to be tough enough worrying my situation is too much for you. Then adding dogs and kids into the equation…"

Michael reaches for me, scooping me up into his lap. "That's better. You're right. I'm just happy. I guess I got ahead of myself."

"I love you. I want all of those things, eventually. Only one at a time. Plus a bigger house takes more upkeep, and I'm not ready for that. How about we try living together for a while, and if we don't kill each other, then we add a dog?" I play with his dark, silky curls and trace my finger along his sharp jawline. "Besides…"

"Besides, what?"

"Well, if we have a big fancy house with a dog and kids, what do I have left to offer worthy of a ring?"

"Oh, having my babies is a bargaining chip, huh?" He chuckles.

"And here I thought the dog would be the better bargaining chip. You are always surprising me, Michael York."

Mick laughs. "Babe. I'm not in a hurry for anything. I have you. I'd put a ring on your finger tomorrow if you'd let me. But you're right. I need to slow my roll and enjoy us. When things with your health have improved, and we're both ready, we'll take the next step."

Bending down, I bite his lower lip, hoping he knows I'm interested in taking this conversation in a different direction. His tongue instantly slides into my mouth, and I want to reassure him how happy I am that this is our new life together.

"So, when you moving your stuff in?" I reach down and stroke his already hard cock through his slacks.

"Ava," he groans.

Sliding down his legs, I perch at his feet and reach for his zipper. The sound of the metal teeth tumbling together as I unzip, making my mouth water. I lick my lower lip and hear another appreciative exhale from above. After I've managed to get his pants pulled down to his knees, I tug down his boxers, allowing his heavy erection to spring free. Not wasting any time, I grab the base and give his crown a lick.

"Ohhh," he moans loudly as his head drops back against the couch.

Stroking slowly, I slide my hand up and down his thick, warm shaft before taking him in deep. I use my free hand to play with his balls, occasionally retracting to lick each of them.

I can tell Mick's coming apart at the seams when he grabs ahold of my hair and starts to push himself in deep, the feel of his engorged cock hitting the back of my throat causing my eyes to water.

"Fuck, Els. I'm going to come down your pretty little throat. Is that what you want?"

I simply nod, my mouth full, trying to relax as he ruts into me.

"Els—"

His voice is cut short as the grip in my hair tightens further, and I suddenly feel spurt after spurt hitting my throat. As turned on as this has made me, there's a sense of pride at bringing this incredibly handsome, sweet, devoted man such pleasure.

"Oh, babe."

"Yes," I answer, wiping my eyes.

"I hope you've recovered from the weekend because when I'm done with you, you're going to need another nap."

Mick

As we begin to build a life together, I greet each day with thankfulness for having Ava by my side. We've been sharing her home, correction, our home, for a few months, and it's been easier than expected.

Ava's daily life has improved after seeing the new neuropsychiatrist. Kendall Kramer's a godsend. Some new preventative therapy as well as more regimented yoga and meditation, have been easing her headaches tremendously. I still think it's all the good loving that's turned around her migraines, but I'll give the pills their due.

The next few months are a blur. I bring Ava, and occasionally her mother, to my family's home for Sunday dinner and have loved introducing her to Zach and Alex. Trevor's moved to Sycamore Mountain, but I think that could be our next weekend trip away.

Ava's my everything. How I was lucky enough to have her stick by me after the way I treated her, I'll never know. But I'll happily spend eternity showing her how much she means to me.

Baseball season remains in full swing, and my team has improved little by little. Ava comes to every game. It warms my heart to see her cheering my boys on from the stands. And they all think she's the baseball fairy after delivering them uniforms and swag. Even though we don't make it to see a major league game often, we've been able to attend quite a few Flying Squirrels games. Luckily, she hasn't gotten too keen regarding the finer details of the sport as I text her regarding our after-work agenda. *It's going to be a great night.*

3:35 p.m.
Mick: I'll pick you up for the Squirrels game at 5:45.

Ava Kennedy
3:40 p.m.
Ava: See ya then! Kissing emoji.

CHAPTER THIRTY-TWO

Ava

"Hi." I greet my handsome man, decked out in our usual baseball attire. I'm wearing a Flying Squirrels T-shirt, tennis shoes, and a short denim skirt, and he's sporting a Washington Nationals shirt and jeans. Who would've thought I would've developed such a love for baseball? Six months ago, I couldn't tell you what the ultimate grand slam was, and now I feel like I'm living it.

"Hi, princess." He scoops me into his arms, kissing me without batting an eye. "You ready?"

We head to his car, hand in hand, before he opens the passenger door and I climb in. It's a Friday evening and the stadium will probably be packed. As we drive the distance to the field, I notice Mick has a tooth popping grin on his face.

"What has you smiling?" I ask, grinning back at him.

"I've got baseball and my best girl. What more could a guy want?" He winks, reaching for my hand again.

Looking out my window as we travel the distance from the office to the downtown minor league baseball stadium, I reflect on how my life has changed since taking a chance on this incredible man at my side. Sure, I had family and friends to spend time with on the weekends. But in hindsight, it feels as if I was just going through the motions. I merely participated in a few social outings here and there to pass the time between work and migraines. I wasn't truly living.

This isn't to say I feel like I need a man to truly live. Don't get me wrong. But I was holding myself back out of fear. Fear of one more rejection. Fear of becoming isolated like my mother. Thank god this magical man in the driver's seat was willing to face his demons as well. For my life has become all the richer.

We pull up to the Flying Squirrels stadium, and I look around, confused. There aren't any cars here. We can't possibly be that early.

"Where is everyone?"

"What do you mean?" Mick asks in total seriousness.

What do I mean? Before I can interrogate further, he's hopped out of the car and come to my door. As it swings wide, I try again to ask where all the people are when I see a handsome man approach. He's wearing a polo with the winged, squirrely visage of Nutzy, the team's mascot, on the upper left portion of his shirt. There seems to be a look of familiarity as he walks toward us, a buoyant smile crossing his face.

"Hey, Mick. Good to see ya."

I watch as the two shake hands and walk ahead of me as if I'm not even here. It's so unlike Mick not to introduce me. He's normally so thoughtful and polite. The three of us continue to walk through the desolate parking lot toward the stadium as if I've somehow missed part of the itinerary. This whole evening is becoming more and more baffling.

Turning to me, Mick says, "Jeremy, this is Ava. Thanks for doing this for us."

"Sure, man, we go way back. I'd do anything for you. Just text me when you're done, and I'll lock up."

I'm so confused that I just smile up at the tall, muscular man in front of me before he turns and leads us toward a side gate. Mystified by these events, I walk in silence beside Mick. Reaching for his hand, I hold it tighter than earlier in the evening. I have to admit, I'm feeling a little nervous about...

"Oh, Mick." I gasp, looking across the ball field. Jeremy has let us in the side entrance to the stadium, and at the pitcher's mound is a small table adorned in a white tablecloth with food and drinks set on it. As we get closer, Mick holds out my chair for me, and I sit in stunned silence that he'd do something so romantic for me. Not sure why after all of the things he's already done. But I'm shocked all the same.

I look about the empty stadium and back to this sweet, handsome man. My handsome man. He may be a rugged, tattooed little league coach and traveling salesman to the rest of the world. But to me, this man is my fairytale prince come to life.

"You like?" he asks with a radiant smile.

"I love."

We eat, drink, and laugh, and I silently thank God above for the gift of this man. It's gone dark, a beautiful night full of twinkling stars. But then again, that could just be the ones put in my shining eyes by Michael.

Suddenly, the jumbotron comes to life, and a picture of a young baseball player appears on the screen. He appears in his late teens or early twenties with big brown eyes, and strands of dark hair escaping from his ball cap. Looking closely, I realize York is printed on the back of the jersey.

"Oh my gosh, that's you?" I ask excitedly, taking him in, my eyes wide with the hotness on display in front of me. Now that I'm looking closer, the beautiful ink on this player's left arm clearly matches Michael's tattoos.

"You said you wanted to know what I looked like in a uniform," he teases.

"Well, I knew you'd be hot. But now I have confirmation." I watch as several other photos pop up on the screen. Done eating, I turn in my chair, entranced by the pictures of Mick in his hay day. Beaming up at the screen, my heart practically stops beating when the pictures of Mick stop, and in their place, a bright red background pops up with 'Elsa, Will You Marry Me?' on the screen. As I spin in my chair, my heart in my throat, I realize he's no longer sitting there. Turning my head, I find he's kneeling by my side. I can't stop the tears from tumbling now. *Is this really happening?*

"Ava, I love you. I never knew I could love anyone as much as I love you. You're my Moonshot. I don't ever want to let you go. Please say yes."

Unable to form words, I just nod, tears streaming down my face.

My prince slides the gorgeous princess cut diamond ring onto my finger and scoops me up into his arms, carrying me from the pitcher's mound to home plate. Both of us now laughing, only my giggles are through tears I can't seem to turn off. I feel like I'm in a dream right now. This can't possibly be real. Standing on home plate, we continue to kiss as he swipes away the droplets on my cheeks.

"Mick. I've never been so happy."

"Really?" He smiles down at me.

"Yes, of course. You're everything I've ever wanted and more. I'll never forget this night."

"Well, it's not over yet," he says with a wicked grin on his face. *I could just eat him up right now.* "Would you do something for me?" he asks, reaching down for my hand and pulling me along with him, never taking his eyes from mine.

"Anything," I say, clutching his arm with my free hand as we walk.

He walks me into the dugout, and I can't help but giggle. I never in a million years would've thought I'd be able to walk into one of these. Sure, I've been in the make-shift ones at the little league field, but this is where big-league teams come to wait their turn at-bat. Where they cheer each other on when they're in the outfield, trying to get back to home plate to place more points on the board. Pulling me into him, he kisses me with a robust passion I wasn't expecting, dipping his tongue hungrily into my mouth as he grips my ass with his strong hands. Pushing his firm erection into my pelvis, I moan at the welcome surprise.

"I need you to lie down on this bench and let me eat your sweet pussy, Ava."

"What?" I gasp. I immediately start looking around, knowing at least Jeremy's here.

"It's okay, baby. Jeremy's in his office. There's no one else here. The Squirrels have an away game tonight, so everyone connected with them is there. It's just us. I'd never let anyone watch me do intimate things to my fiancée." He smiles, waggling his brows at the use of the new descriptor. "Please? I can't tell you how many times I've jacked off to this. How many times I've dreamt of what it'd be like to have you here."

Suddenly, my mouth goes dry. "Have you done this before?" I ask, not really wanting to hear the answer. Hell, he was a baseball player. A college baseball player. Of course, he has.

"No, Els. I've never even pictured doing this with anyone but you." His expression has gone from playful lust to undeniably serious in an instant.

Looking up at his hopeful face, I think of the dream he lost. He's given up so much and now focuses on his little league team to make the best of his unfortunate circumstances. I consider how devoted he is to me and how very much I love him. With newfound determination, I surprise myself by taking a few steps back and rotating toward the bench. As I sit down, I turn and make direct eye contact with my strong, sexy man before straddling the bench and lying down. Reaching overhead, I hold onto the bench for support as well as to calm my quaking nerves.

Michael slowly walks over to me, with a hunger and determination in his gaze I don't think I've ever witnessed before. And I thought I'd seen all of his lust-filled expressions. Dropping one bent knee onto the bench between my spread legs, he reaches under my skirt, finds my panties, and rips the seam of each side until he can lift them off and place them in his pocket. I'm suddenly soaking wet, both in anticipation and at the display of strong, alpha dominance above me. As he drops his face down to the apex of my thighs, I hear him growl his pleasure just as I feel his warm, wet tongue caress my swollen sex. There's no teasing. No sweet kisses to my thighs on the way to his target. He just dives in as if we didn't just have a five-course meal moments ago. I have to close my eyes, or I swear I'll combust.

I feel him spread my folds and lick and suck with abandon. He inserts his large, muscular fingers into me, and I relish the sensation of him gliding them in and out of me while he sucks my clit into his mouth. He alternates using his fingers and tongue to fuck me until I'm unable to sit still. It's only been a few minutes, but I'm already ravenous in my need to come. How the hell have I gotten this turned on in a public place? You'd think my nerves would've prevented me from careening toward the finish line this fast.

"Please, Micky. I need you."

Placing a gentle kiss on my bundle of nerves, he lifts his head, looking up at me tenderly. "You need my cock, Els?"

"Yes," I practically shout.

I can feel his hearty laughter as he stands from where he's been perched between my legs. He walks to stand beside me and pulls me up into a seated position.

"Come here," he orders in a timbre I'm not used to. But it doesn't scare me. I'm even more turned on by his commanding tone. I love how he can vacillate between dominant and affectionate. Gentle and rough. I love them equally, but right now, I need him to take me with a little more force than normal as I'm feeling out of control with the desire he's brought on rapid-fire.

I follow him into the corner of the dugout and watch as he unbuckles his pants, pushing them down until his engorged cock springs forward. He lifts me into his arms, pushing my back into the corner of the enclosed space. I sense him lining himself up briefly before thrusting inside with one powerful stroke. The feeling is made that much more intense, knowing this man has asked me to share this bucket-list moment with him. That he's reserved this kinky little tryst just for me. Knowing there'll be many more unexpected moments with this sensual man in my future.

Hearing his grunts grow louder, I dig my nails into his back just before he bites down into my shoulder. I know it won't be long. I'm already hovering dangerously close to the edge.

"Ah, Mick... I—"

"Elsa, I need you to come for me." He pants, plowing into me with repetitive thrusts against this dark, dingy wall. Each plunge of his hard cock causes his pelvis to strike deliciously against my clit. "You're going to make me fucking come, Els. I need you to give it to me."

My body starts to shake, my thighs tightening around him, and I dig my nails deeper into his back and shoulders, knowing this climax will be powerful. I'm praying he'll keep me pinned against this wall so I don't topple over in its wake.

"Micky, I'm coming. Oh, god." I feel my entire body begin to shake and give in to the rush. I turn my face into his neck, attempting to muffle my cries. The reverberation within the dugout makes our carnal noises sound almost more pained than hedonistic.

Michael's pace picks up, and he lets out an almost torturous growl as he wildly slams into me three more times before he straightens. Compressing my body between his overheated form and the rough cement wall behind me, I can sense the moment he empties into me. I can practically feel the heat as he erupts deeply into my core, my sex still quivering around him.

"Holy, fuck." He exhales as he glides his cock in and out of me in a rhythmic motion as if trying to make this moment last as long as possible. Burying his face in my hair, he lays sweet kisses along the now flushed skin of my throat. "You okay?"

"More than okay." I giggle.

Mick gently lowers me to the ground and slowly withdraws. He kisses me on both cheeks and my forehead before he tucks himself back in and then helps to straighten my clothes. I cringe at the realization of my current state. I'm suddenly aware we haven't used a condom. I'm on birth control, but I'm no longer wearing panties.

"Mick. Please tell me we're headed straight home. I think I'm going to be a mess."

An almost proud, maniacal chuckle erupts from his chest. "Ah, princess. I plan to walk behind you the whole way to the car. I want to watch my seed dribble down your leg and remember every moment of this night. Fuck, I'm getting hard again just thinking about it."

My mouth drops open at his words. I'm marrying a dirty-talking sex-crazed maniac. *And I love it.*

"Come on, baby. Let's go home." He laughs. "I think I'm going to need your help with something when we get there." Taking my hand, he lifts it to his mouth, kissing my knuckles just above my shiny new engagement ring. We walk hand in hand out of the dugout to the side entrance of the stadium, close to where we've parked, like this evening was just like any other spent watching our beloved home team.

Pulling me into his side, his tattoo-covered arm around my shoulders, he chuckles. "So, where does one take Elsa on her honeymoon?"

Smiling up at him, I answer, "Somewhere warm."

CHAPTER THIRTY-THREE

6 MONTHS LATER

Mick

Lying on my side, I take in my sleeping princess. Her platinum locks tumble down her bare porcelain skin as she slumbers peacefully. Leaning forward, I watch how her long dark lashes caress her soft skin as a few unruly strands of hair dance against her light exhales. I've hit the lottery with this woman by my side.

My life hasn't ended up the way I planned. There's no big-league baseball career with a bank account to match. I'm peddling prosthetic medical devices in my travels, not my autograph. I don't have a baller's fancy house, car, or boat. The only trophies on my shelf have Little League Coach inscribed on them. But I wouldn't change a thing.

The richness I've discovered after letting Ava into my life is beyond anything I could've imagined. Rolling back onto my pillow, I stretch my arms, folding them under my head in reflection. We only returned from our honeymoon in Fiji a month ago. While the unhindered time alone with her in a beautiful tropical setting was amazing, I can't help the smile that instantly appears whenever I recall the magical day I married my dream girl.

Our wedding day was perfect. Ava had never attended church with her mother. They'd gone occasionally when her father still lived with them, but her mother became quite the recluse following her divorce. There's no judgment. Carolyn is a good person and did the best she could given her circumstances. The depression and debilitating migraines didn't allow for much beyond the bare necessities.

Ava appeared excited the moment she saw the little house of worship where my mother and I had attended services. It's nothing fancy. A small white church adorned in rich mahogany, deep red wool carpeting, and various scenes from The Bible displayed in stained glass over the baptismal as well as each window on either side of the congregation. I'd taken the pretty place of worship for granted all of these years until I saw the wonder in Ava's eyes as she took it in. "It's perfect," she'd said with tears shining in her eyes.

We married within five months of our engagement. The air was crisp, and the church was adorned in white lights, poinsettias, and Christmas trees strategically placed about the small building. We only had to show up, no additional decorations were required. There were candles all aglow as I stood at the front of the church, awaiting the arrival of my fairytale goddess. As the beautiful memories dance through my mind, I reach over to caress Ava's long tresses, careful not to awaken her.

Zach was a no-brainer for my best man. I was surprised he agreed to stand by me, given his stance on marriage and the like. But he's always been my best mate, and I knew he wouldn't let me down. My family was front and center, Emmaleigh beaming at us like she was starring in a rom-com worthy of Netflix. I guess, in hindsight, she had a lot to do with the union of our two lost souls. I owe that sweet girl so much for never giving up on us.

Ava's friend, Eve, stood by her side as the maid of honor. I love that they're so close, particularly given how I'm on the road several days a week. Eve's accepted a position in the St. Luke's emergency department, and I'm grateful Ava has Eve and Joanie to look out for her while she's at work. Her new boss, Nick, sounds okay as well. A far cry from Dr. Stark, that's for sure. He's already forced her to go home when a migraine took hold. I'm grateful for his understanding. But I digress.

The moment the church doors swung wide, and I finally saw my beautiful girl at the end of the aisle, was surprising. I assumed when my love walked to join me, she'd do it alone with her head held high. She's taken care of herself and her mother for so long. Independent and strong, she needed no one to give her away. When she told me her father, Greg, and his new wife and kids would be attending the wedding, I wasn't sure what to expect. Yet, he respectfully sat in the pews with Lauren and the children as Ava's cousin, Carson, escorted her.

Glancing back down at her now, haphazardly wrapped in cream linen sheets that have fallen to expose the length of her tantalizing back, I picture her as she glided down the aisle of that church like a vision. She took my breath away. Ava was every bit the fairytale princess come to life. Her gown was a simple pearly white long sleeve satin gown that had a scoop neck. Her veil was long and flowed behind her like a cloud. But she could have worn a Flying Squirrels T-shirt and wouldn't have looked less radiant.

Yet the crowning glory was her shining bright blue eyes and her gorgeous hair. She wore it down with small crystal snowflakes artfully adorned in it. The monotone white bouquet, dress, and veil stood to let her deep irises and blushed cheeks steal the show as she practically floated toward me. If Elsa herself had come to life, she wouldn't have been as luminous.

I'd like to say all eyes were on my beautiful bride, but somehow I'd broken contact with Ava long enough to see the hungry gaze of the man accompanying her. I remember following the path of his stare to the maid of honor who was gazing back at him coyly. Unsure if I was making more of this than I should, I chuckle as I recall sharing my observations with my new wife later that evening, and she confirmed she had her own suspicions about the two of them.

"What are you laughing about back there?"

"Oh, I'm sorry, babe. I didn't mean to wake you." I roll over to greet my wife with a gentle kiss on her shoulder. "I was just replaying our wedding day in my head."

"Oh, funny, was it?" She giggles. "Were you laughing about Nacho?"

"No." A robust laugh escapes me at the memory.

Ava had sent Emmaleigh to my room as I prepared for the big day with my wedding gift. As she entered, she held a leash in hand, and I followed it down to the small, large-eared chihuahua that was a doppelganger for Bruno. Emmaleigh had handed me a silver envelope. I laugh at the remembrance of taking a gulp and accepting that if this was my gift, I'd receive it as it was intended. With love from my bride-to-be. Even if it appeared to be more of a gift to herself or Emmaleigh than me.

Dearest Mick, it read.

I wanted to give you something you've waited a long time for. And on the off-chance Zach decides he can't stand up for you, then maybe Chance can do it.

I love you with my whole heart,
Elsa

With a heavy exhale, I'd looked to Emmaleigh, admittedly feeling defeated. Reaching out for the leash, I recall feeling puzzled when she retracted it and yelled, "What're you doing?"

"Isn't this for me?" I point. The tiny dog covered in tan fur had the nerve to tilt his head as if he was offended. *I'm the one who should be offended here. I waited my whole life for a damn dog, and I get you.* I didn't bother hiding my sneer back in his direction, shaking my head. What you do for love.

"No. First, he's not a 'this.' He's Nacho," she announced proudly, bending in her formal wear to pet the haughty little mongrel. "He's my dog." I recall Emmaleigh covering her face to hold back the laughter just before getting herself together and reaching for the door.

Confused, I watched as suddenly a gorgeous black and tan German Shephard pup pushed through the fabric of Emmaleigh's champagne-colored bridesmaid's gown and jumped up onto my legs. This grown man almost cried in front of his baby sister. And here I thought seeing Ava come down the aisle would be my undoing.

"*He's* your dog." Emmaleigh giggled. "Meet Chance."

Bending low to let this gorgeous creature lick my face while I scratched behind his ears, I practically felt like a small boy at Christmas. How could my girl have possibly made this day any more perfect? As I leaned back, I could see he was wearing a collar with a bow tie attached. My eyes flicked up to my sweet sis and her jubilant face.

"He's dressed and ready. But you better get a move on. Come on, Chance. We'll meet the groom downstairs."

The memory of that day is as vivid as if it had happened yesterday.

"So, what've you got planned today, sir?"

"Well, after I give my bride the wake-up she deserves, I think I'm going to go meet Zach and Trevor at the lake. We haven't gone fishing in a while. And Chance will have fun."

"When did Trevor get into town?"

"He's only here for the weekend. Zach said he's been in a bad way since the move to North Carolina. I was hoping the change in scenery would help, but I guess not."

"Is it the job? I guess I always assumed firefighters took care of their own."

"I don't know. I'm sure I'll get more info today. But I got the impression from Zach he's just not over what happened with his girl here and having a hard time moving on."

"Oh, that makes my heart hurt," Ava says, laying her hand over her chest.

"Well, every guy out there can't be as lucky as I am." Lifting her hand to my mouth, I place a kiss on her palm as I pull back the sheets, exposing her creamy soft skin to me.

"What's that look for, Mr. York?"

"Hmm. Breakfast."

EPILOGUE

11 MONTHS LATER

Mick

"Good morning, beautiful," I greet as I enter the bedroom with a breakfast tray for the two of us. I've never been much use in the kitchen, but I can make coffee, spread butter on bakery-fresh croissants, and add some fruit and juice to a tray. Add a flower, and I'm starting this anniversary off in style.

"Good morning," Ava replies, stretching her arms above her head. What've you been up to while I'm still asleep in here?

"Ah, just making my wife some breakfast." Lying the tray on the nightstand, I climb back into bed. Grabbing my wife, I clutch her to me. "I still can't believe it's been a year. A solid year."

"Yeah, you're a lot to put up with, but we made it." She giggles.

"That day was perfect. You're perfect," I declare before nuzzling her neck. "And what's more, today is going to be perfect."

"Oh, I can't wait, Micky. It's going to be such a fun night."

"Well, I hope you can wait. Because I'd like to give you your anniversary present first," I say, pushing my now steely erection into her hip.

"Oh. And here I thought I'd be getting something small after all the money we spent on our party. And our agreement not to get each other anything else."

"I don't do small," I growl as I sink my teeth into her creamy shoulder.

"Don't I know it." She giggles in return. Rolling on her back, she looks up at me with those sparkling deep blue eyes. "I'm ready for my present, sir."

Sliding down her beautiful body, I retract the remaining sheets covering her long limbs and spread her legs wide. Her pussy is bare, and a slight glisten is evident upon the pink folds of her sex. Leaning down, I swipe the flat of my tongue through her opening and feel her hips buck upward. I place one, then two, thick fingers into her tight channel and slowly glide them in and out of her as I tease her tight bundle of nerves with the tip of my tongue. As her moans intensify, I retract my fingers and replace them with my tongue as I reach up to pinch one tight rosy nipple.

"You sure you're ready for a gift this size, Mrs. York?" I ask, sitting back to give my now throbbing cock a much-needed stroke. I know the effect this has on her, usually causing her to beg for it.

"Yes, please," she pleads. "Can I have a little taste before you give it to me? Just to try it out first?" The saucy little minx is cocking an eyebrow at me. Like I'd ever say no to her… or that.

I quickly climb up the bed, straddling her chest, and she reaches for me. Yet, instead of placing my dick in her mouth, she pulls it down in between her soft, sweet tits and pushes them together before bending forward to lick the tip of my crown.

"Shit, Ava." I rock my pulsing cock between her creamy mounds watching as her pink tongue repeatedly darts out to tease my opening as it approaches her lips. I can't take this torture a minute longer. Pulling back from this beauty and her attempts to drive me insane, I slide back down her body so that I'm aligned with her now dripping center. The aroma of her arousal is sending me further over the edge.

"Ah, Mick," she groans as I plunge the full length of my needy cock into her.

Leaning down, I growl into her ear as I thrust repeatedly into her warm, wet body. "Oh, this sweet snatch is just for me. Isn't it? Your pretty tits, that sweet tongue. They're all mine."

"Yes!"

As I buck into her, I readjust my position, lifting her legs up over my shoulders so I can pound her pussy more vigorously. Wrapping one arm around her, I rub her clit between strokes as I thrust in deep.

"Oh, god, Micky. I'm going to—"

"Give it to me, Els. I need to see you shatter before I can—"

Ava lets out a cry just as her entire body convulses around me. The way she gives in to her orgasm is otherworldly. The sight of it alone would make me come, even if I wasn't buried in her tight heat when she began quivering around me.

"Fuck, fuck, fuck." I pant as I continue to plow into her several times more as her body milks my cock of every drop. Rocking my hips back and forth, covered in sweat, I feel something at the end of the bed and still. Looking over my shoulder, I notice Chance has his chin lying on the bed, looking annoyed.

"I'm sorry, big guy. I should've taken you out. But Mama comes first." Turning to Ava, I give her a sexy wink at the double entendre.

"Yes. Yes, she does," she says as she flops back down onto the bed.

⁓

As we drive the distance to the site of our anniversary party, I notice Ava's been fairly quiet. I was expecting a little more jubilance about tonight's events.

"Hey, what's eating you? You've been too quiet today."

"Mick?"

"Yeah, babe?" I take her hand in mine and pull it to my mouth. Placing soft kisses of encouragement against her knuckles, I look over to her in question.

"Are you sure you're okay that it's just the two of us? That I'm nervous about adding kids yet? I mean… most of the people I know who get married start having kids right away."

"What's the hurry? We've got time. I think you're right about waiting a bit. Your migraines are getting better, but I'd like to not be on the road so much when we finally have a baby on the way. I'd be worried about you. And if I don't secure a better job with less traveling, I'd want to know there's someone who can look out for you and the baby if I'm not here."

"Your mom and Emmaleigh have offered. But I hate the thought of putting anyone out on account of my headaches."

"Well, you'd never be putting them out. But my mother already worked hard raising the two of us, me as a single parent. I'm not eager to have her devote her life to another child when she's earned her chance to live a little. Do what *she* wants for a change."

Arriving at the stadium early, we're able to quickly park and make our way to the front gate to gain entrance to our event. I grab Ava's hand as I make my way around the car and pull her into me. This place holds so many great memories. "Whenever it happens, it'll be perfect. But I think it's smart we put it off a bit. And I'm grateful to have this time alone with you," I add before giving her a chaste kiss. So many newlyweds miss out on the time to enjoy this first year of marriage by starting a family right away. I'm savoring every moment I have with my bride.

"Things have been much better at work. I'm not nearly as stressed. I invited Nick to come tonight, but he had plans with his dad. But a few folks are coming from the office," Ava continues.

"I feel like I'll never meet your boss. Well, if Joanie and Allison are here tonight, I want you sitting with them."

"Why?" She giggles.

"With their color commentary, you might get turned on enough I'll get a little action later. Find some place we can relive the hot night in the dugout."

"Oh, good grief. Unless there's somewhere with a lock on it, we aren't doing anything in a ballpark full of people," she declares as we approach the doorway to the box seating we've reserved.

"Happy Anniversary, you two," Jeremy says, holding out his hand to usher us into the large space.

"Thanks, man. It's only fitting we spend it here," I reply, looking through the glass of the box seats onto the stands down below. The view of the Flying Squirrels ball field is fantastic from this vantage point, and there's plenty of seating and food to go around.

"This is going to be great. Thanks, Jeremy," Ava adds excitedly.

Hugging Ava close, I escort her inside and take in the room. It's all cream-colored walls and furnishings so as not to detract from the view outside. The stadium is nearly packed as the fans settle in for a great game.

"Congratulations!" I hear behind me.

"Thanks, Dr. Lee," Ava replies.

"Ava, you can call me Sebastian. We're not at work."

"Sorry. It's a hard habit to break. Mick, you remember Sebastian Lee, don't you?"

"Hell, of course. I owe him a lot, actually." Ava gives me a curious stare. "He's the one who caught you when you passed out that day. He would've carried you to the emergency room himself had I not been there. I'm sure of it." Turning to the man beside me, I extend my hand. This man may be a playboy who looks like he belongs on the cover of a GQ magazine, but he's all right in my book. *So long as he focuses his attention on other women.* "I've never had a chance to thank you."

"You don't need to thank me. I'm glad everything worked out okay. And I'm particularly glad to be rid of Stark."

"You can say that again." Ava laughs. "Nick Barnes is a dream compared to dealing with him."

"Dream, huh?" I tease.

She gives me a reassuring squeeze. I know Ava would never do anything to hurt me. It's my insecurity trying to get a rise out of me, nothing more. I have yet to meet the illustrious Dr. Nicholas Barnes. Looking at Sebastian, I notice an odd expression on his face. Is it our conversation or Dr. Barnes he finds distasteful? Maybe they don't get along. "I'm going to grab a beer. Sebastian, you want a drink?" I realize Zach's managed to come in unnoticed and is in the corner by the bar.

"Sure, I'll join you."

"Hey, man. When did you sneak in?" I shake Zach's hand briefly before introducing him to Sebastian.

"Leave it to you to convince Ava to celebrate her first anniversary in a ballpark. You're smooth. Very romantic."

"Shut up. I proposed to her here."

"Ha. I rest my case." Zach laughs. There's an abrupt shift in his facial expression as I notice him peering over my shoulder. I follow his gaze to a beautiful woman at the door, holding a large sheet cake. I watch as Ava and Eve run over to greet her, large smiles plastered on their faces.

Turning back to Zach, I notice Dr. Lee has his back to us, asking the bartender for a drink. "Want me to find out who she is?" I prod.

"What? Fuck no."

"I'm just saying."

"Look, I'm happy for you and Ava. But those days are over for me. So do us both a favor and drop it. That girl doesn't look like the one-and-done type. And that's the only form of relationship I'm interested in."

"Whatever." Shaking my head, I steal the beer from his hand. Glancing over my shoulder, I watch as Ava carries the white cake box over to a table and lifts the lid. I waltz over to my beautiful bride, who's wearing a magical grin, and drop a kiss on her cheek.

"Who was that?"

"Hmmm?" she asks, still looking down at the sugary masterpiece in front of her.

I almost choke on my beer when I get a closer look. It's a childlike cake, with Elsa hugging Olaf, who has a bubble extending above his head, referring to the line in the movie where he says that some people are worth melting for. Happy Anniversary is printed along the bottom. But instead of Olaf's face, it's mine.

"What the hell did you do?"

"It's perfect." She giggles, dropping the lid and turning to wrap her arms around me, almost mimicking the picture on that damn cake. "You're perfect."

I kiss her on the top of her pretty head. What the hell. I'd give her anything. *Even my manhood, apparently.*

"Who brought the cake," I push. Wondering if there's a chance she's single, and I can wear down my friend.

"Oh, that's Bailey. Her sister just started working with Eve in the

ER. We went out for drinks the other night when you were in Salem, remember?"

I recall her meeting Eve for a girl's night, promising not to drive or drink too much as I know alcohol can trigger her migraines. I didn't want her suffering when I was away. But I admit I had the game on in the background and must've missed any introduction of new names.

"Oh, the game is starting." Ava nudges, pointing toward the field.

We make our way to the front row and sit hand in hand, enjoying this great night amongst friends.

"Hey, guys. Congratulations." I smell Emmaleigh's usual choice in green apple shampoo as she leans in to give Ava and me each a peck on the cheek.

"Hi. Where's Nacho?" Ava asks. "Oh, he's hanging with Mom and Bruno. Dad's not feeling well, so they decided to stay home. Sorry, Mick."

"Oh, it's okay. I hope Rob's feeling better soon."

"It's probably his stomach acting up again. Not too worried. Heck, they may have just wanted a night alone, without me always chattering on."

Suddenly, the crowd gets to their feet as the anthem is played and the game gets underway. As we sit, I wrap my arm around my beautiful wife and look about the room. My sister, my best friend, baseball, and my best girl. What more could I possibly want?

I watch as Ava's hands fly to her face and follow her line of sight to the jumbotron.

I'd marry you all over again, Elsa. I love you. Happy Anniversary.

The End.

THANK YOU FOR READING

It's been my ambition to share the many characters, taking up residence in my mind. I hope you enjoy their adventures, as much as I've enjoyed putting them to paper. Without you, I could not continue to live this dream.

But don't put this book down yet. Keep turning for an excerpt from The Bitter Rival as well as a bonus excerpt from an upcoming work in progress, My Best Shot.

Amazon universal order link for
The Bitter Rival: https://geni.us/7rP7VrA

If you're interested in reading more about Trevor, his book will be released this fall. Naughty & Nice is a novella that will be released as part of the Man of the Month Sycamore Mountain series on September 15, 2022. Amazon universal order link: https://geni.us/NaughtyAndNice

Moonshot is a prequel to The Deprivation Trilogy. Read this angsty, romantic medical suspense to learn all about Dr. Nicholas Barnes and Katarina Kelly. Check out my Amazon author page to read

Deprivation and preorder the extended epilogue as well as Naughty & Nice: https://amzn.to/3xT25BJ

Many of the characters in my books will make appearances in future books or headline their own. To obtain more information on my current books, upcoming work, and special offers, please visit my webpage: www.authorlmfox.com

While you're there, subscribe to my newsletter to receive the latest information straight to your mailbox.

And be sure to visit me on Facebook at AuthorLMFox and my readers' group, Layla's Fox Den, as well as on Instagram, Twitter, and TikTok @authorlmfox

GLOSSARY OF BASEBALL SLANG

Backdoor slider: A pitch that appears to be out of the strike zone, but then breaks over the plate.

Bad-ball hitter: A batter skilled at hitting pitches outside of the strike zone.

Bag: A base.

Bush league: An amateur play/behavior.

Catbird Seat: When a team is in a desirable situation during a game.

Caught napping: When a runner is picked off.

Cleanup hitter: The number four-hitter in the batting order. He often has a lot of opportunities to bring players on-base home.

Cookie: An easy-to-hit pitch.

Curtain call: When a player's performance causes such excitement from the crowd, he returns from the dugout to tip his cap or wave.

Ducks on the pond: When two or three players are on base.

Hill: Pitcher's mound.

In the hole: The batter up after the on-deck hitter.

Moonshot: A long, high home run.

Three-bagger: A triple.

Two-bagger: A double.

Ultimate grand slam: A game-ending hit when the hitter's team is down by three runs in the final inning.
Walk-off: A hit that ends a game.

ACKNOWLEDGMENTS

Thank you to my team! I would not have been able to complete this book without the help of my amazing editor, Kelly, my proofreader, Cheree, and my ever-patient formatter, Shari. Thank you to Jo and the gang at GMB for continually getting my books in front of new readers. And to Linda and the entire Foreword team, I don't know what I'd do without you. Thank you for your tireless support.

I'm so grateful to TL Swan for starting me on this journey. This dream would've remained locked away had it not been for her. I can't believe after receiving your encouragement, I have now published five books. You have my continued unending gratitude for selflessly providing guidance and encouragement all along the way. I love that you're not only my favorite author but one of the most genuinely kind and selfless people I know.

Thank you so much to my beta readers! You're all so patient and motivating and I cannot thank you enough, Denise, Laura, Siri, Rita, and Kelly. All of you help shape my story into the finished product and I love each and every one of you for it.

Thank you to my ARC/Street Team members. Your constant motivation means more than you could ever know. The shares, the graphics, the reviews… I am so very grateful. I've lost count of the many happy tears I've shed because of your posts.

Thank you to the Fox Cubs in Layla's Fox Den and all of the members of my Facebook, Instagram, Twitter, and TikTok Author

pages. Your support means so much to me. I love engaging with you there. I feel like I'm at a fun party, I just don't have to dress up for it.

Ultimately, I would have never completed this book had it not been for the endless love, patience, and support of my husband and my kids. Working full time in the Emergency Room during COVID while writing kept me distant much too often. I thank you from the bottom of my heart for giving me the space to tackle this. I love you all so much!

AN EXCERPT FROM THE BITTER RIVAL

"Thank you," I utter quietly in the direction of the gorgeous man. He's donned in an expensive gray suit and crisp white shirt. The top buttons are undone revealing tantalizing bronzed skin and just a hint of dark chest hair.

"Don't thank me," he replies. "I'm kicking myself I let that guy slither over before I could get the nerve to talk to you."

Unable to help myself, I roll my eyes at this statement. Like this guy would ever need to 'get the nerve' to talk to anyone. I hope he doesn't think I'm falling for that line.

"Awe, come on. You need to dance with me, at least. To keep up the rouse," he winks.

Craning my neck toward the bar, I notice the man in question has already found a new source of entertainment. "I don't think that's necessary." I point a finger in the gentleman's direction, making my point he's completely forgotten about me. I rotate slightly and realize Bailey has slipped back to our table. "Thanks again," I acknowledge before heading in her direction.

"Really? Not even one dance?"

I stop in my tracks, trying to come up with some clever anecdote when it dawns on me. *Why am I in such a hurry to put distance between me and the hottest man I've ever encountered?* Everything about this attractive man screams 'Run.' But it's just one dance. I spin on my heel and look up at him. *God, he's one tall drink of water.* "Okay, one dance then."

His expression shifts from a seductive smirk to a warm, grin. His bright blue eyes twinkle in my direction, like constellations painted across a clear, dark sky. They could easily hypnotize me if I wasn't distracted by that flirty dimple sending me morse code. Not wasting any time, he steps forward and wraps his strong arms around my back, pulling me into him. An immediate hum begins to stir in my loins. *Just one dance, Bella.*

Shocked at his invasion into my personal space, as well as my reaction to it, I attempt to retreat a step until the warmth of his strong hands caresses my lower back. I instantly feel goosebumps pimple my flesh and try to take a cleansing breath to calm my nerves. This action has the opposite effect, as now I've inhaled the most intoxicating aroma. I relent and place my palms flat upon his chest as we move in beat with the music, all the while trying to decipher the incredible notes of his cologne. I quickly determine I should discontinue this investigation before I'm completely inebriated by this man's earthy scent.

As I attempt to pull back, his strong arms pull me closer. I can feel him slide his body down the length of mine in time with the music, placing his pelvis entirely too close to my belly. One firm rock against this incredibly well-built man, and I might start entertaining ways to satisfy my much overdue craving for some hot and dirty sex.

Taking an opportunity to change positions during a transition in the chorus, I twist to dance with my back to him. His hands move to position themselves, not on my hips, but my lower abdomen. As he rocks my body back against his, I can feel his steely erection against my back. *Good lord is that his arm or his dick?*

The song comes to an end, and I seize the opportunity to make my exit. As tempting as it might be to consider a one-night stand with this man, he's way out of my league. Truth be told, I think I'd be nervous considering anything with the likes of this one. He seems a little too hot for me to handle.

"Thank you," I blurt at my dance partner before offering a smile that feels forced. Before he can offer a reply, I make haste to my table to find Bailey. Dropping into my chair, I grab the remains of my margarita and chug it down. *Hell, who am I kidding? I'm going to need an ice bath to cool down after that hot piece of—*

"Uh, Bella? Why on earth would you come back here with me when you could keep dancing with tall, dark, and *fuck me is he sexy*? Jeez, he's the hottest man I think I've ever seen. I almost had an orgasm watching him move his hands all over you. That look on his face. Gah," she utters, fanning herself.

I can't possibly find an answer that will appease her, so I simply shrug my shoulders.

She gives me a blank stare, mimicking my ridiculous motion by drawing her shoulders up toward her ears in question. "What is wrong with you? That man is beautiful."

"Yeah, a little too beautiful."

"Huh?"

"The way he was looking at me, Bailey, and touching me… I was starting to feel like shark bait," I reply as I swiftly look toward the bar for a waiter. I need another drink.

"Well hell, Bella. I'd let him bite me," she scolds, waggling her brows in my direction.

"Bailes, something tells me if a guy like that takes a bite out of you, you won't recover."

Amazon universal order link: https://geni.us/7rP7VrA

MY BEST SHOT

(BONUS EXCERPT)

Colton
Ten Years Earlier

"You all packed?"

"Yeah," I reply, the certainty of this goodbye getting clearer.

"We've spent a lot of years here. It's going to feel odd with you gone, Colt." I notice she doesn't make eye contact with me. This is going to be almost as tough for her as it is for my mother. Meghan's a spunky girl. She's always marched to the beat of a different drummer. Over the years, we've tossed the football, camped in a tent in the yard, spent time at the lake, and spent hours in casual silence together. She's never concerned with appearances. She's not a fussy girl, consumed with makeup and hair like most of the shallow chicks I know. She's not chasing jocks or trying to attend every party. For the most part, she keeps to herself. She's dated a few guys her senior year of high school. She went to prom with my football teammate, Sherman. They were an odd match, but I never felt I'd have to kick his ass for treating her badly. Although Meghan and I are close, we've always had an unspoken rule. We avoid conversations about our dating life.

"You nervous?" she whispers.

"Nah. This has been the plan all along," I reply. My father had been a soldier. I grew up knowing it was my destiny. Unless I was awarded a scholarship for college, the GI bill would pay my way and give me 'the tools to build on,' he'd say. It's a shame the main tool I'd acquired from him was learning how to keep people at a distance. My father's parting gift from the military was a raging case of PTSD. He handled his depression and anxiety with multiple pharmaceuticals swallowed down with a heavy dose of cheap whiskey. Then again, I'm not sure you could say he'd handled anything. He eventually died of an accidental overdose, mixing too much medication with hard liquor. At thirteen, I was suddenly the man of the house.

"I'm going to be lonely without your annoying ass always bothering me," Meghan states, interrupting my unpleasant walk down memory lane.

"One last sleepover, for old times' sake?" I ask.

"Yeah. Sure."

I follow Meghan to the back of her house, a twin of my brick ranch. The biggest difference in the houses was the landscaping. Meghan and her mother were always outside planting something. They had flowers, blooming shrubs, and a vegetable garden. We had a cracked cement patio dotted with broken plastic pots.

"Wait here."

"I know the drill, Megs. Even though your mom could sleep through an earthquake." I don't know why after all of these years, we still tread so carefully. Besides that, Helen Rush is a bright woman. She probably knew we'd spent the night in her room for years. We weren't always quiet, but it was completely innocent. Meg was my best friend, and it was purely platonic. I knew she felt the same.

Hearing the heavy drag of the old wooden window, I look to see Meghan struggling and push it the remainder of the way. Jumping up, I climb in and follow her to her bed. Normally, we'd sit up watching tv or looking at each other's phones, but we both know I have an early day tomorrow. Shrugging off my shoes, I lie down on her twin bed and move close to the wall to keep one of us from falling out. It's been over a year since we've done this, and we've gotten larger. Okay, so I've gotten larger.

Meghan looks down at me and laughs. "You think we're both going to fit on there?"

"Oh, hush it and get your ass over here," I say, grabbing her arm.

She unhooks her overalls and lets the top fall forward. As she bends over to remove her shoes, her shirt rides up and exposes pale, creamy skin and the top of her underwear. I'm surprised I've even noticed as I don't normally consider anything Meghan wears. Spinning around, she slides her overalls down her legs. I take in her lithe limbs, extending from the little white boy shorts she's wearing. My mouth suddenly feels dry as I notice her nipples are protruding into the thin T-shirt she's wearing. *Jesus, man, what's wrong with you? It's just Megs.* I'm sure my emotions are getting the best of me.

ADDITIONAL TITLES

BY LM FOX

The Deprivation Trilogy, Book One: Deprivation

The Deprivation Trilogy, Book Two: Fractured

The Deprivation Trilogy, Book Three: Stronger

The Bitter Rival (the first interconnected stand-alone spin-off from the series)

Upcoming Titles:

My Best Shot: (anticipated release: 2022)

Deprived No More, The Epilogue: (anticipated release: August 2022)

Naughty & Nice: A Man of the Month Club Novella: Sycamore Mountain series
Scheduled release date: September 15, 2022

Mr. Second Best: (anticipated release: late 2022)

ABOUT THE AUTHOR

Born and raised in Virginia, LM Fox currently lives in a suburb of Richmond with her husband, three kids, and a chocolate lab.

Her pastimes are traveling to new and favorite places, trying new foods, a swoony book with either a good cup of tea or coffee, margaritas on special occasions, and watching her kids participate in a variety of sports.

She has spent the majority of her adult life working in emergency medicine and her books are written in this setting. Her main characters are typically in the medical field, EMS, fire, and/or law enforcement. She enjoys writing angsty, contemporary romance starring headstrong, independent heroines you can't help but love and the hot alpha men who fall hard for them.

www.authorlmfox.com

Manufactured by Amazon.ca
Acheson, AB